Heatseeker

Heatseeker

LUCY
MONROE

BRAVA

KENSINGTON PUBLISHING CORP.

www.kensingtonbooks.com

BRAVA BOOKS are published by

Kensington Publishing Corp.
119 West 40th Street
New York, NY 10018

ISBN-13: 978-0-7582-4203-7
ISBN-10: 0-7582-4203-4

First Kensington Trade Paperback Printing: February 2013

10 9 8 7 6 5 4 3 2 1

Printed in the United States of America

In memory of my mom, the woman who taught me that love has more power than hate and to believe in happy endings no matter how hard they are to come by, but most importantly that life offers unexpected second chances and we need to be open to happiness to take them. Thank you, Mom! I love you and miss you! You know you would have loved all the characters in this book and their second chances at happiness. Us girls are working on ours getting healthy and I think you'd be very proud.

Chapter One

It was coming again.

She'd counted out the intervals between the agonizing jolts of electricity, and they were always the same. One hundred and eighty seconds. Three short minutes.

Not enough time to completely stop the involuntary muscle spasms from the last one, but enough time to hope it wouldn't come again.

It always did.

Still, a more experienced interrogator would vary the duration of both the torturous jolts and the time between them, but these were the underlings. Men who were obviously not used to interrogating women. Though they didn't seem to mind hurting Rachel. Nor did they appear to get overt pleasure out of it, the way the man she'd been investigating would.

Abasi Chuma. Egyptian financier and trader with ties to the nomadic people who still carried goods (and, Rachel suspected, intel and illegal weapons) across the desert and country borders on the backs of camels.

Chuma was also a sick, sadistic asshole whose sexual

proclivities ran to inflicting pain to get his rocks off. His young and still innocent fiancée clearly had no clue about that yet. The woman had been Rachel's "friend" and un-witting informant for the past nine weeks. An information asset that Rachel could not betray.

Would not betray.

So she continued to play the nosy-tourist-caught-snooping-where-she-shouldn't-have-been role. And they kept asking the same darn questions over and over again. That in itself was as torturous as the pain racking her body.

Abasi Chuma would arrive tomorrow, and she had to hope he didn't recognize Rachel as the woman who fre-quently had coffee with his fiancée at a café near Jamila's home on weekday mornings. To Rachel's knowledge, Chuma had never actually seen her with his fiancée, but she wouldn't trust the other woman's safety to that belief. If she was ever again in a position to do anything about Jamila's welfare.

That would require getting out of here first. Wherever *here* was. And it had to be soon.

Her captors had let slip that two of the top dogs of their criminal enterprise would be arriving after morning prayers the next day to continue her interrogation. If things went on as predictably as they were now, she just might be alive to meet them.

She was certain one of the men would be Abasi Chuma, but three months of undercover work in Egypt had not yet revealed his partner. Rachel had her suspicions but, so far, no way to confirm them.

Well, she'd know tomorrow. For all the good it might do her, or her agency, The Goddard Project.

TGP had been started during WWII to protect tech-nology assets because of what the Germans had learned spying on Samuel Goddard and his rocketry. It had evolved into a modern-day deep black ops agency technology watch dog, protecting the United States and its citizens from the misuse of home-grown research.

She'd have to escape to pass on the information.

And inexperience in torture techniques on the part of her captors did not necessarily equate to sloppiness in keeping her a prisoner.

An agony of stabbing needles shot through her, and against her will, Rachel bucked against the restraints holding her to the chair in the middle of the dank room. The minor pain of having skin already abraded by the straps rubbed raw added to the agony of the electric shock.

She screamed words that would make no sense to them but that gave her the only comfort she expected to get.

The acrid scent of her own urine mixed with the bile from a vomiting fit brought about by her last encounter with the car battery.

The smells and bitter taste of acid in her mouth registered only faintly as her mind took her to the one place in time when pain wasn't a daily part of her life.

To the time before Linny's death . . . before Kadin Marks decided he didn't love Rachel any longer.

To the sweetness of summer when she was eighteen.

"Abort. Abort." The one word Kadin had not expected to hear in the humidity of Morocco's moonless night came over his earpiece.

"Hold that order," he barked in a whisper. "Why?" he demanded of his second in command, Neil Kennedy, otherwise known as Spazz and a frickin' whiz with computers and all things electronic.

"She's screaming your name, Trigger. They have to know we're here."

If Kadin hadn't been belly down on the ground, commando-crawling toward their target, his legs would have given out on him.

"My name?"

"Yes. The first time I thought she was just screaming something like your first name, but she just shouted, 'Kadin Marks, don't you leave me behind.' She doesn't sound good, boss, but we can't risk going in if they're expecting us."

"They're not."

"But—"

"She's remembering the past, not begging us to rescue her in the present." Rachel Gannon had no reason to believe that Kadin Marks would there for her these days.

He'd given up on being her hero a long time ago.

"Trig?"

"Belay the order to abort. The mission is still on," Kadin said through the communication earbuds.

His five-man team affirmed they'd heard the order, and Kadin began moving forward again. The urge to hurry burned inside him, but he couldn't risk this mission going FUBAR.

Effed-up-beyond-all-recognition was not an option when it was Rachel's life on the line.

He'd let her down enough already for any one lifetime. Kadin had walked away from her when they were old enough to be considered adults but had still been kids, really. At least *she* was still a kid. By the time he was twenty, he'd earned his nickname, Trigger, as a trained and highly effective assassin for MARSOC, the United States Marine Corps Special Operations Command.

A sniper with more kills than he ever wanted her to know about, he'd walked away so the violence of his life wouldn't touch hers.

But, for reasons beyond his understanding, she'd then gone and taken her own path into service of their country, and she had lost more than anyone should have to while doing it.

Her only sister had committed suicide while Rachel was undercover for the DEA. He knew that must have had a devastating effect on her.

He supposed there should be no surprise in the fact that she had taken a dangerous assignment in Egypt following up on the intel his team had garnered in Zimbabwe six months before.

The only true shock was that Rachel had still cried Kadin's name when she was in need. She had to have learned that he was no knight in shining armor ten years ago, and still she'd called for him.

This time he would not let her down.

Rachel's interrogators conferred in a corner of the starkly lit room, apparently unaware that one of the four languages she spoke fluently was the Farsi they were using. She understood another five well enough to eavesdrop but not to converse.

Not that her special affinity for languages was going to do her any good here. Even though she could understand every word her captors spoke, she couldn't do anything about the information she hoped to glean.

The tallest and coincidentally youngest of the three men was shocked she had not yet broken. After all, she was only a woman. He was convinced, therefore, that she was what she claimed to be: a simple tourist who had been foolish enough to be caught in the wrong place at the wrong time.

An older man with clear military bearing, whom the other two deferred to, said she had to have training in anti-interrogation techniques. Which meant he did not believe her overly-curious-tourist story.

The third man evinced no opinion, simply glancing over at Rachel with unreadable eyes. He was the one who had attached her to the car battery and tightened her restraints by tiny increments every once in a while. They weren't cutting off her circulation yet, but they were close.

And it hurt. A lot.

Not enough to make her tell them the truth, though. She *was* a highly trained operative, but her best preparation had come from life. She knew what kind of pain could break a person like her, but they didn't have access to the means to cause it. After all, she'd already lost everyone who mattered.

Her parents and Linny were dead. Grandma was in a home with Alzheimer's and hadn't recognized Rachel in two years. Kadin had left before she lost Linny.

There wasn't anyone left to lose.

And they couldn't break her with her body. Oh, she'd welcome death when and if it came. The torture might be destroying her mind and her perspective, but Rachel would protect her unwitting source of information no matter what they did to her body. Jamila Massri reminded Rachel too much of Linny. An innocent young woman desperate for love, caught up with a sadistic man.

It would take more than physical agony to force that name from behind the barriers Rachel had constructed in her mind.

She'd planned her escape route if those barriers started to fail, and the idiots in the corner had no clue.

All she had to do was tip her chair sideways while the battery leads were connected to her body. She'd fall into the puddle of urine and the water they'd tossed onto it to keep down the smell. The electricity would pass through her heart and, more important, through her brain.

Instant fried cerebral matter.

And if she was lucky, the impact of her head connecting with the cement floor would kill her even before the electricity did.

She hadn't taken her only out yet because the part of her that wanted to do her job wouldn't let go, the little part of her that still hoped, still believed in good winning over evil. She wanted to know who the top players in this undeclared but still very real war were.

And maybe, just maybe, her agency would send someone to extract her in time for her to share that important news.

TGP didn't leave their agents behind, but time was running out, and she wasn't counting on rescue. She never counted on anyone being there for her anymore.

Another bolt of electric agony jolted through her as she forced her mind to go over her "escape" plan again and again, even as she screamed the name of the one person she was absolutely sure she would never see again.

Kadin could now hear the screams through the walls of the facility. His heart stopped in his chest as the agony in that voice paralyzed him.

He'd heard Rachel Gannon's voice lifted in pleasure, he'd heard it broken with pain, but he'd never heard it scream like this. In that moment, he realized it was the one sound that might well break *him*.

"Hey, Trig, you okay?" Cowboy asked as he drew level with Kadin.

Kadin jerked his head in a nod and started moving again. He had to be all right, damn it. He couldn't let himself get distracted. Rachel's life depended on his keeping his head in the game. Hearing the proof of what was happening to her could not get in the way of that.

Not even when it came special-delivery with his name on it.

One damn thing he had never expected was for her to call out to him in her time of need. It had to be a mind game she played with herself to keep her real secrets locked inside, but hell if it wasn't wreaking havoc on his brain, too.

Rachel was on count 720 when she realized it had been longer than three minutes since the last shock. She opened her eyes slowly, but even so, it took a moment to focus. Her vision was so blurry at first, the room appeared completely dark. But it wasn't. The single lightbulb in the ceiling was still on, and the stark illumination it cast revealed that the men tormenting her were no longer in her cell.

She hadn't heard them leave.

That was not good. Maybe she was farther gone than she'd thought.

Had the time come to take her escape route?

She took several deep breaths, trying to assess her condition and how close she might be to revealing something she did not want to without realizing it.

As Rachel contemplated her options, limited though they were, the door opened, and an old woman shuffled in. She muttered a prayer in Farsi under her breath as she offered a cup of water to Rachel to drink.

Rachel didn't bother asking for help. This woman was as trapped as she was. The first couple of sips of liquid tasted as bitter as the acid in Rachel's mouth, but then the clear, cold flavor of well water took over, and Rachel's eyes stung with gratitude.

The woman helped her drink the whole cup before stepping back.

"Thank you," Rachel croaked out in Farsi.

With a nod of her cloth-covered head, the older woman turned to leave.

"Wait." The word cost Rachel, coming out of a throat raw from screaming.

The woman turned, her eyes filled with resigned sadness. "I can do nothing else for you."

"You can tell me where we are."

Though Rachel could make a good guess based on the way the woman was dressed.

"We are in the mountains, far from any city."

"In what country?"

"Morocco."

Okay, that was a lot farther from Helwan, the small city outside Cairo where she'd been conducting her investigation, than she'd expected. She must have been out cold a lot longer before arrival than she'd thought, or they'd flown her here.

Either way, she now understood why she'd been left alone for, at best guess, almost a whole day after being dumped in this less-than-hospitable room. The fact that the big dogs hadn't arrived yet made more sense, too.

Moving her to Morocco was smart, but hopefully not as clever as the locator chip in Rachel's hip that Vannie at TGP headquarters had installed.

"Thank you. What is your name?"

The woman shook her head and left without answering.

"Mine is Rachel," she croaked out as the door closed. Her head dropped, the last, tiny reserve of energy draining from her.

She had no doubts her people would find her, but she was fairly sure at this point that it wouldn't be alive.

Moments later, the door opened again, this time silently. Only the shift of air in the room gave the movement away. So, *not* her captors' return.

But who? Had her agency sent a rescue team? Hope seared through her as worry rose up to meet it.

A man stepped inside, closing the door behind him with an economy of movement and absolutely no sound. She would not know he was there if she could not see him with her own eyes. Big, both tall and broadly muscled, he wore the newer black digital camouflage. His face was covered by a cotton ski mask, but his eyes were eerily familiar.

She blinked her own, unable to process what her brain was telling her. Her rescuer had Kadin's eyes.

She knew with every particle of her remaining sanity that it couldn't be Kadin Marks. Not here. Not now. Just her fantasies playing tricks with her mind. This was much worse than losing track of time during her torture. Reality was colliding with imagination, and that terrified her.

She had to keep her mental faculties together. Her brain was the only weapon she had left. And apparently she needed to stop using old memories to fight the horror of the present.

"Kadin?" she whispered, almost silently, the fear she'd refused to give in to up to this point nearly overwhelming her.

The man heard her. His head jerked, but he didn't say anything. He moved forward on quick, silent feet, dropping to one knee beside her. He flicked open a lethal-looking blade and put it against the zip tie holding her wrists together.

"Wait!" she gasped.

He stopped. "Don't worry, Rachel. I'm not here to hurt you."

It was Kadin's voice, saying her name. Her mind *had* snapped.

Even knowing that, she asked again, "Kadin?"

"Yes."

Impossible, but he'd just said he was Kadin. Maybe her rescuer would have agreed to anything; maybe men like him were trained to deal with delusional torture victims like her that way. One thing she was certain of. The man, whoever he was, was here.

"I'm not dreaming." She said it aloud because she

needed to convince herself. She was fairly confident that she was in too much pain to be dreaming, though. Besides, in all her dreams, Kadin had never shown up in commando gear.

The Marines had taken him from her; she wasn't about to have fantasies of him dressed like a soldier.

"No." He brushed her cheek with a black-gloved hand. "You're not dreaming."

That voice again. It could not be, and yet, somehow, her nearly broken mind kept insisting that it was. "It's you. Really."

"Yes." Never one for long speeches, her Kadin.

No, wait. Not hers anymore. Not for a very long time. "How?"

"It doesn't matter. We have to get you out of here."

"No."

He made a sound a cross between shocked gasp and growl. "Yes."

"No. Two of the top guys in the organization are coming tomorrow." One of them was an expert in interrogation. And she was sure she knew which one held that dark claim to fame in his underlings' eyes. "I know one of them but not the other. We need that information."

So, okay, her brain was still functioning. Which meant this man really *was* Kadin Marks, because she wasn't so far gone that she was turning fantasies into reality in her mind. She hadn't done that for almost as long as Kadin hadn't been hers.

"Then get it another way," he growled in an almost subvocal whisper directly against her ear. "You are not staying here to be tortured anymore."

"They're finished for the night." At least, she hoped they were.

"Bullshit. They're giving you a chance to think it's over before coming back and trying to break you."

A more experienced interrogator might do that, but these guys? She was hopeful not. "They haven't broken me yet."

The sound of plastic snapping came from behind her, and then Kadin's big hands were on her arms, massaging them as he slowly allowed them to relax downward. "Your limbs are going to hurt like a sonofabitch, but you can handle it, angel."

The pain started then, and she didn't bother wasting breath on trying to argue or demanding that he never, *ever* use that endearment again. She had to handle this, and a lot more quietly than she had her torture. Yelling out Kadin's name right now could get them both killed.

Once her arms hung at her sides, he made quick work of the ties holding her legs to the chair, and then he swept her up into his arms. "They aren't getting the chance."

"Chance for what?"

"To break you."

"And I won't get the chance to identify the other major player, either."

"I'll leave a team to do surveillance."

"There's no guarantee the head honchos will show once it's discovered I'm gone."

"Is she for real, boss?" someone asked, and Rachel realized Kadin was wearing an earbud communicator.

She wouldn't have heard the voice through the comm-link except her head was right next to Kadin's. He should be carrying her in a fireman's lift, so he had one hand free.

The fact that he wasn't messed with her head in a way the torturers hadn't been able to.

"Boss?" the voice asked again.

"Yes." Kadin didn't sound happy when he said it, either.

"Tell her we'll take care of it," said another voice, this one with a distinct Texas twang.

Another day, another time, Rachel would have demanded to know how, but right now? It was taking every single one of her stay-with-it molecules to keep from passing out, puking, or ignominiously doing both.

Chapter Two

Rachel slept on Kadin's bedroll in his tent while Cow-boy briefed him on the nighttime activity at the enemy compound. "Looks like she was right, Trigger. Those sorry bastards are all sleeping, along with everyone else in that compound except for a single guard on the perimeter."

"They're relying too much on their remote location for security."

"Don't sound so disgusted. If they were as good as we are, it would have taken a whole lot more effort to break in and rescue your girlfriend."

"She's not my girlfriend." There was a time when she'd been even more, but those days were gone.

And it had been his choice to jettison their relationship. He'd done it for her sake, but he doubted she'd ever believed that. Women didn't. And Rachel was more convinced of her own invulnerability than most.

"Sure sounded like your girlfriend, screaming your name."

Kadin surged to his feet, ready to deck his friend.

Cowboy stepped back, hands up in surrender. "Don't get pissed at me, Trig. You know I didn't mean it that way."

Kadin nodded once, his throat too raw to speak for a second.

"All I'm saying is, she sure looked like your girlfriend,

too, the way you were carrying her and all." Cowboy had taken a few steps back before adding that bit of opinion to Kadin's already screwed-up night.

He was never going to get the sound of Rachel's screams out of his head.

"Why? Is that the way you carry *your* girlfriends?" Spazz asked Cowboy with an edge to his voice Kadin didn't get but had no interest in figuring out right now.

Cowboy frowned, all evidence of humor gone from his expression. "I don't have any girlfriends."

"Right." Spazz didn't sound as if he bought that.

Kadin wouldn't, either, except he knew something about his old friend and former fellow MARSOC soldier that Spazz clearly wasn't privy to.

Cowboy's shoulders bunched, and he sat down away from both of them. "Leave it alone, Neil."

"*Spazz*. Everybody calls me *Spazz*."

"I like *Neil*."

Well, piss and damn. Maybe Spazz had more of a clue than Kadin thought. It didn't matter.

"I do not need my team sniping at each other. Knock it off." Kadin raised a hand when it looked as if Spazz would argue. The little guy had guts. Most wounded grizzlies would know better than to argue with Kadin right now, and a sane man should. "Both of you."

Spazz subsided with a muttered, "Sorry."

Cowboy didn't apologize, but he didn't open his trap again, either.

"Spazz, you got one of those tech-dealies that can jam signals?" Kadin asked the wiry blond.

Former Navy, the guy could do anything and everything with a computer and most technology. He was a kick-ass fighter, too, though, which was why the Atrati had recruited him.

"I do." Spazz went all-business, the man a soldier first.

Just like the rest of them, even if they didn't technically answer to Uncle Sam anymore. "My newest little toy will even work on a satphone transmission."

Kadin nodded. Given the remoteness of the location, satellite phones were likely in use. "What's the radius?" he asked.

"Half a click, but it will block everything, including our own transmitters."

Kadin nodded again. That was to be expected.

"Why?" Cowboy asked.

"In the morning, someone is going to figure out that Rachel isn't in that room. We don't want them communicating that fact to the men coming. She wants them identified."

"I heard. That little gal is as crazy as you, Trig," Cowboy said, his voice laced with admiration.

Even knowing what he did about his teammate, Kadin had to stifle a growl welling up inside.

"You don't think the brass are going to get suspicious when they can't get through to their little compound in the mountains?" Cowboy asked.

Kadin hoped not. "Areas like this, technology is spotty, even satphones."

Spazz agreed with a nod.

"Wouldn't it be best to make sure Rachel's disappearance isn't noticed in the first place?" Cowboy asked.

"You have a plan to make that happen?"

"Drug the guys who were doing the interrogation. While they're sleeping. They won't wake up early, and by the time their bosses arrive, no one's had a chance to figure out that the prisoner isn't in her cell."

It wasn't a bad plan, but it left a hell of a lot up to chance. "And if someone else checks on her or wakes the kidnappers?" Kadin asked.

"Besides the three guys doing the interrogating, there are only two guards. One's on watch. One is asleep. SOP would be for them to switch places sometime in the night. It's not likely that either of them is going to check on the others."

Was standard-operating-procedure among terrorists enough to rely on? "What about the old woman who feeds them?" he quizzed Cowboy.

"She's not going near that cell without orders."

"And if she does?"

"Then Neil's little gizmo stops them from raising the alarm."

Spazz pulled a protein bar from his pocket and opened it. "As long as one of the guards doesn't hike out to spread the alarm," he commented.

"If he does, I'll be waiting for him." Cowboy was damn near as good with a rifle as Kadin.

"Do it," Kadin ordered.

Spazz flinched and tried to hide it by taking a bite of his food. The look of worry he gave Cowboy wasn't lost on Kadin, either.

The tough Texan who'd let his hair grow shoulder length after leaving the Marines seemed oblivious, though, as he got up to gather what he'd need for the assignment.

"I don't think Cowboy should go in without backup," Spazz said.

The techno-geek was right; Kadin had had no intention of sending Cowboy in alone. "You go with him. We'll want listening devices planted so we can track movements."

Spazz nodded, jumping to his feet.

"You'll both stay to jam the communications if necessary and take recon on the arrival of the men in charge. I want face shots and names if you can get them."

"You got it, Trigger," Cowboy drawled.

"We'll maintain camp here until tomorrow night." They were far enough away from the secret compound not to be detected, and Rachel needed rest before she was going to be up to the hike back to their transport.

"No one will expect us to stay in the area after rescuing the prisoner, that's for sure." Cowboy's tone made it clear he shared a little of that disbelief.

"Unless they bring troops with them, they aren't going to have the manpower to search for us, either," Spazz added, both men giving their tacit approval of the plan.

Not that Kadin needed it, but it was nice to know his team didn't think he was an idiot. He'd only taken over lead when their former captain, Roman Chernichenko, got promoted to management.

Being in management worked for a man who was getting married, but Kadin couldn't imagine leaving the field. He had nothing to stay Stateside for, anyway. He'd given up on dreams of home and family a long time ago.

About the last time he'd seen Rachel Gannon standing under the big oak tree outside her grandmother's house in their hometown.

"We'll break camp under the cover of dark tomorrow." By then, he hoped Rachel would be able to walk without passing out. If she couldn't, he'd carry her, but he'd rather have his hands free in case he needed to protect her.

"I'm going to check on Rachel and then grab a few *z*'s. Peace is on guard duty." Maluakeakua was a man who said he fought for peace . . . with his fists. Kadin had seen the laid-back Hawaiian in action too many times to doubt it. "Check in with him every fifteen. Report to me when you're done with tonight's assignment and in position for tomorrow morning."

Spazz and Cowboy nodded, both men already putting together the gear they needed for the revised mission.

As he crawled into his tent, Kadin didn't think about the fact that there wasn't another person besides Rachel Gannon who could have convinced him to change his mission directive from retrieval to espionage.

He crowded the small space already occupied by Rachel and their team medic, Eva. "How's she doing, Doc?"

"Her vitals are good, but I'll feel better after we get her checked out at a decent medical facility."

Kadin looked down at the woman who had haunted his dreams and waking fantasies for ten long years. There were a couple of livid bruises on her face, along with one on her neck that showed above the light blanket covering curves he could still feel in the palms of his hands if he closed his eyes and thought hard enough.

She used to tease him about what he saw in her, calling herself average. But to him she'd been anything but. And still was. He supposed at five-foot-five she was average height, but she'd always seemed small beside his big six-foot-two-inch frame. Her light brown hair might not be considered exotic, but he had loved running his fingers through it.

Her pale blue eyes meant she had to wear sunglasses even on overcast days, or she'd squint in that adorable way of hers, but he could see everything in them. Her eyes had never hidden anything from him, and he'd been determined not to fill them with the horror that knowing what he'd become would do.

Her lips were what he remembered the most often, though, their bow shape curved in a smile or open just a tiny bit, inviting a kiss. Images of the lips that were now cracked with dryness used to wake him in the middle of the night in a cold sweat. And he'd ache for what he couldn't have.

Her hair was a frazzled mess around her face, but she

smelled better than she had when he'd found her. The sharp scent of disinfectant indicated that Doc had bathed Rachel with wipes and had probably just finished.

Kadin frowned at every little proof of what those bastards had done to her. "She won't leave until we get the information she's after."

If he wasn't so pissed, he would smile. Even in sleep, Rachel's slightly squared jaw was set in stubborn lines.

"She's obstinate." Doc shrugged. "Like someone else I know."

"You mean every member of this team, right?"

Doc smiled and saluted in a *touché* gesture. "Maybe."

"We'll get the intel tomorrow, and then we're out of here."

Unlike his other teammates, Doc didn't look as if she approved of that plan. "Can't Spazz get the pictures with one of his handy gadgets while we take Miss Gannon down from the mountain and get her proper medical treatment?"

"I suggested that to her." When they'd gotten back to camp. "You were there."

It hadn't been a suggestion, either, but Rachel had argued with what little strength and voice she had left. Batting away his hands and those of the medic, Rachel had refused medical treatment, or to even lie down, until he agreed she could stay until the men were identified.

He'd finally given his promise. Something he would not break unless he had no choice.

"*Acho men.* So she refused. Since when do you let the extractee tell you how to do your job, *jefe*?" Eva demanded.

The woman was seriously irritated when she broke out the Spanish cuss words. Though *damn it, chief* was pretty mild.

But Kadin's answer was a simple one. Since that extractee had become Rachel Gannon, the one woman—hell, the one person—on the planet he didn't know how to say no to and never had. Except the one time he'd made it count.

He reached out, wanting to touch Rachel but knowing he shouldn't. His hand hovered just above her arm. "She's not up to the hike out, anyway."

"One of you could carry her." Eva gave his immobile hand a worried look. "It wouldn't be the first time."

"It will be better for her if she gets some rest first, even if I do end up carrying her." The idea had sounded reasonable in his head but not as convincing out loud.

The look on Doc's face said she was of the same mind. "It will be *better* for her to get to safety."

"Rachel came to Africa to do a job. She's not going to leave without doing it."

"If you indulge her."

"She deserves a little indulgence after what she's been through." Damn. What the hell had the woman been thinking, taking this assignment?

But that was a question he'd been asking himself ever since discovering that the agent who'd come to Africa to pretend to be Tanya Ruston six months ago was Rachel. And he didn't expect to get an answer anytime soon. Not that he wasn't going to ask her when she woke, but he had a feeling Rachel wasn't going to think she owed him any explanations.

Doc sighed, her Latin temper calming a little. "I can't argue with that."

"Good."

"Damn it, Trigger, I didn't mean—"

Kadin cut Eva off. It was really bad when she started swearing in English. "You're the medic. Tell me she wouldn't improve with some rest and nourishment."

"That's not the point. Until we get her on a plane back

to the States, she's at risk for recapture. This organization she's been gathering intel on isn't some fly-by-night operation. They had an in with the Zimbabwean army and no doubt have all the connections they need here in Morocco."

"Then I'll just have to keep her safe, won't I?"

"*We*, Kadin. We're a team. Remember?"

"I remember."

"*Fuche!*" That meant *phew*, or something like it, and Kadin let out a breath of relief, but Eva wasn't done. "Roman wouldn't have let the mark dictate the plan for evac."

"Roman isn't our captain anymore. I am."

"Then act like it."

"I am. I made the call. We're leaving tomorrow. Deal with it."

Eva frowned, no doubt cursing him out in Spanish in her head, but not a word of it passed her lips.

He forced himself to say, "If you're okay in here, I'll go get some shut-eye."

He didn't want Rachel out of his sight.

"This is your tent, and don't think you're going to take over mine. She's stable. You can watch over her while she sleeps as easily as I can."

"You're the medic."

"And you have a calming influence on her."

"She looks plenty calm."

"Exactly." Doc sighed. "Ten minutes ago, she was having nightmares. She was so tense, she looked like she was having convulsions. I tried to calm her, but I didn't want to sedate her, you know? Her entire body went lax when she heard your voice, telling the boys to chill. And she's stayed calm the whole time we've been talking."

He shouldn't have been loud enough earlier for his voice to carry. It just went to show that this rescue had him seriously rattled. And no matter how much he'd known that was going to happen, he'd still insisted on taking the assignment.

He had refused to trust Rachel's rescue to anyone else.

Eva scooted around him and pushed up the tent flap. "My advice, as team medic, is for you to settle your ass down beside Miss Gannon and give her a sense of safety. I don't think she's had much of that lately."

"Shit."

"Not inside the tent, please."

"Smart-ass."

"I *am* smart."

Kadin ignored the last, knowing, with Eva, chances were good he wasn't going to get the final word. He went to lie down beside Rachel, doing his best not to jostle her.

Her eyes fluttered open as he settled beside her. He doubted she could see him well in the shadows cast by the low tent light, but she smiled as if she recognized him. As if she was glad he was there.

Go figure. She was probably still disoriented.

Though weak, the smile remained. "Hey, Marks," she whispered.

Amazing, resilient, incredible woman.

"Hey." He wanted to reach out and touch her so badly, his hands literally ached with the need.

"Didn't think I was ever going to see you again."

"Me, neither."

"Glad I was wrong," she slurred in a barely-there whisper.

For a moment, he was too stunned to reply. Finally, he forced out a gruff, "Me, too."

But she'd slipped back into sleep as fast as she'd come out of it, and he didn't think she'd heard his last reply. That was okay. She had to know he was glad to have gotten her out of that hellhole.

Even with their past, that had to be a given.

Giving in to his need, he wrapped his fingers gently around her badly abused wrist so he could feel her pulse. Only when he'd detected the steady thrum of her heartbeat did he let himself doze, listening for trouble even as he sort of slept.

Cowboy and Spazz were silent as they hotfooted it through the forest back toward the enemy's compound. Neil took care of checking in with the double click that indicated all was well every quarter hour.

The former squid might be a technology geek, but he moved with the stealth of a well-trained soldier. Just as he had when they'd been on the same team together right after they'd both been recruited into the Atrati.

Neil Kennedy had requested and received a transfer from that team after the first year.

Cowboy had missed the other man every day since, until Wyatt had been assigned by his request to Kadin Marks's team after Roman Chernichenko's promotion. Not that Wyatt had said as much to Neil. The other man wasn't about to listen.

Not after the way their relationship had ended, hacked to death by Wyatt's pride and need to stay in the closet completely. So damn completely that he'd dated women as a smokescreen and let his daddy talk him into getting engaged to one before he finally came to his senses.

But it had been too late to save what he had with Neil.

And the sexy computer geek wasn't giving Wyatt any signs he might be open to offering him a second chance. In fact, he'd made it damn clear he wanted nothing to do with a closeted gay man from Texas.

Breaking into the enemy compound proved as easy the second time around as the first. Cowboy located and drugged Rachel Gannon's captors with hypodermics, pretty damn pleased to discover a whiskey bottle that had clearly been shared before the men had taken to their racks. That promised excellent possibilities.

Meanwhile, Neil planted his listening devices, clicking over their comm-links as each one was successfully deployed.

This enemy organization might be a big ol' nest of vipers, but a bite could only be as poisonous as its successful strike rate. And even the fastest snake among them wasn't likely to win against a man with a gun.

Or a Texan with a needle, in this case.

Neil wasn't there to meet him outside the building when Cowboy was done, though, and he felt dread make the hairs on the back of his neck stand straight up. Where the hell was his squid?

It took twelve more minutes, two extra clicks, and a double-click check-in that only marginally comforted Wyatt before Neil showed up.

"Where the hell were you?" Cowboy demanded in a whisper.

Spazz shook his head, refusing to answer aloud. While Cowboy understood the man's caution, he was fit to burst by the time they'd gotten enough distance between them and the compound to converse safely if quietly.

He repeated his question, this time grabbing Neil's arm to stop the other man from moving until he answered.

Neil glared up through the gloom under the trees that the moonlight barely penetrated. "I was doing my job."

"What the hell? You only had a couple of listening devices to install."

"I wanted to put up a couple of spy-cams, too. They're so tiny, unless they've got way better counterintelligence than security, they're never going to find them. But I ran into the other guard and had to wait for him to move on before I could get out of there."

"You were only supposed to go in and get out, not host a damn tea party."

"I wasn't serving tea, you redneck idiot."

"You tryin' to insult me, darlin'? I remember a time when you used to call me *redneck* as a term of endearment." Wyatt moved closer to Neil, letting the other man's nearness just wash on over him.

"I wasn't using it as an endearment just now, asshole." Neil's breathless tone belied the insult.

"You scared me, sailor-boy. You owe me something for causing me such distress."

"What are you, a six-year-old girl, getting all worried when your friend doesn't meet you on the playground right when you expect?"

"So, we're friends again?" Wyatt asked, tugging Neil just that much closer.

"Stop. No . . . damn it, Cowboy."

"Shit, baby, call me Wyatt like you used to do."

"No way in hell." Neil wrenched his arm from Cowboy's grasp and moved back. "Those days are long over."

He fast-marched several feet away and then swung back and faced Cowboy. "And don't call me *baby,* asshole."

He was going to start hearing the insult as an endearment if his man kept saying it like that. Oh, the anger was there in Neil's voice, but so was something else, something Wyatt knew the blond computer geek would be pissed as hell to know Wyatt had heard.

"Don't scare me like that again, and I'll consider it." *Like hell.*

"How I handle my assignments is none of your damn business."

"You go on believin' that, darlin', if it makes you feel better."

With an expletive, Neil turned and started through the forest in the direction of the spot they'd agreed to set up

surveillance of the road leading to the compound. Cowboy followed, his senses on alert for any danger, since his
man seemed a little too upset to be paying the attention he
should.

Chapter Three

Rachel woke to intense pain at odds with the sense of safety that told her the gentle hold on her sore wrist was friendly.

Not willing to trust that sense, she focused on remembering where she was and how she'd gotten there. Memories of being tortured for information in a small dank room flooded her mind as her body tensed in irrational preparation for flight. The exhaustion in her limbs said she wasn't going anywhere.

More memories came back: the impossible rescue by a phantom from her past. Had she dreamed it? Kadin Marks wasn't really here. He couldn't be.

Letting her eyes open slowly, she squinted into the low lighting in the small tent she was in and had no trouble making out a man-shaped shadow beside her.

Kadin?

Her mind rejected what her eyes told her was true, but his big body was so close, she could smell a long-forgotten if all-too-familiar scent.

Once she'd accepted years ago that Kadin Marks was never coming back, she'd done her best to forget everything about him. The speed with which sensory memories flooded her now was proof of how difficult—and fruitless—her efforts had been.

But it was also further proof that last night had happened as she remembered it.

"Rachel's captors won't wake before midmorning. They'll feel and act like they're hungover. I found a bottle of their whiskey—seems they like a drink before bed—so they shouldn't question their condition too much. At least not immediately." The voice with a Texas twang came over a communications unit beside Kadin's head.

Rachel realized that was probably what had wakened her.

"What bad Muslims, partaking of harsh spirits," Kadin replied quietly but with sarcasm.

"It worked to our advantage, anyway. The three glasses next to the bottle indicated they'd all imbibed before bed."

"Lucky."

"Yeah. And so was Spazz, getting out of there. He decided he wanted to put in a couple of webcams and nearly got caught by the guard getting ready to go on duty."

"Webcams?" Rachel croaked. "We're going to get visual?"

Kadin's fingers on her wrist tightened and then loosened immediately when she made a soft sound of distress. "Yes, angel. We'll find out who the bigwigs are for you."

Her heart contracted with an old pain she only wished had been dead as long as her hopes. "I'm not an *angel*, Ka—Trigger. Not anymore."

She was nobody's innocent sweetheart these days. She had too much blood on her own hands for that. And he wasn't *her* Kadin. He was now called Trigger, a soldier who didn't know the woman Rachel Gannon had become any better than she knew this hardened warrior.

"You're a damn fine agent, ma'am," the Texan who'd been talking to Kadin said.

"They caught me." She'd been where she wasn't supposed to be and hadn't been able to talk her way out of it.

She still wasn't sure why. The two men who'd discovered her in the back rooms of one of Abasi Chuma's holdings had seemed to buy her nosy-tourist-in-the-wrong-place ruse—she could tell. At least, she'd thought they had.

But they'd still abducted her. After a heck of a fight, which she'd hoped they'd interpret as a desperate woman fighting out of terror for her life, they'd knocked her out.

She'd woken in that cell with three men standing over her whom she'd never seen before. They weren't Egyptian, but she hadn't realized they were Moroccan, either. Though, just because they were in the mountains of Morocco, that didn't mean her interrogators were local.

"I bet you fought like a tiger," the Texas twang opined.

Kadin grunted a sound of agreement, and she wanted to touch him, just to see if he was real.

"I did," she agreed. "I still lost."

"It happens," Kadin said.

Kadin. He was really here. Wasn't he?

The need for reassurance of her sanity overwhelmed her, and she reached out to touch the man lying beside her. But something tethered her hand, and when she tugged against it, it stung.

She must have made a sound, because his hand was there, holding hers in place. "Don't pull, Rach. You've got an IV, and Doc says it stays in until you've taken the full bag."

"Okay." She remembered the medic, a beautiful woman with Hispanic features and a slight Puerto Rican accent who had handled Rachel as efficiently as any doctor she'd ever been to.

"Yeah. We don't mess with Doc." The cowboy stretched the word *yeah* out as if it had two very long syllables.

Rachel understood that. "Back at the agency, nobody messes with Vannie, either."

"She's your tech-wizard, like our Neil, right?" The Texan chuckled. "Our boy has a hard-on for Vannie's toys, that's for sure."

"Yes." The word came out on a croak, Rachel's voice failing under the stress of trying to talk with strained vocal cords.

"Hush now, angel." Kadin's voice sounded kind of strained itself as he pressed a big finger against her lips. "No more talking."

"Or Doc's going to have all our hides," the cowboy's disembodied voice added.

"You and Spazz get some shut-eye while you can," Kadin instructed the other man.

"Roger that." And then silence.

Kadin's hand slipped down to cup Rachel's cheek. "You, too, angel."

She opened her mouth to remind him she was anything but, but his finger traced her lips in silent command not to speak anymore.

And she found herself drifting off to sleep again, feeling safer than she had any right to in a tent in the mountains of Morocco.

Kadin leaned down and kissed Rachel's soft lips. And in her sleep she responded, her mouth curling into a smile as his name whispered past her lips. He'd lost the right to call her his when he made his first kill, but damned if he wasn't going to make sure she was safe from herself as well as the world before he walked away from her again.

"I don't have a 'hard-on for Vannie's toys,' " Neil said as Wyatt climbed into their tent.

"Heard that, did you?"

Neil didn't bother to reply.

Cowboy climbed into his sleeping bag, his body thankful for the chance to rest, no matter how short the break might be. "Don't worry, baby. I won't tell anybody else about your toy fetish."

"I do not have a 'toy fetish,' and stop calling me *baby*."

"I don't know. I seem to remember you liking certain toys, sure enough."

The growl that came from the other man was pure frustration laced with a sexual need Wyatt was damn sure Neil was hoping the Texan hadn't noticed.

"Why did you request the transfer to my unit?" Neil asked after several seconds of charged silence.

"You can't make a guess?"

"No." Neil sighed. "You can get ass anywhere—you sure as hell don't need mine. It comes with too many requirements you can't fulfill"

"You sure about that?"

"I am."

"That's why you left our team?"

"I left our team because the man sleeping in my bed got himself engaged to a woman." And didn't Neil sound plenty pissed about that still?

"I made a mistake."

"So did I. I trusted you."

"You'll trust me again."

"No."

"Yeah. You're my one and only, and I ain't lettin' you go again, darlin'."

"Stop talking like a redneck."

"You like it when I let my twang show."

"Not anymore, asshole."

They'd see about that. They surely would. "Get some sleep, darlin'. We've got plenty of time to go at it. I'm not going anywhere."

And neither was his man. Not this time.

★　★　★

Kadin woke with his arm draped across Rachel's midsection, his hand curved possessively at her waist. Dawn's early light filtered through the tent, and he luxuriated in the ability to gaze at this woman once again.

Her eyelids fluttered and then opened. Dark brown eyes blinked up at him, incomprehension giving way to memory in a matter of seconds. Cowboy had been right. The woman was a damn fine agent with an agile brain.

She was also one of those rare brunettes with *blue* eyes.

"Shit. You're wearing contacts." And they had to be pretty damn dry about now.

She nodded with a minuscule movement of her head, as if doing even that hurt.

He grabbed his comm-link and barked, "Doc."

"Sí?" The woman sounded tired, but then, she'd checked on her patient every couple of hours through the night.

"Rachel's wearing colored contacts for her cover. I couldn't tell last night in the dark." He thought her light brown hair was a few shades darker, too, but hair dye wasn't about to hurt her.

Contacts left in too long could do some damage, though.

"I'll get a saline wash ready."

Kadin didn't bother to reply, figuring the medic was already busy pulling her supplies together.

"Thirsty," Rachel croaked.

Kadin grabbed his water bottle and brought it to her lips. She drank deeply, and he let her. By the time she was done, Eva had arrived.

She washed Rachel's eyes with the saline for several long seconds before instructing her to blink rapidly.

Doc repeated the process until there was a wet spot on the small pillow under Rachel's head and the smell of salt water permeated the air. "Okay, I think it should be okay to take them out."

Rachel nodded and reached up to do it.

Doc pushed her hand back down. "Let me."

Rachel did, and a second later, her pretty blue eyes, bloodshot but looking otherwise okay, were staring up at Kadin.

"That's better," he said gruffly, glad to see her unhindered pale gaze once again.

"I kind of liked the brown," she whispered with a wry smile.

He shook his head decisively. "Blue is better."

"I didn't know you had that preference, Trig," Doc said as she packed up her stuff. "No wonder you never made a move on me."

"I didn't make a move on you because I knew you could slice my balls off in my sleep, and I like the boys just where they are."

Doc laughed, but Rachel looked between them as if trying to figure something out.

He brushed his fingers through the damp hair at her temple. "What?"

Rachel just shook her head.

"Did you need the contacts for vision, or were they simply cover?" Doc asked Rachel.

"Cover," Rachel replied quietly.

"Is there something you can give her for her throat, so she can talk more easily?" Kadin asked.

"If she needed it, I could give her a steroid shot, but she's better off just letting her vocal cords heal. Try to keep her from talking, and definitely no yelling." Doc gave him the stink-eye.

Kadin frowned. "You act like I pick fights with everybody."

"Don't you?"

"Hell, no."

"Oh, really?"

"Really. You ever hear Peace yell at me?"

"Peace doesn't yell at anybody."

"Kadin still likes to poke at people?" Rachel asked the medic.

Doc frowned at Kadin. "You're saying he's always been like this?"

Rachel nodded, a world of words in her eyes.

"Good job," Doc said.

Rachel gave her a questioning look.

"Not talking. I can tell there's plenty you want to say. Don't worry, you can tell us all his secrets tomorrow or the next day."

A frown settled over Rachel's features.

"What's wrong, Rach?" Kadin asked, only to get identical glares from both women.

"You're not helping by asking her questions like that. If she's got something to say, she'll say it."

Kadin's communicator sounded a soft beep in his ear, and he answered. "Marks."

"How's your little gal gettin' along this morning, boss?" Cowboy's Texas twang was entirely too happy for O-dark-thirty after hitting their racks as late as they had.

"Our extractee is showing signs of voice strain and some impairment in movement."

"She any more reasonable about leaving?"

"Negative."

"You fixin' to give her the lay of the land?"

"It wouldn't do any good." He'd known Rachel longer than anyone else in his life except his family. She did "stubborn" better than a CEO hanging on to his stock options.

"You sure about that, son? I've heard of seasoned warriors who pissed themselves when they had to go toe-to-toe with you, Trigger."

"That's because they realize I can kill them in their sleep and leave behind no evidence. But Rachel knows she's safer with me than anyone else on earth." At least, he hoped she did.

After the way he'd disappeared from her life, maybe she didn't trust him any more than she did the man she'd been spying on. He wished it could be different between them.

He wished so many things were different, starting with the way he'd given her up all those years ago and ending with her becoming a spy instead of a nursery-school teacher, like they'd always planned.

"Is that right?"

"Yes." The growl in Kadin's tone said, *drop it.*

If Cowboy didn't get the message, they were going to tangle when the other former MARSOC soldier got back.

"We're still on for the information-gathering this morning?" Cowboy asked, showing he was smarter than he acted sometimes.

"Roger that."

"Spazz has a nest with a clear view of the road."

"And you?"

"I've got eyes on the compound."

"That's damn risky, Cowboy."

"Yeah, well, your lady love isn't going to leave here without photos of whoever shows up today. Spazz is good, but there's no guarantee he'll get a clean face shot with his toys."

"I'm assuming wherever you are, there is."

"Yep."

Well, shit. As much as he appreciated the other man's dedication, there was only one way Cowboy had a clear view that would guarantee a face shot. "Spazz know you're back inside the compound?"

"I may not have mentioned the exact plan, no."

"That's a good way to get your ass kicked." Especially if

what he was beginning to suspect about the two men was true.

"It should make for some lively discussion, yes." There wasn't a speck of worry in the anticipation lacing Cowboy's tone.

"It's your funeral, buddy. Especially if Spazz decides your actions indicate you don't trust him and his toys to get the job done."

"Well, now, it sounds like we're fixin' to have a proper tie-up for sure." If anything, the Texan sounded plenty happy at the prospect.

Crazy fool.

"As soon as you get visuals, I want you back here." He siphoned all the *friend* from his voice and injected a healthy dose of *obey-orders-or-your-ass-is-mine.*

"I might be a tad late."

It had been a hell of a lot easier to deal with when Cowboy pushed the boundaries of direct orders when Roman Chernichenko had been the one giving them.

"Why is that?" Kadin asked with fatalistic calm.

"I might have set things up to look like Rachel got away on her own. I'll want to lay a false trail for when they go a-searchin'."

"You think they're going to buy that scenario?" Not that Kadin didn't like the sound of it, because he did.

"Into every soldier's life, some luck must fall."

"Counting on luck will get you killed."

"We already got the luck. It looks like those boys are in the habit of indulging in their after-dinner drinks pretty heavily. Their superiors are going to have no trouble believing the carefully laid evidence in front of their eyes."

"And Rachel's interrogators won't remember anything from last night, so they can't deny it." Not after the drug cocktail Cowboy had dosed them with the night before.

"I almost feel sorry for them."

Screw that shit. "I don't. If it had been my assignment to administer the ketamine, those bastards wouldn't have survived it." Not after what they'd done to Rachel.

"You like her." Cowboy didn't bother to say who *her* was, but he didn't need to.

"There was a time when I used the word *love,*" he admitted. He didn't even know if he was capable of that emotion anymore.

Before he had learned to take life, Kadin would have given his for Rachel in a heartbeat. Weapons could not afford to have emotions, though, and that had been the key factor in Kadin's decision to walk away from the woman he'd promised to marry.

She'd been such an emotional, vulnerable girl, and she'd deserved better than a paid killer for a husband. Even if Uncle Sam was the one doing the paying back then.

"She could do a lot worse than you," Cowboy offered quietly.

Kadin just snorted his disbelief. "Keep me apprised on any movement."

"Roger that."

They cut the communication, and Kadin turned toward Rachel. Her eyes were open, but barely. He didn't know how much she'd overheard, not that it mattered. He'd always been lousy at keeping secrets from her. If he had been able to, they might still be together.

But she deserved better than a half life with him built on lies.

He reached out to brush her hair from her face, the exhaustion of her body caused by torture even more apparent in the natural light of morning.

She flinched so readily, the reaction seemed long-standing rather than a response to what she had just been through.

"You don't like to be touched?" he asked, making no effort to hide the shock he felt at that reality.

The Rachel he remembered was a cuddler. She liked holding hands, nuzzled right in to watch movies on the sofa, and loved casual brushes of affection.

This woman gave off the vibe that she'd prefer that even Doc keep her hands to herself.

Rachel shook her head, mouthing the word *no* in case there was any question about her answer.

"Now or ever?"

She shrugged, her expression asking if it mattered.

"It matters. If something happened to you that has significantly altered your personality already, your post-assignment debriefing is going to have to be adjusted for additional psych work."

Rachel just shrugged again. As if it didn't matter, as if the fact that there was such an event in her past was of no importance.

Looking into her eyes, he saw something he had never expected to see there. Apathy. Her eyes had burned with need when she'd told him they couldn't leave this area yet, but when it came to her own welfare, Rachel showed little interest and even less concern.

The feeling—or lack thereof—was too familiar for him not to recognize it.

And damned if he was going to let that stand.

"When your throat is better, we're going to have a full debriefing." And then some.

He was getting to the bottom of this new Rachel Gannon, and he was going to fix what was broken, damn it. After their past, he owed her.

Because a world where his Rachel had lost all passion for her own life wasn't worth living in. Seeing the same shell-shocked apathy in Rachel's beautiful blue gaze as he had in so many brown eyes in Iraq was totally unacceptable.

Why the hell had he joined the Marines in the first place if it wasn't to protect the people he loved from that very type of thing?

She stiffened and gave him a stubborn look he'd never forgotten; the pain and fear lurking in her eyes were new, though. With a decisive shake of her head, she turned on her side, away from him.

Like hell. He might have let her down in the past, but this time she was getting everything she needed from him. Even if she didn't want it.

"If you were returning Stateside right away, it could wait."

That stubborn chin jutted, and she jerked her head in another negative.

"Okay, then, you debrief with me."

"Someone else," she whispered with clear effort.

"No." He didn't bother explaining himself to Rachel. She wouldn't agree with his reasoning, but this wasn't something he was budging on.

He dug through his rations pack and found an envelope of protein-drink powder. He mixed it up with water and handed her the cup. "Drink this. You need the calories."

Rachel drank, showing her less-than-approving reaction to the taste with a wrinkling of her cute little nose.

Kadin grinned. "Yeah, it tastes like shit, but it's got all the essentials to help your body start healing."

When she was done, he handed her a bottle of sports drink to replenish her electrolytes.

She gave a significant look at the I.V.

"You need to replenish your electrolytes. And the sooner you're drinking and passing fluids, the sooner you can get that needle out of your hand."

"Good point," she mouthed without sound, and she

gulped down half the bottle before setting it aside. "Sleep," she breathed, and then she did just that.

He'd like to indulge himself and just stay in the tent to watch her, but there was too much to do to ensure her safety and that of his team.

The first thing was making a sat call to Roman Chernichenko to update the chief on the change in their objective.

Chapter Four

"You didn't tell me you two had a past when you took this assignment," Roman said in a neutral tone.

"Me demanding you send my team didn't give it away?" Kadin asked with pure sarcasm.

Like hell Chief had not realized Kadin had a personal interest in Rachel Gannon's extraction. The man was too smart to claim ignorance now.

"I may have had an inkling. When a war machine like you shows emotion, it makes a man sit up and take notice. Last time I saw emotion burning in your eyes like that, you were stupid drunk and going on about your 'Sunshine.' I didn't figure you were talking about the song."

No, not the song. In another lifetime, Kadin used to call Rachel Sunshine. "I don't remember that."

"The powers of copious amounts of alcohol."

"I don't drink."

"Not often, no, you don't."

"I had just found out that Rachel's baby sister, Linny, was dead," Kadin said, knowing that was the last time he'd been drunk.

"Reason enough to tie one on."

"Yeah."

Roman sighed. "So, what happens after you get the intel?"

"Ideally, we'd head home."

"But you don't think that's going to happen?"

"Rachel's been using an unwitting information asset in Egypt. She babbled a lot about the young woman when we first extracted her from her kidnappers. She's not going to want to leave this girl behind." Not after saying over and over again that Jamila was just like Linny.

Kadin didn't know the full story behind Linny's suicide, but he could guess what a burden of guilt Rachel would carry over it. Protecting her baby sister had been what Rachel was all about as a teenager, especially after they'd lost their parents.

"Would it do any good to order your sorry ass home?" Roman asked with exasperation but without the lethal edge that could chill his communications to below freezing.

Love did that to a man, Kadin guessed, and his boss deserved his happiness.

But Kadin wouldn't be adding to it today. "Nope."

He was here as long as Rachel needed him.

"Rachel may get her orders sooner than she expects. Washington is in a furor of political posturing right now."

"When isn't it?" And Roman might think orders were going to sway Rachel, but Kadin knew better. They weren't leaving Africa until Rachel was convinced Jamila Massri was safe.

Roman just chuckled and rang off without saying goodbye.

Rachel woke to the sound of low voices outside her tent. She recognized those of Kadin and the doctor, Eva, but she could also hear a smooth, melodic male voice that was unknown to her.

She couldn't make out all the words; they were being too quiet, but she thought she heard "Cowboy" and "picture." She noted the empty glucose bag hanging from a tent pole above her and decided it was time to take out her I.V.

She'd done it before, but it never made the doctors happy. The nurses, either, for that matter. She couldn't help the fact that an I.V. line always made her feel tethered. Once the feeling of being trapped set in, she got a little irrational.

It had always been that way. Ever since the accident that killed her parents. And the accident's aftermath.

Better to get rid of the I.V. before the inevitable panic set in.

She carefully withdrew the needle, wincing at the pain but managing to stifle her gasp. Blood ran in a thin rivulet from the place the needle had been. She looked around for something to blot it away and spied a pack of wipes. She opened it and yanked one out, vaguely remembering the medic using them to clean her up the night before.

She pressed the wipe against the tiny wound until the blood stopped, and then she looked around for something to wear. Her soiled clothes had been removed at some point, though she couldn't remember exactly when.

Things had been pretty hazy right after her rescue, Rachel's discordant sense of reality in no way helped by the presence of the one man she had resigned herself to never see again.

She still didn't understand how Kadin Marks could be her rescuer; the mere idea was worthy of a drug-induced hallucination. She'd had those once, after a mission that ended badly, with her recovering in a hospital on narcotic painkillers. She hated hospitals.

The zipper on the tent opened as Rachel sat up despite her muscles' screaming protests. She yanked the cover over her, glad she had when her visitor turned out to be Kadin, not the female medic.

He noticed her missing I.V. immediately, his eyes narrowing, his gaze focused on her hand. "What did you do?"

Right. *Ask a stupid question,* she snarked in her head.

"Took it out, *Capitan* Obvious. What does it look like?" Okay, maybe she should tone down the sarcasm, if for no other reason than because her throat, though better, was still strained.

Kadin didn't appear fazed by her detour to Snarkville. "If Doc wanted the shunt removed, she would have done it."

Rachel shrugged, unconcerned by the possibility. She had enough to worry about already. The medic's reaction to Rachel's necessary action didn't even make it onto the bottom of her A-list.

"Maybe she'll want to administer meds through the I.V. line," Kadin said in clear censure.

Well, that was hardly impetus to have left the shunt in. "No meds."

"Your body took a lot of abuse."

And her muscles wouldn't be forgiving her for a while, but that wasn't the most important factor to consider. "I don't need to be loopy."

"You can afford to get some relief. I'm watching out for you." *Now* he looked offended.

"I stopped trusting someone else to take care of me a long time ago." She was careful to keep her voice modulated, but the words refused to stay inside.

That he'd been the one to teach her that lesson remained unsaid, however.

He frowned as if he'd heard the unspoken caveat and really didn't like it. "You can go back to being the Lone Ranger when we hit Stateside. For now, I've got your back."

No long-term promise, but then, she hadn't expected one. Kadin had stopped making forever promises to her about the time she stopped believing in them. It wasn't a coincidence.

Cause and effect, more like, and it was about to bite them both in the backside. She could feel it.

Maybe because she knew that "for now" was going to be shorter than *she* wanted and *he* expected. It wasn't going to last past her refusal to leave Africa without Jamila.

Rachel was under no illusions that the Old Man— Andrew Whitney, head of TGP—would approve bringing the young Egyptian woman in. Rachel had already requested it once and gotten turned down for well-articulated reasons, but that wouldn't stop her from trying again.

She had to. Jamila deserved to be safe. Rachel hadn't been able to protect Linny, but she wasn't going to let down another vulnerable girl who should be able to count on her.

"No drugs," she repeated firmly, letting Kadin know she was taking his assurances as seriously as he'd taught her to.

Which was not at all after he broke the most important promise he'd made to her: to love her forever.

Tension filled him, but he did a darn good job of hiding it. Too bad for him that she knew his tells and had been trained to notice. The slight tightening around his sherry brown eyes and the way his breathing hitched belied the casual stance he tried to portray.

"Have the bigwigs arrived?" She still wasn't convinced Chuma and his cohorts would show at all once they realized she was gone.

"Cowboy and Spazz both worked to get pictures."

"They did?" Her breath caught in excitement, and she winced at the immediate pain tensing her muscles caused. "Face shots?"

"You're hurting."

She waved that off with one hand, demanding with a look that he answer her.

"Yes. There were four men in the jeep. Between Cowboy and Spazz, they got all four in full frontal face shots."

"Impossible."

He frowned, as if something bothered him, but only said, "My team does what they have to in order to get the job done."

Someone had to have gotten dangerously close to get those pictures, though. "Thank you."

She shifted, unable to hide another wince, and his scowl darkened.

She sighed. "The human body is not meant to withstand the convulsions accompanied by electrocution."

"Your muscles seize just as much during orgasm, but the endorphins and adrenaline protect you from residual pain."

"I can guarantee you, being hooked up to a car battery is nothing like sex." Rachel found that if she kept an even and low tone, it didn't hurt too much to talk.

It was Kadin's turn to wince. "I didn't mean it like that."

"I know." He just had a habit of spouting useless facts when he was nervous.

"What are you worried about?" she asked warily.

What wasn't he telling her?

"Spazz wired them for sound."

"So?" That was a good thing, right?

"Jamila Massri's name came up, but without enough info to know if she's in any trouble."

Her entire body tensed, and she didn't waste energy on hiding the pain that caused her. "What, exactly, was said?"

"One of the men asked, 'What about Jamila?' Your target replied that she was nothing to worry about."

Cold chills went down Rachel's spine. Abasi Chuma

was not a man to dismiss a potential threat to himself. He had to have a plan for Jamila that would eliminate any threat she might pose. The least disturbing of which, but by no means without danger to Jamila, was moving the wedding date forward.

The fact that the young woman's name had come up at all in this context could imply that she was now under suspicion, whether because of Rachel or because of something else did not matter.

"Stop," Kadin ordered. "I know what you're thinking, and that's why I didn't want to tell you about this. You don't know what Chuma was talking about. He's engaged to the woman. It would be strange if her name *didn't* come up."

"But—"

Kadin pressed one callused fingertip against her lips. "*But* nothing. Stop assuming worst-case scenarios."

That was easy for Kadin to say, but she'd bet he never took his own advice in that regard. Assuming "worst case" was something they both had to do in their jobs.

No matter what, Rachel would not allow Jamila Massri to become collateral damage.

Surging to her knees, Rachel ignored the pain spiking through her muscles at the movement, though she could do nothing about the way her body swayed. "I need to get to her."

"Calm down. You're not going anywhere right this second."

She glared. *That's what you think.*

Instead of looking worried, he chuckled, the sound warm and too familiar for comfort.

"What's so funny?" she asked with enough censure to put some strain on her vocal cords.

"Well, you're not exactly dressed for a hike down the

mountain." His gaze had warmed considerably, and there was a message there she did not want to see.

But his words registered. "I need clothes."

"You *need* to check in with your boss."

Kadin probably expected her to insist on getting dressed before calling Andrew Whitney, but she wasn't the naïve girl he'd grown tired of all those years ago.

She put her hand out. "Give me your satellite phone."

His eyes flared with surprise as she'd expected, but it didn't show in his tone. "No can do. It will be safer to make the call once we're in Marrakech."

"I need Whit's approval to bring Jamila in." She kept her voice even with effort; she had to settle for letting her urgency show in her expression.

"Do you think he'll give it to you?"

"He'll have to."

"Maybe. Maybe not." His unconcerned words were belied by the intensity of his gaze.

"She's just like Linny, Kadin. So innocent, ready to wed a sadist, and clueless."

He frowned, his expression showing he had questions about Linny, but all he asked was, "Isn't it an arranged marriage?"

"It is, but she seems to want it." Clearly the dutiful Jamila had no idea about the real nature of the man her father had told her to marry.

"Maybe she's into it."

"She's not!" Jamila was young. Innocent. And totally ignorant of her fiancé's sadistic bent. "Her father must know, though. He has to. He and Chuma are friends as well as partners in business."

Rachel had long suspected Dr. Massri of being one of the key players in Abasi Chuma's organization, but she hadn't been able to turn up anything conclusive linking him to Chuma's illegal dealings. She told Kadin her suspicions.

"You insisted on staying here just to confirm something you already knew?" Kadin didn't sound remotely happy about such a possibility.

"No." Her throat, which had been doing better since waking, grew tight. "Not if I'm lucky."

"You were hoping the other honcho would show so you would have all the names," Kadin guessed, proving he still knew the way her mind worked . . . or that he would make a darn good spy himself. Maybe both.

But she liked the idea of his being a good spy better than his still knowing her that well. It would mean that too much of the innocent girl she'd once been still existed inside her.

She nodded her agreement to his supposition, regardless of how he'd come to make it.

Kadin didn't lecture her on the foolhardy nature of her plan. He just shook his head with a wealth of meaning. "Cowboy will catch up to us on the hike to our transport. You can look at his pictures there. See if you recognize any or all of the men."

Again she nodded, figuring she'd pushed her vocal cords far enough.

Kadin handed her another one of those foul energy drinks. "Your breakfast."

"I like your French toast better," she said with a grimace as she took the drink.

Kadin chuckled. "I do, too. Now stop talking. You need to drink some water after that." He indicated the drink. "Especially after taking out the I.V."

She ignored the pointed remark and forced herself to down the energy drink.

It tasted just as awful as the one the night before, but it didn't upset her stomach.

Considering the amount of stress-induced acid roiling in there, that was saying something.

She didn't argue when he traded her now-empty cup for a water bottle, but she imbibed in sips, not gulps. Both beverages had soothed her throat.

A slight relaxing in the tension around Kadin's eyes indicated he approved. She didn't like the pleased feeling that accompanied that realization.

Her brows furrowing, she asked the question that had been bothering her since she'd come to accept that the Kadin Marks who had arrived in her temporary prison was not an apparition created by her fever-ridden mind.

"How?"

"The Atrati get called in by The Goddard Project almost as often as the CIA," he answered, doing her the courtesy of not pretending he didn't understand the question.

"Not the Marines?" she asked, surprised he'd left behind his military career.

It was the dream he'd decided to keep when he'd dumped her and their dreams of a family and a future together.

"The Atrati recruited me. They . . . *we* do things for Uncle Sam when a sanctioned military force would cause problems. I'm still a weapon, but in the Atrati, I'm more than the finger that pulls the trigger."

There was something in there, something beyond what he had said, but her thoughts were still too disjointed for her to get it. Maybe later.

"I get the Atrati, but why *you*?"

"I requested the assignment for my team when I heard who the extraction was." He started packing up things from around the small tent. "I didn't know you'd transferred to TGP."

"You knew I was DEA?" He'd known more about her than she'd known about him and the changes in his life.

But then, since Linny's death, Rachel had made a concentrated effort to forget Kadin Marks even existed. And,
mostly, it had worked.

"I kept track of you."

Why? He'd made it clear she didn't matter to him anymore.

"Never called." Or wrote. Or even e-mailed. Except for
one sympathy card. She'd believed absolutely that he'd
walked away that devastating summer day and never
looked back.

For all intents and purposes, that's exactly what had happened. Whatever vagary of thought had prompted him to
keep up with her career hardly mattered. Not after Linny.

"I wasn't a part of your life anymore."

"No." By his choice.

"I found out about Linny after the fact. I'm sorry."

"Your card said." Delivered in an envelope without a
return address.

Stupidly, she'd hoped it meant Kadin would contact her
again. She'd believed that maybe out of the horrible
tragedy of Linny's death at least that much good would
come.

Rachel had felt guilty for that hope. When she discovered it was a false one, she'd convinced herself that she deserved the pain that came later.

"What happened?" Kadin asked.

Rachel shook her head, not up to explanations.

"Is that when you left the DEA?"

That much, at least, she could answer. "Yes."

"You must have impressed Whit. He runs a pretty select crew."

She shrugged, the slide of the cover against her bare
breasts reminding her that she was still naked. The blanket
slipped down to reveal the upper curves of her chest, and
she tugged it higher, but Kadin had already noticed. Of

course he had. The suddenly heated look in his eyes said he liked the view, too. And, despite everything, desire pooled deep in her belly.

He'd always had that effect on her. Every other emotion seemed to have died inside her with Linny's suicide, but not this one. Not desire.

It was like the cockroach of feelings, and right now all she wanted was a guaranteed exterminator.

He looked away first, cursing under his breath. "I'll get you some clothes."

"Thank you."

His shoulders jerked in what could have been a shrug as he backed out of the tent. The sound of him barking an order for something to dress her in was followed by Eva coming into the tent, a bundle of khaki cloth in her hand. It turned out to be scrubs, and Rachel was grateful.

The loose-fitting clothes didn't rub any abrasions or make her feel constricted, but they did make her feel safely covered, regardless of the fact they did not come with underclothes.

Rachel didn't mind. Her breasts weren't so large that she couldn't comfortably go without a bra. And the very idea of trying to get one on with her sore muscles made her cringe inwardly. Same for the thought of having to pull underwear over her hips.

Just getting the scrubs on had been hard enough, leaving her panting, with beads of sweat on her forehead and trickling down the center of her back. It would have been easier if she'd accepted Eva's offer of help, but Rachel wasn't so good at letting others do anything for her these days.

Another legacy of her many losses.

The less she relied on others, the less chance she would be hurt again. She always had a personal exit strategy, one that didn't rely on the cooperation or help of anyone else.

Her mind grappled now with one for her and Jamila Massri, in case the Old Man remained firm on not bringing the young Egyptian woman in.

Kadin's thoughts were in a turmoil as he helped Peace pack the camp with efficient movements.

How could he have gotten turned on by Rachel's bare shoulders and that peek at the upper swell of her breasts when her face still bore the marks of someone hitting her and her wrists were bandaged because of the deep abrasions there? What kind of man was he?

The kind he'd always known he would be if he didn't get out of Rachel's life completely. One who wanted her and everything she represented to him almost more than his honor. His honor *almost* was his personal salvation. He couldn't afford to give it up now.

But damn . . . it was close.

"Your *wahine* okay to hike?" Peace asked, his Hawaiian accent thicker when he didn't get enough sleep.

"She'll insist on it." Even if Rachel wasn't up to hiking on her own. "I'll let her try."

"You make allowances for dis one."

"She deserves them."

"After what she been through? I think you are right, but it's more than that, brah."

On this mission Kadin had found himself being more emotionally honest with his team than ever before, but he owed it to them. He was making choices with that stone in his chest he called a heart, and they had a right to know it.

Besides, he wasn't the only soldier recruited into the Atrati with a past full of regret. "She was my one and only."

"Was?"

"When we were kids." And innocent.

Before the Marines made him a weapon, a man who had lost his humanity.

"*One and only,* that don't expire, brudder."

"It does when one of you changes into something else."

"Something like a MARSOC assassin?" Peace asked knowingly.

"Yeah. Something like that."

"You aren't that guy no more, brah."

"You call me *Trigger,* just like everyone else does."

"So you good with a sniper rifle. You a captain in the Atrati now. We specialize in protection and extraction."

"But we still wage war, still kill." He'd killed as a member of the Atrati, too—maybe not as often as a Marine, but Kadin was still a weapon.

"Warriors have been necessary since the beginning of time." Peace shook his head, as if he was thinking that Kadin had a stupid bone. "There is no shame in being a soldier."

"No, there isn't." But Rachel deserved better than him, better than a man who could and would kill on an order without ever letting his enemy look him in the eye.

"We're damn fine men, Kadin," Peace said without a trace of his usual Hawaiian laid-back manner. "Don't you doubt it."

Kadin nodded, because on one level, he completely agreed with Peace. The men he most admired were all soldiers, or former soldiers.

That didn't change what he wanted for Rachel, what she seemed to have spent the last ten years trying to make sure she would not get. A decent, *normal* guy. Kadin had been knocked straight onto his ass when he found out that she'd gone to work for the DEA out of university. And not in the administrative sectors, either, but as an agent.

He didn't know why she'd given up her dreams of

teaching in a nursery school until she could save up the money to open her own. Rachel loved kids, but she sure wasn't going to work with them as a government agent.

And now she was TGP, taking ultra dangerous assignments out of country.

Losing Linny could have done that; Rachel didn't have anyone Stateside to keep her there anymore.

But what had changed his sweet and gentle lover into a woman who carried a gun and could withstand the kind of torture she had without breaking?

Chapter Five

Feeling so pissed that red hazed his vision, Neil took lateral guard position.

When Wyatt caught up with them, Neil was going to give the damn Texan a verbal smackdown that would leave his ears ringing.

What the *hell* did the man think he was doing, going all *cowboy* on them? What did Wyatt think? He was running his own mini-op, or something?

Shoving his anger down with the rest of the emotions he'd been stuffing for the past year, Neil erased all evidence of the team's movement through the forest.

The TGP agent was leaving the most markers. The stubborn woman was barely able to stand without assistance, but she'd insisted on walking on her own.

Neil expected that to last another thirty minutes—an hour, tops—and then Kadin's patience was going to run out like the minutes on a burner phone.

Moving at their current pace, it would be near dusk before they reached their transport. That would leave them driving down most of the mountain in the dark.

No way would the captain let them use headlights until they were in a populated-enough area that doing so wouldn't give away their position or otherwise make them memorable.

It was a damn good thing Peace had eyes like a mountain cat's.

It was a whole forty minutes later when Rachel stumbled for the third time in as many minutes, and Trigger raised his hand to indicate they needed to stop. Because of their slow progress, Neil caught up to them within seconds rather than the minutes it should have taken him.

The female government agent stood swaying slightly and blinking, as if she didn't really comprehend what was going on.

The captain's expression was hard enough to crack concrete. "Peace, help Rachel onto my back."

That brought the woman's head up, her eyes narrowing despite the exhaustion pulling at her features. "That's not necessary."

Her voice was barely discernible, and Trigger's expression tightened. "The hell it's not. You're done walking."

She shook her head but winced when the movement clearly caused her pain.

Kadin made an animalistic sound that Neil understood only too well. Wyatt brought the same sound from his lips often enough.

The stubborn bastard.

"You need to ride," Eva said, her tone brooking no argument.

"No."

"If you'd rather Peace carried you . . ." Eva let her voice trail off.

Rachel took an infinitesimal step nearer Trigger, though she seemed wholly unaware of doing so. "I can walk."

"We need to pick up our pace, angel, and we can't do that with you walking on your own," he claimed.

"He's right," Neil said as he tossed a broken twig she'd stepped on into the brush. "I'll be able to move faster clearing our six if you're not leaving behind so much trail, too."

Trigger glared at Neil as if he'd insulted the agent's mother rather than pointing out the obvious.

Rachel frowned. "I'm sorry."

"Nothing to apologize for. You're trained as a spy, not in covert wilderness ops."

She gave a barely-there nod, but Kadin was still scowling.

Neil shook his head. "Pick her up already, Trigger. We haven't got all day."

Especially if they wanted any hope of traveling down the narrow mountain road with some daylight.

Rachel sighed, her eyes bloodshot from not enough sleep and what she'd been through. "Fine. I'll piggyback on Kadin."

Like anyone thought she'd choose to ride with someone else.

She moved around the big former Marine, even more obviously unsteady on her feet than when they'd been walking.

Trigger made another sound of frustration and looked like he wanted to just pick her up, but the stubborn set to the woman's features seemed to make him hesitate.

Eva ended up helping Rachel settle into a piggyback position on Kadin; Peace was too damn smart to lay a hand on his captain's woman. Even to help.

They started off again, their pace increasing significantly. Neil wasn't worried about Trigger keeping it up with the woman on his back, either. The captain had slogged through way worse conditions than this for a hell of a lot longer than they had to hike now.

Neil let the others get far enough ahead that he could monitor their trail without fear of missing something. If he was lagging just a little to give Wyatt a chance to catch up, he wasn't going to admit it to anyone.

Not even himself.

He didn't like how long it was taking the other man to reconnect with the team, but Neil didn't let himself get too worried. Wyatt had checked in with a steady, evenly spaced set of clicks over their comm-units.

An hour later, Neil sensed eyes on him. He slowly moved to better cover as he scanned the area without moving his head.

There, movement in his left periphery.

Moving around a large tree, Neil stopped on the other side, giving his pursuer a chance to catch up with him.

His hand was raised to deliver a debilitating blow when he recognized Wyatt's gray eyes in his camo-marked face. Neil nearly let the punch fly, anyway, but held back and swore instead. "What the hell? Why didn't you comm in your location when you got close enough to make visual contact?"

Wyatt smiled, his eyes filled with amusement. "Wanted to surprise you, sugar."

"I nearly surprised you with a chop to your windpipe."

"Nah, you're too good to mistake a teammate for the enemy."

"Asshole."

"There you go, using endearments again."

For some reason Wyatt's amusement set flame to the tinder of Neil's temper, and he took the swing he'd stopped himself from earlier.

His ex-lover was good. The blow didn't connect. He didn't lose his look of amusement, either.

And that just pissed Neil off even more. He swept his foot out and knocked the other man off his feet.

Wyatt managed to tangle their feet and bring Neil down

with him. Neil landed on top of the Texan, before Wyatt rolled and reversed their positions.

"Now, this has possibilities. Too bad we've got to get off this mountain."

"We're on assignment," Neil growled, ignoring the hard-on pressing against his thigh and the one trying to crawl out of his own pants. "Get the hell off me."

"You feel good." Wyatt rocked his pelvis against Neil, leaving no doubt just how good.

Neil bit back a moan and glared up at the other man. "Wyatt, damn it . . ."

"Say it again."

"What?" But he knew what the other man wanted to hear, and no way was he giving in.

"My name."

"Cowboy, get your lazy ass off me. I'm not your bed-roll."

"Ah, sugar . . . I'd give a lot to be in a bedroll with you right now."

"Stop it." Neil shoved the other man, hard, but the oversized idiot wasn't going anywhere.

Wyatt leaned down and touched noses with Neil. "I want to kiss you."

"No." But damned if his voice didn't sound almost breathless.

"You're right. Now isn't the time." Cowboy got up, putting a hand out to Neil.

He slapped it away and jumped to his feet. "We need to clean up."

"There was a time you said that in entirely different cir-cumstances."

"That time is over." Neil started working on removing evidence of their little skirmish.

"No. It's not."

That had him spinning to face his cowboy. "Yes, it is. It ended when you got engaged to a woman."

"I'm not engaged anymore."

"You're not out of the closet, either."

"I'm a damn sight closer to the door."

The pain that went through Neil at those words staggered him. He hid his reaction by getting back to the task at hand.

"I'm not giving up on us, sugar."

"You already did." Wyatt had chosen his family's acceptance over Neil, and Neil wasn't stupid enough to ever forget that.

He couldn't even really blame the other man. Wyatt had always been close to his dad and brothers; the whole Texan way was ingrained in him to the bone. And that way had kiboshed any idea that it was okay to be gay.

Hell, according to Wyatt's daddy, it wasn't okay to be single past your twenty-fifth birthday. Hence the fiancée who had ended Wyatt and Neil's relationship.

But understanding and acceptance were two different things.

Neil knew what it meant to pay the cost of being true to himself, and he would have given up anything, *except* his self-respect, to be with Wyatt.

Despite all the times she'd said a mother's love was unconditional while Neil was growing up, his mother hadn't spoken to him in ten years. Not since he came out to her and his father as a teenager. She'd told him then that she'd never accept what she considered his "deviant lifestyle."

She never had, and she'd never accepted him again, either.

His dad, on the other hand, had taken the news hard at first but ultimately decided that God didn't make mistakes and no way was he cutting loose his son for being true to himself. Neil knew he was lucky.

His dad just wanted to know when Neil was going to settle down and stop traipsing around the world trying to get himself killed.

Wyatt helped Neil clear the area of track before they started moving again. ❝I made a mistake.❞

Neil just shrugged. Some mistake. It had been hard enough having Wyatt hide their relationship from others like an ugly, dirty secret he was ashamed of. It had destroyed Neil to realize that Wyatt had been hiding things from *him,* too.

Like his casual dates with the woman from Texas he'd ended up engaged to.

Wyatt walked silently beside him for several minutes before saying, "I knew it was a mistake when I did it, but I was convinced the only way to have the future I wanted was to do what Daddy was pushing for."

Neil didn't bother to reply. They'd been over this before, albeit a hell of a lot more loudly, two years ago. That pain and anger were old enemies Neil wasn't going to tangle with today.

Instead he focused on why the man had him so infuriated. "What the hell were you doing, going off orders back at the enemy compound?"

Wyatt made a sound of frustration. "We're talking about *us.*"

"No," Neil said very carefully, very succinctly. "We are not."

"You're more stubborn than a wild bull coming into pasture."

Neil just gave Wyatt a sidelong glance and repeated his question, this time with fewer words and a lot more meaning.

Wyatt spied a mark of the others passing and cleared it. "Our targets weren't going to believe my little setup if they didn't have a trail to follow out of there."

"That's another thing: who told you to set the scene in the holding cell?" Neil demanded.

Wyatt countered, "Who told you to plant extra surveillance equipment?"

"It wasn't anything big."

"Neither was staging a false scene. A little fraying where Kadin cut the ties holding her, giving her chair a sharp edge where the blood from her wrists had stained it already. It wasn't exactly my first rodeo, yeah?"

"And what if they'd caught you laying the false trail?"

"I'm too good to get caught."

"So you think."

"So I know."

"What happens when they get to the end of the trail?"

"They keep looking. I ended it at a little stream."

"How'd you know it was there?"

"I studied the satellite images on the way over in the plane."

"You're smarter than you look," Neil acknowledged grudgingly. "In some things, anyway. But it was still a hell of a risk."

"It's my job," Wyatt said way too complacently.

"Your job was to drug the guards so Rachel's rescue wasn't discovered immediately."

"And yours was to plant listening devices, not to lay those extra cams."

"Would you stop harping on that?"

"Only if you do." Wyatt's gray eyes challenged him.

"You took an unnecessary risk—that's all I'm saying."

"So did you." Wyatt's expression and tone held none of the amusement usually lurking there. "You take too many of them."

"Like you said, it's my job."

"You've got a reputation in the Atrati."

"When it comes down to it, a lot of us do."

"Not like yours."

"Old soldiers gossip worse than old women." Neil knew his reputation, and he wasn't interested in talking about it.

Even among the select members of the Atrati, he was known as fearless, or just plain crazy.

"Yeah, well, you give them plenty to talk about. In the past year, you've taken too damn many risks."

"I'm still alive, aren't I?"

"Luck."

"Skill."

Wyatt grabbed his arm, stopping Neil's progress forward. "Damn it, Neil, you've got to stop living like you don't care if you die."

The concern in Wyatt's gaze touched something inside Neil he didn't want touched. Not anymore. Not by this man.

"How I live is not something you need to worry about." He yanked out of Wyatt's grasp and started moving again, his focus on the forest floor.

If losing Wyatt had hurt enough that there had been a few assignments when Neil hadn't cared whether he came home or not, that was no one's damn business but his own.

"That's where you're wrong, honey. How you live, that you live at all, is something I care about more than you want to know right now." Sincerity rang in the other man's tone.

Neil had believed that sincerity once and had ended up with a broken heart. He'd never known pain worse than he'd felt when he'd learned that the man he loved was engaged to be married. The betrayal had destroyed Neil's ability to trust—and hope.

He wasn't going to be fooled again. "Bullshit."

Wyatt had made his choices, and they'd pierced Neil's heart with the power of armor-penetrating bullets.

Kadin felt it through his whole body when Rachel relaxed enough to let her head fall against his shoulder. Her hold on his jacket didn't loosen, but everything else did, her legs dangling limply over his forearms.

It felt just like the trust he'd vowed that Rachel still had in him.

And that about took his legs out from under him.

He didn't deserve that trust, but he'd die himself and take out the enemy on the way before he betrayed it again.

Having her body pressed against his back recalled memories he couldn't afford to dwell on, but even in her current state, Rachel got to him like no other woman ever had or ever would.

And as much as he hated the fact that she was so used up that she needed to be carried, he let himself revel in the stolen closeness of holding her. If she'd taken Eva up on the idea of piggybacking on Peace instead of him, he figured somebody would have ended up with a black eye.

Or worse.

Knowing that didn't make him proud, but he had never been entirely rational where Rachel was concerned.

Faster than he expected and without incident, they made it to their hidden Land Rover. Rachel's eyes barely fluttered as Kadin set her carefully on the backseat.

Eva pushed him aside to assess her patient and nodded to herself as if satisfied. "She's looking better despite the hike."

Rachel hadn't technically hiked all that far, but Kadin didn't bother saying so. Doc was happy with the other woman's progress, and that was all that mattered.

They'd kept Rachel hydrated with sports drinks and his favorite protein powder. It tasted like crap mixed with water but had the right balance of nutrients and vitamins. He'd tested it plenty of times in the field himself.

"Doc, you and I will sit in the back with her. Spazz, you take point with Peace. And, Cowboy, I want you in the cargo deck, keeping an eye on our six."

After stowing their gear in the back, leaving just enough room for Cowboy and his rifle with a scope, the rest of them took their positions, and Peace headed the Land Rover down the mountain.

They were coming into a more populated area when Peace asked, "The airport or the safe house, boss?"

"Safe house. Rachel's not going to leave Africa without Jamila Massri."

The tension in the truck ratcheted up.

"She needs proper medical treatment," Eva said mildly, though her expression belied any sense of relaxation her voice might have implied.

"Rachel's priorities are the job and that girl."

"And what are your priorities?" Spazz asked from the front without taking his eyes off the rapidly darkening landscape beyond the windshield.

Cowboy shifted just slightly in his position behind Kadin, but his rifle remained at the ready. "Our orders were to bring her out."

"I'm not leaving without her, and she's not leaving without the Egyptian woman."

No one said anything to that. And Kadin wasn't sure what the silence meant.

If Roman had made that announcement, there would have been no doubt in his mind that they all would have followed the other man wherever he led. Chief had inspired that kind of loyalty.

Kadin, on the other hand, wasn't sure where, exactly, he stood with his team. They'd been together in the same

Atrati squad for two years, some of them longer than that, but he'd only been their captain for the past six months.

Before that, he'd just been one of them, a damn fine weapon and teammate but not their leader.

Part of him breathed out a sigh of relief when Peace passed the turnoff to the airport and headed toward the safe house.

Cowboy silently camouflaged his weapon, keeping it lowered but still at the ready while the other team members peeled off outer layers of clothing. Grabbing scarves and other items that made them look more like tourists than an extraction team, they prepared for driving through the streets of Marrakech.

All the while, Rachel dozed beside him, her breathing soft and regular.

In the midst of an op he could not afford to screw up, he was assailed by memories of a time when that sound had been what drew him into his own sleep.

Sleep not haunted by the eyes of the dead. From the time before killing became his calling card.

Cowboy was a damned fine marksman, but Trigger was better. He could shoot anything from a Glock to a grenade launcher with deadly accuracy.

What he couldn't do was jettison memories that were more hindrance than help and always had been.

Their Land Rover didn't arouse any interest that he could see on the crowded streets of the city bathed in the artificial light of night.

Peace pulled the truck into the alleyway behind the safe house. Spazz got out and did quick recon before signaling the rest of them that it was safe to exit the vehicle.

Rachel woke, blinking, her breath speeding up as she acclimated herself to her new surroundings. Kadin was impressed by how silent she was as she did it. Not so much as a gasp passed her lips.

"Where are we?" she finally asked in that ruined voice that made him want to kiss her and make it all better.

But he was a warrior, not a miracle worker, and even the most mind-blowing kiss wasn't going to erase Rachel's memories or her pain as she healed.

"Safe house."

She relaxed a tiny bit, though no one else would have noticed it. Kadin, tuned in to the slightest nuance with this woman, was glad. He knew she had been worried he was still going to try to extract her from Morocco without Jamila Massri.

She let him help her into the house and voiced no protest when he swung her into his arms to carry her up the narrow stairs to the second floor.

Like most houses in Marrakech, this one was built on multiple levels with an expansive living area on the roof. The interior rooms were narrow and long, divided by thick walls and even narrower hallways.

The Abduls, the couple who cared for the house and those who used it, showed no surprise at their arrival. The man, a Moroccan of indeterminate years somewhere between his forties and sixties, explained that he'd been informed to expect them.

Roman.

Kadin was grateful the other man hadn't left orders to evacuate. Chief might not like that Kadin had decided to stay in Marrakech, but Roman Chernichenko wasn't the type of man to undermine his new captain's orders.

And it was a damn good thing, because whatever Roman had said, Kadin wasn't leaving Africa without Rachel, and Rachel wasn't going anywhere without the young woman, Jamila.

There were empty bedrooms on the second floor. Kadin didn't even bother doing mental calculations before carrying Rachel into one of them. His team could sort themselves out, but he was staying with the woman he'd come to Morocco to rescue.

Looking over his shoulder to Cowboy, Kadin asked, "Can you get my pack?"

"Sure thing, Trig." Cowboy dumped a pack inside the door with a smirk.

The other man must have grabbed it with his own when they got out of the Land Rover. Kadin wasn't even surprised. They were Atrati, after all. *Semper paratus, semper fatalis. Always ready, always deadly.*

Kadin nodded his thanks and carried Rachel to the bed. Eva was right behind them.

The doc examined a barely-awake Rachel, taking her blood pressure before changing the bandages over the abrasions on her wrists. "These look better. She probably won't need the gauze after tomorrow."

"Good."

"Without proper medical facilities, I can't run the tests I'd like, but it looks like she's doing fine." Eva turned to face Kadin. "She needs sleep more than anything else right now."

"She'll get it."

"You could use some, too." Eva's voice held censure.

Kadin just shrugged.

"Don't have to watch over me," Rachel slurred from the bed.

He turned to face her, wanting to rage at the vulnerability in her pale eyes. "It's a pleasure, angel."

She shook her head, wincing in pain from the movement.

Eva's eyes narrowed slightly. "Your muscles sore?"

"Yes."

"That's to be expected." Eva gave Kadin a measured look. "A massage would help, though."

Chapter Six

"You think I should give her a massage?" Kadin asked, glad that in his tone, at least, surprise overrode the other emotions cascading through him.

"It will help her muscles recover from the shock-induced contractions."

Kadin knew that his field medic was right, but his sudden fear made him want to continue protesting, anyway. He couldn't even touch Rachel without feeling things he'd spent the best part of a decade avoiding.

Oh, he hadn't been celibate or anything, but neither had he touched another person with tenderness and care in all that time. Sex was just that. Sex. Screwing. Stress release.

Emotion hadn't entered into him since the last time he'd been with Rachel. He didn't show or receive affection from anyone but his family, and he'd kept them at a distance about the same number of years.

His mom never gave up, but Trigger did his best to be on assignment for all the major holidays. The people he loved, whom he'd fought his entire adult life to protect, deserved something better than to say grace over dinner with a killer.

This wasn't a family dinner, though; this was something a hell of a lot harder.

Touching the one woman who had ever laid claim to his heart was something he knew he should not do.

"If you'd rather, I can do it." Eva cocked her head, studying him, her eyes questioning.

She was a woman. She was a doctor. And still Kadin found himself growling out his refusal. "I'll do it."

Eva didn't seem surprised as she nodded her agreement and then stood up and moved toward the door. "I'll get the caretaker's wife to send up some soup. Try to get her to eat."

He'd dismissed the medic from his mind before the door shut on her retreat.

A sound of protest from the bed had Kadin fixing his attention back on the scrubs-clad woman lying so still.

Her brown hair was messy, her blue eyes were bloodshot, there were bruises on her cheeks, and the scrubs did one hell of a job hiding any feminine attributes, but Rachel was still the most beautiful woman he'd ever seen.

Her bottom lip protruded in a purely unconscious but adorable expression. "Not hungry."

"Maybe you'll feel more like eating after the massage."

"No massage," she slurred. Even in exhaustion, there was a stubborn tilt to her chin.

Kadin shook his head, finding himself smiling despite the situation, and shifted until the bed brushed his calves.

Built into the wall with decorative scrollwork around the base, it was as narrow as a double but longer and a lot closer to the floor than his bed at home.

He lowered himself to the futonlike mattress and gave Rachel his best *do-what-the-hell-I-say-or-else* look.

She just glared back, her mouth moving into a mulish line.

He brushed her hair away from her forehead, noticing she didn't flinch this time. "You want to stay in Morocco?"

"For now." Her eyes narrowed, as if she was trying to figure out where this was going.

He knew damn well what she was thinking, and it wasn't that she'd go back to the States sometime soon, either. The woman intended to go wherever Jamila Massri was, and Kadin's best guess was, that would mean a return to Egypt for Rachel.

"You want to stay, you let us do what we can to help you heal. That means you eat the soup when it comes up, and you sleep tonight without trying to sneak out of bed to find a computer to do some research."

The way Rachel's blue eyes flared, he knew he'd hit a nerve with that one.

"And you let me give you a massage."

"Eva can do the massage. She's the doc."

"And I know your body better than she ever will."

Rachel's sharp intake of breath put a sharp pain into his own chest, but she didn't argue the point. She just looked at him as if he'd betrayed her all over again.

He looked back, letting his own "stubborn" show. He didn't know why this was so important to him. He had no claim on the woman lying on the bed, but that didn't stop him from needing to do this for her.

"Not fair, Kadin."

He nodded, making no effort to disagree. "I can be a real bastard."

Her blue eyes widened and then narrowed. "No. The men who did this to me? They're the bastards. You're just a pain in my backside."

"Good to know." That inexplicable urge to smile was back.

"Yeah, well . . ." Her voice trailed off.

He leaned over her, his hands fisted on either side of her hips, the heat from her body calling to him. He did his best to ignore the message. "The massage will be easier and more effective with skin contact, but if you want to leave your scrubs on, I'll work around them."

There. Look at him, being all reasonable and shit.

That gut-wrenching vulnerability washed through her eyes again. "I . . ."

"It's okay, Rach. Whatever you want."

She took a deep breath and looked at some point over his shoulder, the wheels turning in her head so loud, he could hear them. "No scrubs," she finally whispered.

He was so shocked by her decision, it didn't register at first. But when it did, his body had a wholly unacceptable reaction. He'd thump himself, but he wasn't about to draw her attention to his condition.

"Okay, then. Will you let me help you?"

An infinitesimal nod was his only answer.

Kadin pulled a thin blanket from where it was folded at the foot of the bed. "Let's put this over you, all right?"

She didn't answer, but neither did she push the covering away as he gently laid it over her.

He reached under it and took hold of the elastic waistband on the scrubs. "Can you lift your hips?"

Rachel didn't bother to answer Kadin with words but tilted her pelvis so he could slide the loose-fitting pants down her thighs.

Her throat was still sore, but that wasn't why.

Acknowledging any of this verbally was beyond her. She'd fought him on doing the massage, but all the while she'd known she wanted *his* hands on her and no one else's.

He made her feel safe like no one else could do right now or maybe ever again.

When he'd asked if she wanted skin contact for the massage, she'd realized that she didn't just want it, she *needed* it. The connection of one human being to another.

The feel of his big, strong hands giving comfort when her body had known so much pain.

Deep inside, where her soul resided, she knew that if she didn't let someone touch her now, she'd never let *anyone* touch her again. And since the thought of anyone besides Kadin touching her made Rachel's stomach cramp in preparation for heaving, Kadin Marks was it. No matter what she'd said to the contrary.

Rachel had known he wouldn't let the doctor do the massage, just as he'd known that ultimately Rachel would cave on his doing it.

Ten years of separation didn't change some things. No amount of time could.

Like the fact that, at his core, Kadin was a decent man who would protect her with his life. Equally certain was the fact that while she might have made mistakes in the past, Rachel wasn't a woman who could walk away from Jamila Massri and the train wreck waiting to happen to her life.

Kadin was careful as he removed her top, both to protect her modesty and not strain her muscles in any way. He'd always been capable of a gentleness at odds with his hulking muscles and often-acerbic nature.

That care took about five times as long as it did when she undressed herself, but she wasn't complaining. He'd managed to get both bottoms and top off with minimal discomfort to her.

Even after the muscle relaxers and anti-inflammatories Eva had given Rachel, her entire body ached.

The slightest movement sent twinges of pain zinging along her nerve endings. Yet even with the discomfort, her body responded subtly to Kadin's nearness and his touch.

Rachel's nipples tightened in peaks that pressed against

the light blanket he'd laid over her, her body craving a touch that had little to do with healing massage. It was insane.

Yet he had always drawn forth this intrinsic, nearly atavistic sexual reaction from her. When they'd been young and in love and she'd trusted him with more than her life, with the deepest recesses of her heart, too, she'd believed that kind of sexual desire normal. It was all she'd known.

He was her first. And the only man she'd given more than her body.

But she'd learned the truth over time. Rachel had never experienced that natural sensuality with another man, not even anything remotely similar.

Regardless, if it weren't happening again right now, Rachel would have thought this response of her body impossible. She had believed that such a reaction was beyond her now.

It had been so long since she'd wanted someone, since before Linny's death, and never the way Rachel used to want Kadin. After what she'd been through, the very last thing she should feel now was the stirring of desire.

And yet there was an emptiness in her core that she knew instinctively only he could fill.

She shook her head in denial. This could not be happening.

Kadin misunderstood and stopped, his hands on her stilling in their initial ministrations to her feet. "Do you want me to get Eva?"

"No."

"You shook your head."

"Ignore me."

"That's never going to happen, angel."

And she knew he meant it. He would push to get his own way, but ultimately, if she said no, he'd respect that.

"You're a different kind of man, Kadin."

It was his turn to shake his head. "You don't know what I am."

"I bet I can guess." And though she would have been clueless ten years ago as to what that look in his eyes meant, she wasn't anymore.

She'd spent enough time around hardened agents, the ones who had been forced to kill in the line of duty, to know what that particular expression meant.

Kadin had gotten the name *Trigger* for something other than being fast on the draw sexually. In fact, as quick as he might be to arousal, the man took his time getting off.

Or at least he used to.

Kadin's expression turned troubled. "Yeah, maybe you can, at that."

She closed her eyes and without comment rolled onto her stomach under the light blanket. They were not going to get into her choices and why she'd made them.

Not now. Not ever, if she had anything to say about it.

She didn't know what quirk of fate had brought Kadin back into her life, but she was too smart to think it was anything but temporary.

She'd given up on the hope of having Kadin in her life. Not right away. Not ten years ago, but she had eventually gotten it. Stubbornly believing they were meant to be together and doing the one thing she thought would prove that to him had cost her the other person in her life Rachel had loved with her whole heart.

Even if she could forgive Kadin for walking away, she'd never forgive herself for the choices she'd made after he was gone.

That this man had been the one to rescue her just proved what a cynical, vicious bitch fate was.

"We're going to talk, Rachel." Kadin re-started his massage of her feet, strong fingers pushing firmly into her arches. "Don't you doubt it, angel, but not right now when your throat needs to rest more than I need answers."

"Small mercies," she quipped.

The husky quality of her voice made it sound like she was flirting when in fact she'd only intended to be a smart-ass, hiding pain that had nothing to do with being tortured behind sarcasm.

His chuckle said he knew her intention and appreciated the result regardless.

That ready, throwaway laugh sent a shiver of fear through her. There had been a time when this man had known her in ways no one else on earth, even her sister, could come close to doing.

Rachel didn't want any indication that maybe he still did. Even on the most superficial level.

Her love for this man had cost her everything.

She had nothing else to give.

"They were amateurs," he said in a tone between relieved and something she couldn't quite name. "They left your feet alone."

She agreed with a short jerk of her head. Her interrogators might not have been experienced or trained in the fine arts of torture, but the electric jolts through her body had been enough. To hurt her badly. To make her consider death before she broke.

Something in the quality of her silence must have gotten to Kadin, because he paused with his hands on her ankles. "They nearly broke you."

"How do you know they didn't?" she asked in a bare whisper.

"I know."

Another zing of atavistic fear went through her. "You think you do."

"Yes, angel, I do."

She was going to protest the nickname but knew it would be a waste of breath, and she only had so many words right now.

It wasn't words but groans of pleasure-filled relief that came out of her mouth a moment later as he began working on her right leg with both hands. The tension that had been holding her muscles rigid and in pain, even when she slept, began to seep out of her.

"Good?" he asked, clearly not expecting a reply.

And she didn't give him one.

Her body was aware of who was touching her on the most primal level, and because of that, she found herself relaxing to a degree she had forgotten was possible.

No matter what had gone between them, she knew in the deepest recesses of her being that she was safe in Kadin Marks's hands.

That knowledge was dangerous to her head and her heart.

"That's right, angel. Let yourself go. You'll feel a hell of a lot better for it later." He continued rubbing the stiffness out of her leg with steady, careful movements.

Old memories melded with the present. A young man who dreamed of being a soldier putting his hands on a young woman's body, a woman who dreamed only of loving him.

Kadin had made it bearable after she lost her parents, made her believe that life wasn't all about loss and pain. They'd learned about passion together, had dreamed of the future they would share, and they had brought Linny into those dreams. Rachel wasn't the only one devastated when Kadin said he wasn't coming back.

For the first time in years, those final memories took a backseat to what had come before, and Rachel found it easier to breathe if she just let them.

Rachel slipped into an almost trancelike state as Kadin worked her muscles and reminded her body that touch did not always come with pain.

Kadin could sense that Rachel wasn't sleeping, but he didn't think she was completely aware, either.

And he was damn glad.

If she had been, she might have noticed the ridge in his pants, or the way his own breathing had gone rough even as his fingers ached with the need to do more than massage the smooth skin under them.

He wanted to touch and caress her, bring her pleasure the way he used to. Back in the days when he had the right to touch her with intimacy, not just healing.

Despite his own lust-filled discomfort, he exulted with each sign that her body was relaxing and letting go of the pain from the torture.

There were burn marks where the leads had touched her, but other than that, her beautiful skin was mostly unmarked.

And so damn soft. Perfect.

She was thinner than she'd been as a teenager, but her curves were more womanly, and her muscles were toned in a way that spoke of a serious fitness regimen. Or training.

He pressed into the muscles between her shoulder blades, increasingly grateful with each knot he felt loosening under his fingers. "You lift weights."

Rachel just made a noncommittal noise.

He smiled. "Time to turn over."

He didn't wait for her to answer but gently rolled her, preserving her modesty with the blanket as he did so.

Her eyelids fluttered and for a brief moment opened, revealing the pale blue gaze he'd spent the last decade remembering in the darkest hours of the night. "Thanks."

Then her eyes fluttered shut again, her body boneless against the bed.

He went back to her feet, starting the massage again, determined to give her front as much attention as he had her back.

His cock hardened to the point of pain as he was allowed to touch but not caress the woman who starred in every one of his fantasies. Both sexual and of the family he knew he was never going to have.

Desire coursed through his blood like hot lava, making him sweat, and he had to breathe shallowly or start panting.

Her eyes slid open, the pale blue filled with a hazy concern. "Are you okay?"

He almost laughed, but he kept his cool and managed a nod. "Sure."

"You sound . . ." Her voice trailed off as her gaze slid down his body and snagged on the damn painful bulge in his trousers. "Oh."

"I'm fine."

"You want me." He couldn't read her tone.

Did that disgust her? Please her? Not affect her at all?

He was disgusted with himself enough for both of them. "I know. I'm a real bastard, getting excited by touching you after what you've been through."

"No."

He shook his head, refusing to accept her denial.

She frowned. "I want you, too." She paused as if gathering her thoughts . . . or enough voice to go on. "Just old memories."

"No." It was his turn to offer the stark denial.

"You left . . . didn't want me anymore." Her face set in concentration. "Maybe you want the new me. It worked, then." She sighed, turning her face away. "Too late."

He didn't know what she was talking about.

She said it as if she was no longer the girl he'd once known. And maybe she wasn't, but essentially? At the core of her being, Rachel Gannon would always be the angel of his dreams.

She was right about it being too late for them, though. It had been too late the day he took a kill shot that led to an innocent man's death. He'd been exonerated of any wrongdoing— his superiors had put it down to bad intel— but Kadin would never forget that the enemy wasn't always the only bad guy.

And shooting people was still his job.

"I never stopped wanting you," he said, returning to the present.

"You dumped me."

"I wasn't worthy anymore."

Her eyebrows drew together, the hazy relaxation almost completely gone from her features. "What?"

He wanted her to go back to that relaxation, but he didn't know how to *not* have this conversation. "You were so innocent and pure." Too pure for him.

"You were my white knight."

"No. The Marines made me a killer."

The confusion in her beautiful blue gaze grew. "For your country."

"You deserved something better."

"Than a military hero?"

"There's nothing heroic about shooting the enemy from behind the scope of a sniper's rifle." No matter what his pile of medals tucked away said.

She didn't say anything for several long seconds, just looked at him with eyes that used to see into his soul. That was one of the reasons he'd left.

He didn't want her looking and finding the black mark there.

Rachel gave a tiny shrug, and he took it as a win that

she didn't wince in pain from the movement. "Doesn't matter."

He'd believed that for ten years. That the truth didn't matter. He'd walked away, and that was what was important.

"Kiss me."

Shock jolted his body with the strength of a falling power line. *"What?"*

"No more talk. Kiss." Her voice sounded rough. "Need to remember."

"The passion between us?" he asked in disbelief.

"That not all touch is pain."

Oh, shit. How did he respond to that?

All the reasons that giving in to her was a bad idea went through his head even as his head lowered of its own volition. "Just a kiss."

She licked her lips with unconscious sensuality, her head dipping in a tiny acknowledgment.

He wanted to ask, why a kiss, damn it, but knew he owed this woman whatever she wanted. Had for a very long time.

Their mouths barely brushed, but damn if it wasn't good. Too good.

He let out a breath he felt like he'd been holding for a decade, and she matched it with a small sigh, her expression unreadable.

Chapter Seven

Kadin pressed down for another kiss, because that was what *he* needed, when a soft knock interrupted, immediately followed by the opening of the door.

Eva carried in a tray of food for them. "I was going to ask how my patient is doing, but it's pretty apparent she's feeling better." Eva gave Kadin a look with a single raised eyebrow.

He couldn't remember the last time his face had heated with a blush; before he'd left the Marines, for damn sure. But he was blushing now. "I thought you were going to have the food sent up."

"I needed to check on Rachel once more before hitting my rack."

Kadin nodded, moving to stand, but Rachel's hand on his arm stopped him.

She didn't say anything, but her expression spoke eloquently. She wanted him to stay.

She felt safe with him. And safer when he was within touching distance.

Not something she'd ever admit aloud, he'd bet, but he wasn't going to ignore the message in her pale gaze.

He changed his movement to one of lifting her into a sitting position. The blanket slipped, but he tucked it back around her, doing his best to ignore the creamy flesh exposed temporarily.

"Did the massage help?" Doc asked as she set the tray with two bowls of lentil soup between them.

"Yes," Rachel answered, her voice soft.

"Good."

The sound of yelling male voices came from down the hall. Rachel jerked, her eyes skittering to the door.

Doc just smiled and patted Rachel's shoulder before sliding a blood-pressure cuff onto her. "Don't mind them. The boys are arguing about who gets their own space and who has to share."

"You're not worried they'll leave you in the shared room?" Kadin teased.

Eva grinned, her expression just short of evil. "They know better. I can dose their breakfast with something that'll keep them in the latrine for most of the day."

Rachel let out a small laugh.

Kadin just shook his head. "You think she's kidding. I know she's not. I'd pit Doc against any man on my team and guarantee she'd come out the winner."

"Even you?" Rachel asked, a glimmer of familiar mischief glowing in her tired gaze.

"No comment."

Eva snorted. "I'm a sneaky bitch, and they all know it."

Rachel's smile felt to Kadin like getting the drop on the Taliban, but she didn't say anything as Eva finished her quick examination.

"Well, your massage brought down her blood pressure. Which I would not have expected, considering what I walked in on." Eva tucked her blood-pressure cuff and stethoscope away.

"It was just a kiss." And a damned innocent one at that.

"I didn't think you knew how to kiss, Trigger."

Rachel's eyes widened and then narrowed, and Kadin realized how Eva's words could be taken.

"We've been drinking buddies. I'm not known for romancing my dates."

"You're not known for dating. Hooking up? Yes. Though not nearly as often as Peace. That soldier is a man-whore for sure. But dating? Not Kadin 'Trigger' Marks, superwarrior and damn fine leader."

Kadin realized Eva was doing her own version of talking him up to Rachel, and he was unexpectedly moved. "Don't get soft on me, Doc."

The beautiful Puerto Rican grinned again, her expression purely evil now. "Not going to happen."

"Good to know."

The sound of a door slamming reverberated through the room, and Eva grabbed her bag. "That's my cue to find my room and make sure no one is stupid enough to be in it."

"She's tough," Rachel said after Eva had left, closing the door firmly behind her.

"She is."

"You like her."

"I do."

Rachel nodded, looking down at her soup. "Good to know."

Well, shit. This woman had always been more complicated than any other female he'd known. "Not like that."

Rachel just took a spoonful of her soup. Her hand shook a little, but she managed to get the lentils into her mouth without spilling.

Kadin waited until she was done chewing before placing his hand under her chin and bringing her head up so their eyes met. "There is nothing between me and Eva, and there never has been."

Rachel shrugged, the movement bigger than before, and winced.

Damn it. "You need pain meds?"

"Maybe."

"Eat your soup first. It'll make it easier to keep them down."

He ended up feeding her and then giving her the meds with a water bottle. She was falling asleep sitting up by the time they were done.

He helped her under the covers and over to one side of the bed. "I'm sleeping in here tonight."

"Okay."

He looked at her sharply but didn't see any disagreement with his pronouncement in her expression, either.

"Someone needs to stay with you. I could get Eva."

Rachel could have made a joke about the other woman making it clear she wanted her own space, but she didn't. His angel looked at him with eyes too damn jaded and vulnerable at the same time.

"I want you to stay," she said simply.

He nodded, getting beneath the covers. Calling Roman again could wait until the morning. Kadin positioned himself so he was lying on his side facing Rachel and put his arm across her stomach.

She seemed to relax, her breath going shallow in sleep almost immediately.

Well, this assignment had gone FUBAR for sure, and he couldn't even make himself regret it.

Wyatt leaned against the door, watching Neil. The sexy blond man was as volatile as a vial of nitroglycerin.

"I am not sharing this room with you," Neil growled.

A totally inappropriate smile took over Wyatt's face. And didn't he just know that was going to piss the other man off something fierce?

"We slept in the same tent last night. That was a smaller space than this." He indicated the room with the sweep of one hand.

There were two narrow beds and another one almost as wide as a double under the grill-covered window. It was pretty typical for a house in Marrakech and a hell of a lot nicer than a lot of places the men had been forced to sleep on assignment.

"Get out of the way." Neil's tone was as aggressive as his words, but he stayed on the other side of the room.

As if he was afraid to get too close to Wyatt.

Come on, baby, get closer.

"I'm not going to attack you in your sleep," Wyatt promised. As if the man didn't know him well enough to know that.

Oh, they were going to end up in bed together again, but not without Neil admitting he wanted it.

"I never said you would." The blush of guilt across the techno-geek's cheekbones indicated otherwise, though.

"Seriously?" Damn it, this man, of all men, knew Wyatt better than that. "Sugar, when have we ever done anything that we both didn't want?"

"I didn't want you to date a woman and end up engaged to her." The anger in Neil's voice couldn't compete with the pain in his eyes.

Wyatt had spent the last year regretting that mistake, but it was time they both moved on from it. Not just for his sake, but Neil's, too. In all this time, the man hadn't gotten over Wyatt, and Wyatt was never going to get over Neil.

He'd been a dumb shit, but that didn't change one inconvertible truth: they belonged together. Forever.

Wyatt gave Neil the best honesty he could. "Me, either."

Neil could have said something cutting to that. Wyatt would deserve it.

But instead his squid just sighed and shook his head. "What happened?"

"I felt like I didn't have a choice. I had dreams." Dreams of running the family ranch with his brothers, living the "family" life in East Texas just like his daddy and his daddy's daddy before him had done.

"I don't mean that. We already hashed out the why a year ago."

The problem was, they really hadn't. Oh, they'd tied one on for sure once he'd told Neil about the engagement, but not a lot of intelligent discussion had happened then. And sure as hell not since.

"What did you mean, then?" Wyatt took a cautious step away from the door and toward Neil.

"You're not married."

"No."

"Are you still engaged?"

"After leaving the bride at the altar? I don't think so."

"You what?"

"You telling me your intel didn't include that tidbit?"

"I've done my best *not* to keep tabs on you."

Hearing that hurt, though it was no less than Wyatt could have expected or deserved. "I couldn't go through with it."

"You left her at the altar?" Neil asked with disbelief. "That was cold."

"I tried. Damn, I really did."

"What stopped you?" Neil asked, as if Wyatt's answer didn't matter at all to him. The intense look in his dark blue eyes said otherwise, though.

"You. I dreamed about you the night before my wedding."

Neil's expression turned cynical.

"Not a sex dream, though the good Lord knows I've had plenty of those. You were old, sitting on the front porch of my family ranch. Another man was in the rocker next to you, giving you a look that said you were his."

"You?"

"No." And, waking from the dream, Wyatt had been sweating as if he'd had a nightmare worthy of a Hollywood B movie. "It was someone else, and I could see you were both happy."

"On your parents' front porch?" Neil asked, sounding strange . . . almost amused, but something else, too.

"Yeah. It was messed up. That should have been you and me. I wanted to kill the other man."

"There is no other man."

"But there would have been. If I didn't get my head out of my ass, I was going to lose you forever. And on the morning of my wedding, on the cusp of having what I always thought I wanted, I realized that was the one thing I could not stand."

"You'd already lost me. You threw me away."

Wyatt couldn't deny it, couldn't change it, but he wasn't living in that place anymore. "I screwed up. And maybe another man wouldn't forgive me. Another couple couldn't make it past that kind of mistake."

"But you think we can?" Neil looked at Wyatt as if he'd lost his mind.

"I know it. What we have . . . it's too big for my Texas-roots prejudices, or even my old dreams, to keep it buried."

"Those prejudices are all over the place. Too many people think I shouldn't have a right to love you."

"But you do, anyway."

"I didn't say that."

"You didn't have to."

"If I let you in again, you could destroy me."

"But I won't." Wyatt covered the distance between them, pulling Neil to him. "Trust me, sweetheart, please."

Neil shook his head. "I can't."

"You will. I won't give up."

Neil didn't believe Wyatt. It was in every inch of his tense frame, but he didn't say it.

Wyatt was grateful for small mercies.

"If we share a room, you're not touching me." There was no give in Neil's voice.

"Okay," Wyatt agreed. "For now."

Neil nodded, clearly smart enough to realize that was the best he was going to get. "Let me go."

"One kiss."

Neil opened his mouth, and Wyatt just knew he was going to refuse.

"Please." Wyatt's pride had cost him this man once before. He was never going to let that happen again.

Neil stilled, his body relaxing the tiniest bit toward Wyatt. "Not a sex kiss."

They were all sex kisses, because for them sex was love, and their love made for damn good sex, but he knew what the other man was saying. And Wyatt would comply.

This time.

Their lips brushed, and electricity arced between them, the charge so intense, Wyatt's eyes burned from the power of the moment. He didn't press to deepen the kiss, didn't push their bodies closer together, didn't take advantage of the arousal saturating the air around them.

Wyatt kept his mouth closed as he moved his lips against Neil's, relearning the contours he'd craved for every day of the year they'd been apart.

He didn't want to stop the kiss, but if he didn't, he was going to break his promise to Neil. This kiss was going to go carnal in about one second, and they would be in bed a heartbeat after that.

But that wasn't what Neil wanted, or what Wyatt had agreed to. And he wasn't going to break his word to the other man ever again.

Using all the self-discipline he'd learned as a Marine and later in the Atrati, Wyatt stepped back.

Neil's eyes opened, their indigo depths hazy with an emotion Wyatt was hesitant to name. "You didn't push the advantage."

"I said I wouldn't."

"You used to say I was it for you, but you were dating her on the side."

"I never had sex with her. Not once." Hell, they'd never even come close.

"Didn't she think that was odd?"

"She wanted to wait for marriage."

"You hurt her, walking out on the day of your wedding. Like you hurt me."

"Yes, I hurt her, but not like I hurt you. She didn't love me like you do."

"But she did love you."

"She thought she did, but she didn't know me, so how could she?"

"She loved the man you let her see."

"Yes." Wyatt would regret using a good woman and a good friend like that until his dying day, but following through on the marriage only would have added to his sins, not mitigated them. "What I did wasn't fair to her, but marrying her would have been worse."

Understanding and agreement burned in Neil's gaze. "You didn't love her."

"Oh, I loved her . . . like a little sister. I wasn't *in love* with her." A major disaster had been avoided on what would have been their wedding night—and all the nights thereafter.

"Do your parents know?"

Wyatt stepped back, needing distance if they were going to have this discussion. "Why I called off the wedding?"

"Yes."

"They do."

"And?"

"Daddy said he didn't raise any of his sons to use a woman like I used Candace." Wyatt turned away and grabbed his duffel, dropping it onto one of the smaller beds. "He's disappointed in me."

Not because he was gay, as Wyatt had expected, but because his daddy had raised him to man up, and, well, he hadn't. He had now, but he'd never be able to erase the look of disappointment in his daddy's eyes from his memory. He wished he could.

"He still loves you," Neil said with certainty, a lot closer than he had been a moment before. Wyatt turned, and Neil was there, his hand reaching out to squeeze Wyatt's arm. "You're still his son."

Wyatt nodded. His daddy would never deny him, but things weren't the same as they had been, either. "I'm not one of his heirs, though. Not anymore."

"What do you mean?"

"He's leaving the ranch to Jericho and Travis." Exactly what he'd expected his daddy to do when he heard the news his middle son was gay.

"I'm sorry. Maybe he'll change his mind after he's had time to think."

"He's had six months, and I don't see him changing even if I gave him six years." Wyatt shrugged. It didn't much matter, anyhow. "I knew I couldn't go back there and live like I'd always planned, not and have a male partner."

"It's a pretty conservative place."

"It ain't Houston, that's for sure. Or even Austin, for that matter."

Neil sighed. "I never wanted you to give up your heritage."

Wyatt knew that. Just like he knew that, as a man, he

had to make choices about how he was going to live his life. He could spend a lifetime lying and pretending to be something that he wasn't, or he could be honest about himself and live with the consequences.

It had hurt like hell to do the latter, but he didn't regret it. Couldn't. "Mama says she'll pray for my soul, but I'm not welcome for Christmas this year."

Neil paled, hurt covering his handsome face. "That's not right. What did your dad say?"

"Daddy rules the ranch, but Mama rules the house. He won't go against her."

"I'm sorry." Suddenly, shockingly, Neil pulled Wyatt into a hard hug. "I know how much that hurts."

Wyatt wasn't about to turn down the contact. "True. *Your* mother is an idiot." He'd always thought so. How any woman could write off a son as honorable and loving as Neil was beyond Wyatt's ability to understand. "At least my mama still sends me my care packages."

She'd told him she loved him but couldn't agree with his choices. Since he hadn't *chosen* to be gay, he figured she meant his decision to stop hiding it.

"There is that," Neil said with a suspicious-sounding laugh.

"Yeah, sugar, there is that. I saved you some pecan cookies from the last one. They were always your favorite. I put them up in the freezer."

Neil laughed again, and this time the sound was even more strangled. "I'm not sure your mama would approve."

"She'll love you once she meets you, and maybe she'll learn to accept me this way, too."

"You really want to try again?" Neil stepped back, and Wyatt made himself let the other man go.

"Yes."

"I don't know if I can."

"Think on it." To Wyatt's way of thinking, neither of them had much of a choice.

They were each other's one true thing. It was time they celebrated that truth instead of fighting it.

After forty-eight hours of forced inactivity, Rachel was ready to go AWOL. And with the help of Kadin's boss, Roman Chernichenko, she just might get away with it.

Kadin had refused to give her a situation report except to say that Abasi Chuma and his muscle were still on the mountain looking for her, convinced a woman could not truly have gotten away from them. Especially a woman who had spent the day before her disappearance hooked up to a car battery.

Rachel wanted more information than that. She wanted to know if Jamila Massri was safe. She wanted to know what the man's plans for his innocent fiancée were.

Rachel needed to get Jamila out of Egypt before Chuma went home and started putting the pieces of the puzzle together. She couldn't rely on his remaining ignorant of Jamila's newly developed friendship with a woman from the West.

The man was a sadistic monster, but he wasn't a stupid one, and Jamila herself might well give the game away with her own innocent comments. And if Chuma questioned her, that would be even worse. The young Egyptian wouldn't know any better than to answer him with complete honesty.

She still thought the man her father had chosen for her to marry was charming and sophisticated. She had no idea where the man's tastes ran and what life married to him might be like.

Just like Linny.

And just as Arthur Prescott had done with Linny, if Chuma had his way, he'd chew Jamila up in his twisted pleasures and then spit her out a broken woman.

Rachel swung her legs over the side of the bed. It was time to find out exactly what was going on. With both her case and Jamila.

Kadin's commander had called in for a sit-rep, and if she was quick about it, she might get a chance to listen in.

Moving a lot faster than she had been able to two days ago, Rachel crept from the room on silent, bare feet.

The hall was unsurprisingly empty, but she could hear faint voices from one of the rooms on that landing as well as Kadin's rumbling tones from somewhere below.

She snuck down the narrow stairway, Kadin's voice growing more discernible as she did so. He was in a room right off the bottom of the stairs, talking on his satphone.

"No, she hasn't talked to Whitney yet. She's still recovering."

Silence while the other man spoke.

"Well, he'll just have to wait. She's not talking on the phone until Eva gives the go-ahead. Rachel's voice box was strained from screaming while she was tortured, damn it."

Another silence, this one longer.

"No. I take full responsibility for not returning Stateside yet. It's my call, and I made it."

Rachel could just imagine how well that was going to go over with the Old Man, much less Kadin's boss.

"That's not going to happen, Chief."

This time the other man's response wasn't so quiet, because Rachel could hear the raised, angry tones if not the actual words coming across the satphone.

"That's not going to happen," Kadin repeated in a tone Rachel knew too well.

It was the one that said he wouldn't be moved. Full stop. Period.

So, he wasn't going to force her to return to the States without Jamila. Today, anyway. She'd take that and let tomorrow worry about itself.

Realizing that Kadin and his chief's focus was going to be on his orders—to get her safe and out of Africa—she stepped back from the door. She'd heard what she needed to on that count. Now she wanted answers about Chuma and Jamila.

And she *didn't* want to get caught disobeying Kadin's order to rest. He wasn't her boss, but he hadn't figured that one out yet, and right now she was reliant on his good will. So, she wasn't going to spend a lot of time disabusing him of his faulty notions of authority.

When the appropriate time came, he'd learn the truth.

She snuck down the hallway toward another doorway.

"We need to let Kadin know," a thin blond man was saying to someone not in her line of sight through the partially open door.

Chapter Eight

Even though it was a safe house, Rachel wasn't sure she would have been as quick to talk with doors open, but then, she'd learned the hard way to be overly cautious.

"He knew the ruse wouldn't keep them on the mountain forever. Even a West Texas tumbleweed-humper would have cottoned on eventually," the unseen man said with a pronounced Texas twang.

The thin blond turned slightly so he faced the other speaker. "It worked for two days, and that's twenty-four hours longer than I thought it would."

Rachel moved a silent step to her right to keep herself out of the man's line of sight.

"Only because that Chuma guy seriously underestimates what a woman is capable of doing. My granny woulda had his guts for garters afore he knew what hit him."

The blond shrugged, his face cracking into a smile. "No doubt, if she was anything like you. But I don't mind that Chuma's sexism worked in our favor."

"That it did." The other man, a big guy with shoulder-length brown hair, moved into her view, his hand reaching out as if he was going to touch the blond.

The blond tensed and shifted so the hand did not connect with his face, his smile slipping. But there was warmth in his indigo eyes she had a feeling he didn't know was there.

The over-muscled body of the other man jerked, and a look of pain tightened his features before the corner of his lips tilted slightly. "You've got an amazing smile, sugar."

"And you are so full of Texas bullshit, you could fertilize your daddy's hay fields." The words were harsh, but the tone wasn't, and those indigo depths were still warm with emotion.

If his wince was anything to go by, the big man with gray eyes didn't notice the tone or the emotion in the other man's gaze.

There was some history here, and if Rachel wasn't so worried about Jamila, her curiosity would have her working to figure it out.

She hadn't just gone into the DEA to prove something; she'd realized her curious nature could work for more than figuring out the latest news even before the most accomplished gossips in her hometown did.

"Find out anything interesting?" A large hand landed on her shoulder, while Kadin's other pushed the door all the way open in front of her.

Rachel maintained her composure, but just barely.

Ignoring the sounds of surprise at her presence coming from inside the room, she looked up at Kadin. "I didn't hear you coming down the hall."

It bothered her. She was definitely not operating her A-game yet.

"You were too interested in what was going on in this room. I have to wonder, though . . . were they talking about Abasi Chuma or fighting with each other again?"

She didn't bother to answer but was unsurprised that Kadin realized there was something going on between the other two mercenaries, as well. The man had always been too observant to be fooled by anything but his own self-delusions.

Kadin ushered her into the room. "In case you don't remember meeting them before, this is Neil Kennedy." Kadin pointed to the blond. "Our resident computer and technology geek. We call him Spazz."

"Spazz?" she asked, thinking the name didn't match the man, who could have fit in at any corporate computer lab with his Van Halen T-shirt (from the David Lee Roth era) and loose-fitting jeans.

"I get a little wired when I drink too much coffee."

"Yeah. Anything over half a cup," the Texan interjected.

She smiled and dipped her head, wishing she could pretend she hadn't seen the hand extended toward her. "Nice to meet you." She forced herself to reach out and brush his fingers with her own before jerking her hand back to her side. "Rachel Gannon. But I'm sure you knew that."

"Yes, ma'am."

Neil let his hand drop without any evidence of offense at the marginal handshake. "This behemoth is Cowboy, name self-explanatory as soon as the man opens his mouth. Though his parents still insist on calling him Wyatt."

Cowboy tipped his hat, not offering his hand, and she had to stifle the urge to thank him.

"There's no call for name-callin'," Cowboy grumbled at Neil.

A wicked gleam came into the dark blue eyes. "Hey, I can't help that you and Kadin are the brawn and I'm the brains of this outfit."

"What does that make Peace?" Kadin dryly asked.

The computer geek grinned and winked at Rachel before answering. "In a class all his own, man."

Cowboy's laughter was rich and warm, reminding Rachel that not all men were evil. Even if they let you down when you needed them most. Her gaze slid to Kadin and got caught there.

He was looking at her as if he was reading her mind again.

"So, I was just telling Cowboy that Chuma and his men are coming into Marrakech," Neil said, bringing Kadin up to date on her aborted attempt at eavesdropping. "They're hypothesizing that Rachel must have made it to the road and hitched a ride with someone."

"It took them two full days to come to that conclusion?" Kadin asked, his tone tinged with disbelief.

Cowboy moved to lean against the table Neil had his computer set up on, his hips resting inches from the other man. "Chuma doesn't think much of a woman's fortitude, Trigger."

"He finally decided his men had lied about how much torture they'd subjected her to." Neil looked like he wanted to move but wouldn't let himself.

Rachel understood that need to show no weakness. "That's not a bad thing, Mr. Kennedy."

She wasn't going to call him *Spazz*. This man might get wired on coffee, and his lethal edge showed in glimpses here and there, but *Spazz*? It just didn't fit. The technology specialist was too controlled.

"No *Mr.* Anything here, ma'am. Just call me Spazz. Everyone else does."

"I don't," Cowboy said with a defiant glint in his gray eyes.

Neil acted as if he hadn't heard, but the way his nostrils flared told a different story. He looked almost panicked as the other man shifted just a tiny bit closer.

Wanting to take the attention off the man she was feeling an unexpected kinship with, she said, "Call me Rachel, please."

"We'll work on it, ma'am, but you know how the old

saying goes," Cowboy replied. "You can take the man out of the military, but it's not so easy to take the military training out of the man."

"I understand that." She shot a sidelong glance at Kadin, registering clearly now that the black fatigues weren't standard military issue.

Close but not exactly, and the gray-on-black insignia of a stalking panther with *Semper Paratus, Semper Fatalis* under it didn't resemble any military badges she'd seen.

She hadn't noticed earlier because she had been so certain Kadin would never leave the Marines. So her mind had supplied her with the information that the fatigues were military, but the truth was, only black-ops agencies clad their people in black, even in a war zone.

"So, what, exactly, are all you guys, you Atrati, if you aren't military?" She'd originally assumed they were all Marines.

Another oversight she could blame on her prior expectations. It certainly didn't jive with her current observations. Cowboy's hair, hat, and boots were hardly the norm for a jarhead.

"We're Atrati," Kadin said simply when the other two remained silent and speculative in the face of her question.

"Yes, but what, precisely, does that mean?"

"We're a private black-ops company the government and others contract for specialized assignments."

That statement still told her nothing concrete.

"Like TGP?" she probed.

"Not really. Like I said, we're privately run, and we aren't a spy agency so much as a black-ops force. The Goddard Project calls us in when they want to control the outcome on an op rather than releasing it to the CIA or FBI." Kadin's expression went flat. "But we don't take our orders from the U.S. Government or its agencies."

"I don't imagine either of our bosses is feeling 'in control' of this op right now."

"No, I don't imagine they are." Kadin didn't seem too worried about that prospect.

"Are you in trouble because of me?" she still asked.

"I make my own decisions."

She nodded, accepting the non-answer for what it was. Kadin took responsibility for his choices, regardless of whether or not his superiors agreed with them.

And she was frankly less worried right now about either her or Kadin's careers than she was about Jamila Massri. "We need to determine Jamila's whereabouts and Chuma's plans for her."

"That would be Marrakech," Neil Kennedy said, succeeding this time in shocking Rachel right into sitting down.

It couldn't be that easy, could it? "She's here?"

Why had Chuma seen fit to bring the young woman to Morocco? Were Rachel's worries founded? Had Abasi Chuma sussed out the connection between Jamila and Rachel?

"Or will be shortly." Cowboy reached for some papers and shuffled through them, finally pulling one out. He pointed to a highlighted line. "Chuma said something about Miss Massri's father coming to Morocco and bringing her with him."

"But why would he bring her here?" Rachel asked, worry tightening her gut even as her analytical mind began working on the reasons for Dr. Massri's arrival in Marrakech. "Unless he suspects she's part of an information leak."

"Or he wants her company," Neil said in a tone that said he wasn't sure that was an improvement on the situation.

Rachel agreed wholeheartedly. She shifted on the wooden chair, fidgeting with the hem of her scrubs top.

No matter how Rachel looked at it, this could not be good. Jamila's wedding wasn't scheduled to take place for another three months, but that didn't mean a man like Abasi Chuma would want to wait that long for intimacy. No matter what the cultural norms.

If her father really cared about Jamila and her future, would he have contracted with a monster for her hand in marriage?

"So, she's on her way here?"

"That's what the man said," Cowboy agreed.

"Spazz?" Kadin prompted, as if he expected something more.

"I tracked her and her father on a commercial flight from Cairo. First-class. They flew into Menara," Neil said, naming the airport on the outskirts of the ancient city. "And have reservations at a privately held hotel here in Marrakech that caters to the rich and famous."

"Chuma is footing the bill, I bet," Rachel said with disgust.

"No takers on a sure thing." Neil typed on the ultrathin laptop in front of him. He made a sound of surprise, his brow furrowing. "An entire block of rooms is being paid for by Massri, not Chuma. They've been reserved for use for the past forty-eight hours even though they've been empty. Or at least there's no record of anyone actually checking in."

Cowboy looked smug. "Chuma expected to be back in the city the day he arrived in Morocco."

"It looks that way," Neil agreed, the lethal edge to his demeanor pronounced for a brief moment.

"So, we go in and extract Jamila before Chuma gets down from the mountain." Rachel wasn't letting that sadist get his hands on the young innocent.

"You don't have clearance to bring her in, or to break cover to reveal the truth to her," Kadin pointed out.

"I need to call Whit."

"Are you sure you want to do that?" Cowboy asked.

Neil nodded as if agreeing with a statement rather than a question, his expression understanding. "Sometimes it's easier to ask for forgiveness than for permission."

She looked up at Kadin to see how he was taking the talk of insubordination from his team, but he was looking at her. And the only expression on his face was one of interest.

"I won't compromise the operation without warning him first." She wasn't going to leave Jamila to dangle in the wind, but Rachel's loyalty to her agency was too deep to take any steps without at least giving Whit a heads-up first.

Besides, she believed in her boss. He would finally see the need to bring Jamila in. He had to.

Kadin nodded.

Neil said, "I'll set the call up."

"Why can't I just use your satphone?" she asked Kadin.

"Extra protocols are in place for communications with TGP. Your agency hasn't kept its invisible status in Washington by accident."

"Don't know how invisible it's going to be with the recent audit of the State Department going on. Those Tea Party politicos have got it in for the Oval Office and Whitney's agency for sure. And their investigator has sickening skills on the computer," Neil said as he typed furiously on his laptop.

No one said anything to that. Politicians were always putting one agency or another on the bubble. Sometimes rightly so; sometimes it was nothing but political grandstanding. Rachel personally loved the president and had little time for the Tea Party.

She knew other agents who felt different, but no one got into it over their political beliefs. Not in TGP offices, anyway. Whit had a strict no-discussion of religion, politics, or personal diets policy in place.

Even though everyone knew he wasn't a fan of any of the grandstanders, and particularly not the Tea Party. His wife, on the other hand, had her fingers in a lot of political pies. The woman was downright scary, and Rachel shuddered to think what would happen if she ever found out about TGP.

But TGP had weathered the McCarthy years, the Nixon fiasco, and the Clinton scandal without discovery. Surely, this latest burst of political interest would swirl around and over them, too.

Interrupting her thoughts, Neil handed her a headset. "It's a direct line to your director's office."

She'd barely gotten the earpiece to her head when she heard the Old Man's voice barking, "Whitney here. Where in the *h-e*-double-toothpicks is my agent, Marks?"

"It's Rachel Gannon, sir."

"Rachel." A soft sound came over the headset, as if Whit had sighed in relief. "How are you feeling, agent?"

"I'm doing better than I was three days ago, sir." She didn't have to fake the slight break in her voice.

She was better, a lot better, but her voice box had been strained to the point of whispers and pain.

"No doubt. No doubt. You're being called in from the field. Another agent will take over the investigation."

"That's not necessary, sir."

A snort of disbelief came through the phone, and then a no-nonsense tone saying, "It is. Absolutely. Your cover is either blown or, at the very least, compromised."

"But I got most of the information we needed." Or Kadin's team had. "We have photos."

"Send the digital files in; we'll start running facial-recognition software immediately." He didn't ask how the pictures had been obtained or whom they were of.

Andrew Whitney didn't waste time on what he considered unnecessary dialogue.

"Yes, sir."

"When will you be Stateside?"

"Sir, there is still the matter of Jamila Massri."

"What matter? Has something significant changed on that front?"

"I'd say my capture was significant."

"Did your captors give you reason to believe that Chuma had twigged on to your connection to his fiancée?"

Rachel wished she could lie, but to do so with her boss would betray her sense of integrity. She didn't have much left of her humanity, she thought sometimes, but this she did have. "No, sir. Though they'll figure it out eventually."

"You're founding this belief on what?"

"I met the woman for coffee almost daily for weeks."

"But you were careful not to be seen by Chuma, and you said she wasn't being shadowed."

"He might be sucking her in with a false sense of independence."

Whit didn't reply to that, but what could he say? They both knew that Abasi Chuma was a bad, bad, *bad* man. But only she was convinced that evil was going to leave its mark on Jamila Massri before TGP had a chance to move in on Chuma and his cohorts. Working the angles they did sometimes meant getting other governments involved in taking down dirty information brokers like Chuma.

All of that took time, time Jamila might not have to maintain her innocence in the face of the evil her future husband embraced.

"I need to bring her in, sir."

"We've discussed this, Rachel." Whit sounded tired and almost apologetic. "She's a field asset without the intel to justify an involuntary extraction."

"She'd come voluntarily if I told her the truth about Chuma." But even as she said the words, Rachel wasn't sure she believed them.

She'd been so sure she could have saved Linny if only she had been paying attention, if she'd discovered the truth about Arthur Prescott and told her sister before Linny got in too deep. If Rachel had even *known* about Prescott.

The past weeks with Jamila had shown Rachel how far an innocent woman would go to believe the best of a man who was rotten to his very core.

"Maybe. Best-case scenario, yes."

"So I tell her."

"You're in no condition to fly to Cairo."

"She's in Marrakech."

"No." Unequivocal and stark.

Rachel opened her mouth to argue, but Whit didn't give her the chance. "It's too dangerous. Worst case, she doesn't believe you and goes to him with a story about the crazy woman trying to ruin his reputation."

"We don't know that."

"It's our job to consider the worst-case scenario always and prepare for it." His words were so like her earlier thoughts.

Tension ratcheted up Rachel's spine. She hated having her own certainties turned back on her. "But, sir—"

"And in no scenario can you see or be seen with Miss Massri there in Morocco," Whit interrupted. "If you've managed to maintain any semblance of your cover, it will be blown wider than the gates of Baghdad, and any hopes of keeping Chuma ignorant of our investigation with it. I don't need to tell you we can't afford to give him time to cover his tracks."

"Whit, we can't leave her to him." They just couldn't.

"She's an adult. She's made her own choices."

"Her father made the choice for her."

The sound Whit made could have been exasperation, but it could also have been one of grief. His words were unbending, however. "She doesn't disagree with it."

"It's not right, Whit. You know it's not right."

"We don't always get the chance at *right*; sometimes we have to settle for bringing down the bad guys."

"You're talking about collateral damage."

"You're not stupid, Rachel."

"No, I'm not, but I won't let her fall into that pit, either."

This time, Whit's sigh couldn't be taken as anything but impatience. "I need you Stateside, Rachel."

"Whit . . . no . . . please . . ."

"Look, can you flip her, do you think?" he asked, his tone saying he didn't have a lot of hope she'd agree.

"What do you mean?" She knew what it meant to flip a spy, but Jamila? "You want her to spy on Chuma on purpose? How is that going to keep her safe?"

"Keeping an informer perfectly safe is not in our charter. We are charged with protecting vital information from reaching the wrong hands."

"The individual is still important, sir." Jamila was important.

"But she cannot take precedence over the operation."

"She deserves our protection, just like anyone else."

"You cannot protect an adult woman from her own decisions." There was a message in her boss's words, but Rachel wasn't going to hear it.

"I need to bring her in, sir." That was the message *he* had to hear.

"You cannot approach her in Morocco." Whit's voice dropped several degrees toward icicle. "You *will* not approach her in Marrakech."

"We have to do something!" Rachel's voice broke again, this time simply giving out as the attempt at yelling cost her a big chunk of the progress she'd made so far.

"Rachel . . ." Whit's voice trailed off, sounding more tired than she'd ever heard the director. "Come back to Washington, and we'll work something out."

She saw the promise for what it was; unfortunately, it wasn't enough.

"We can't leave her just yet, sir," Rachel tried to explain. "We don't know what Chuma will do."

"Marks's medic recommended another twenty-four hours of rest before your long flight back, I think he said," Whit equivocated.

"I'm not supposed to be out of bed *now,* sir."

"Twenty-four hours, Rachel. That's all I can give you."

"I've got vacation time accrued, sir."

"I can't approve that at present."

"Sir?"

"Twenty-four hours."

"I hear you, sir." But she was careful not to agree.

"Take care of yourself."

"Yes, sir."

"Tell that Atrati captain that I want you on the plane in twenty-four hours. No later."

"I'll tell him, sir." But she wasn't promising to go.

"I'll tell him myself," Whit said in a tone that implied he had noticed her lack of verbal commitment to his plan.

"If you say so, sir."

"Put him on."

Rachel didn't bother to answer but pulled the headset off and passed it over to Kadin.

Chapter Nine

"Your boss not agree with you staying in Morocco?" Neil asked.

"He gave me twenty-four hours."

"It shouldn't take that long to get the girl." Cowboy looked like he was trying to figure out why Rachel didn't seem happier.

"Whit forbade me to see or be seen with Jamila Massri in Morocco."

"Yeah, that tracks," Neil mused aloud. "Chuma and his goons are still undecided on whether or not you're intelligence or just a very nosy tourist."

"Apparently the man can't figure out a female spy who doesn't use a come-on to get what she wants, and since you never approached him for sex . . ." Cowboy mused aloud.

"Therefore, I can't be a spy." Maybe Abasi Chuma was dumber than she thought. "And if I *was* just a tourist?"

"Didn't matter. Their plans were to kill you either way once he was sure he'd gotten all the answers from you that you had to give."

Rachel felt sick to her stomach at such a quick dismissal of human life. "And Whit wants me to leave Jamila at the mercy of that man."

"Your boss doesn't want the investigation compromised," Kadin said as he took off the headset. "He expects you on a plane home—"

"In twenty-four hours. I know." But she wasn't going. Not without Jamila.

"He also said that we are specifically denied permission to extract Ms. Massri as a hostile witness."

"In other words, he wants the little lady left exactly where she is." Cowboy's twang didn't give away his opinion of that reality.

"That's not going to happen," Rachel said with more vehemence than she should have. Her voice started to give out again.

Kadin's eyes flared with concern. "That's enough talking for now."

"I'm fine," she denied, but she was careful to keep her tone and volume modulated. "You need to understand that I'm not leaving Morocco until I know Jamila is safe."

"It could take days—weeks, even—before your agency and/or its allies are ready to make their move."

"Then I stay for weeks."

Kadin didn't argue with her or ask if she had a plan. He just nodded.

Cowboy and Neil didn't say anything, either, but the looks they gave Kadin spoke volumes about their commander's sanity. She'd understand it if the look was directed at her, but it wasn't.

"I'm not leaving Africa with Jamila in jeopardy," she said, in case there was any question left in any of their minds.

"Yes, ma'am, we did get that impression," Cowboy drawled.

"So, why are you looking at Kadin like he's the one who's nuts?" she asked before she could think better of it.

"Because Kadin is perfectly capable of drugging you and putting your stubborn ass on a plane regardless, but the man's got no plans to do so." Cowboy frowned at Kadin. "Even though his orders are clear."

Kadin's jaw hardened. "Andrew Whitney does not write my orders."

"He does when TGP contracts our services."

"No." That was all Kadin said, but the word left no room for misinterpretation.

Rachel's boss was not *his* commander, and that was that.

"Roman isn't going to be happy if you disobey a direct order from the head of TGP."

"I've pissed him off before. I'll do it again."

"That's for damn sure," Neil said under his breath.

Kadin didn't appear to take offense.

It was Rachel who couldn't help asking, "Why?"

Suddenly Kadin's attention was fully and completely on her. "Because I'm just that kind of guy."

"That's not what I meant, and you know it."

"Why not force you back to Washington?" Kadin asked, his expression unreadable.

"Yes. And why help me?" Because she knew he was going to.

"I owe you."

Rachel's mouth opened; nothing but air came out. She took several shallow breaths before turning away without another word and heading off to find the kitchen.

She was hungry.

She was not going to overthink what Kadin had said. She just wasn't. He had walked out of her life ten years ago without a backward glance. He'd walked back into it when she'd been pretty sure all hope was lost.

She was not going to question his reasons for helping her protect Jamila.

Whatever made Kadin feel like he owed Rachel some kind of debt was working in her favor. He wasn't drugging her and tossing her unconscious behind onto an airplane headed for the States. Right now, that was pretty much the best she could hope for. With Jamila's life and innocence on the line.

Besides, while Rachel might be years past believing Kadin owed her anything, no matter what he claimed, he did owe Linny.

They both did.

Wanting to follow Rachel, Kadin turned to Spazz instead. "What else do you have?"

"Not sure." Spazz's eyebrows drew together, his expression thoughtful. "But they're freaked about something."

"Not just finding Rachel where she wasn't supposed to be?"

"No. Chuma still isn't convinced she's anything more than she claimed—a nosy tourist caught in the wrong place. But something has got him acting level-four paranoid."

"What do you mean?"

Spazz shrugged. "Look, despite the way Chuma devalues women, I'm not sure his underlings would have reacted like they did with Rachel if the big man wasn't so tense about whatever's about to go down. Yes, tourists disappear every year, but a kidnapping could still bring attention Chuma can't want."

"If TGP has their shit together, they're already taking advantage of the opening the political situation in Egypt has caused," Cowboy mused aloud.

Kadin nodded. Roman had said as much; so had Whit when he'd spoken to Kadin and tried to order him to bring Rachel Stateside immediately. "You can bet on it."

"It's pretty clear that the men who kidnapped Rachel were acting on orders given *after* they found her snooping." Spazz shook his head and typed something into the computer. "Chuma had to want her out of there worse than Whit wants her back in DC, and I'm thinking there's a reason."

Kadin had to agree. "Something big."

"And that something is still in Egypt." Cowboy tipped his head back, his eyes going cold. "I'm thinking whatever that something is, Chuma having it is not in the U.S. of A's best interests."

"Yeah." And Kadin's world just got a little more complicated.

They might not work for the government, but almost every member of the Atrati had been in the military at one time. He and his team had all defended their country with their lives, and that wasn't something a man forgot because Uncle Sam's name dropped off his paycheck.

"Shame." Cowboy frowned. "Timing sucks for your little gal. She might'a got away with the whole dumb-tourist routine if Chuma's boys weren't on high alert."

"Maybe." Unlike Spazz, Kadin wasn't convinced of that.

All the intel they had on Abasi Chuma painted him as a true sexual sadist. A man like that, who enjoyed inflicting pain, especially on the unwilling, was always looking for excuses to do so and would make them up if he had to.

"So this *thing?*" Kadin prompted. "What is it?"

"Not sure. They've mentioned a Tyfer tank," Cowboy said, his forehead gathered in a frown.

"A tank?" Kadin asked, confused. "Are we talking new technology?"

There were dozens of tanks in warfare today, but anti-tank missile technology was getting more sophisticated by the month. Some were even positing an end to tank warfare, though Kadin didn't buy that. Ground combat had been the primary format for war throughout history and still was.

Had Chuma discovered significant improvements some-one had made in the armored vehicles that could combat the newest missile technology in a significant way?

"Don't ask me. When I first heard it, I thought they were talking about a stock tank," Cowboy said with some humor.

Spazz smacked the table and cursed, grabbing the head-set and putting it on, then doing something on the computer.

"What is it, sugar?" Cowboy demanded.

Kadin raised an eyebrow at the endearment, but Cowboy just gave him a *deal with it* look.

Kadin made a gesture with his hand that the other man would recognize from their days in the Marines that meant, "It's all good."

Cowboy smiled, but Spazz was swearing again, this time at himself. "I can't believe I didn't see it. Or hear it."

"What?" Cowboy asked again.

Neil waved him off.

Kadin wasn't so patient. "See what?" he demanded in his command tone.

Spazz sighed and yanked off the headset. "It wasn't a Tyfer tank. Chuma was saying *Treffert* tank."

Cowboy didn't look any more enlightened, but Kadin's gut tightened with the feeling he got just before something went FUBAR for real. "You mean that Treffert guy . . . the one who's doing all the research on savant syndrome?"

"What the hell is *savant syndrome,* and who is this fella Treffert?" Cowboy was sounding more than a little impa-tient now.

"You've heard of an autistic savant?"

"I've heard of an idiot savant, but my mama would'a washed my mouth out with lye soap if I ever used that term."

"Your mama . . ." Neil's expression saddened as he looked at Cowboy, but then he shook it off. "Dr. Treffert argues pretty convincingly that neither term is fully correct. Not all savants are retarded mentally or autistic, though statistics would suggest that one in ten autistic people is a savant of some kind."

Still not sure where Spazz was going with this, Kadin added for Cowboy's benefit, "Which is why they used the term *autistic savant* for so long."

"What? You reading medical journals now, Trigger?" Cowboy asked with a smirk.

"My sister makes sure I keep up with the news on this particular topic, since my oldest nephew is autistic, but it's not exactly a state secret."

Spazz typed something into his computer. "No, but it's also a very specialized area of study and not common knowledge."

Kadin shrugged. Considering the number of autistic people in the United States, he thought maybe it should be.

"What does savant syndrome have to do with Abasi Chuma?" he asked Spazz. "*Chuma* sure as hell isn't one."

"No. The man has a smart criminal mind, but he is not a savant. Not by any stretch," Spazz said with disdain.

Kadin would find the technology geek's attitude amusing under other circumstances. "No arguments here."

"Right. So, Dr. Treffert is the acknowledged expert on savant syndrome, and he estimates that there are only about fifty true savants alive today." Spazz's tone and attitude seemed to imply that what he'd just said was significant.

"So?"

"What if he's wrong?" Spazz asked.

"And the other savants are part of some kind of think tank," Cowboy said, proving he, at least, was catching up fast.

Kadin hadn't made that leap yet, though the lag might have more to do with the fact that thoughts of Rachel were interfering with his concentration on this conversation.

Kadin forced himself to focus on the topic at hand. "You think Treffert has something to do with it?"

"Doubtful." Spazz was still concentrating on his computer screen. "The man's too public. My guess is, someone lacking imagination borrowed his name as a moniker for the think tank, believing they were cleverly hiding what it really is."

Cowboy wasn't looking too happy. "And Chuma got an in to it."

"Or just some breakthrough the think tank has made," Kadin suggested, finally back in the game mentally.

Spazz nodded without looking up. "It's his business to acquire and sell information and technology that could be very dangerous in the wrong hands."

"*Acquire* . . . How has he acquired this information?" Kadin didn't like any of the scenarios his mind came up with.

"I don't know, but I have some ideas." Spazz looked up then, his blue eyes narrowed in a way that said he wasn't too pleased by his own thoughts on the matter. "Now that we know what we're looking for, I can do some digging, though."

"And what are we looking for?"

"Information on a Treffert tank, for one," Cowboy answered for the other man.

"And any link Chuma might have to its output or someone involved with it."

Kadin didn't like it. This wasn't their normal type of assignment and required specialization outside his expertise and control. "That's a big order."

"For someone else, maybe," Spazz said with well-earned arrogance.

"That's my man," Cowboy said with pride in his Texas twang.

Spazz jolted as if he'd been shot with a Taser and glared at Cowboy. "I'm not *your* anything, and you're not *out.*"

"I am to Trig, and you keep telling yourself that, sugar, but we both know the truth, and sometime soon here, you're gonna admit it, too."

Spazz looked at Kadin. "You know?"

That Cowboy was gay?

"Sure." Kadin shrugged. Like it mattered.

"And you don't care?"

"Should I?" Though if Cowboy and Spazz were planning to cohabitate, that information was something a team leader needed to know.

Roman would want to know, too. There were no rules about Atrati agents not being in relationships, but the truth was, most field team members were single. It was just the way it worked.

Spazz shook his head. "I've got work to do here."

In other words, get out of the technology geek's hair. "You've got less than twenty-four hours."

"I read you loud and clear, Trigger," Spazz said as he turned his attention fully to the computer.

"You think TGP will change their directive for their agent if we can prove there's a current case to work beyond her identifying Chuma and his cohorts?" Cowboy asked.

"Maybe. We can hope."

"You don't sound confident."

"That shit going down in Washington could tie Whit's hands."

"There's always shit going down in Washington," Cowboy said with a snort. "But TGP slides under the radar."

"Not this time."

Spazz nodded, proving he'd been listening though he'd already started doing whatever it was that led to the amazing results he always got. He probably knew more than Roman or Whit about what was going on in Washington right now.

The man was more than a little smart, and he kept his ear to the ground in a way that was damn scary sometimes.

"What do you want me to do while Neil is researching this think tank angle?" Cowboy asked.

"You're with me on Jamila detail."

"What about our listening devices? Daredevil here bugged one of the satphones. If they take it with them when they leave the mountain, we'll still have ears on them."

Kadin was glad his men were all the type to take the extra initiative. Not so popular in the military, that attitude went a long way in the Atrati.

Though Cowboy didn't sound too happy with Spazz's having taken the extra risk. "Peace, Rachel, and Eva can work out a schedule to monitor whatever we get."

"You think that's a good idea, Trigger?" Spazz asked, proving the man was still listening despite his swiftly typing fingers.

"If we don't give her something to do, she's going to sneak out to watch Jamila Massri herself."

Cowboy whistled low. "Your little filly is damn stubborn."

"She's not mine." Why the hell didn't saying that hurt less today than it had ten years ago?

Whoever had been stupid enough to claim that time healed all wounds had never had a Rachel Gannon in their life . . . and lost her.

"Whatever you say, boss."

"Spazz, you got any more of those listening gizmos?" Kadin forbore continuing the argument.

And if that argument was about something more than the simple fact that Cowboy could be a stubborn sonofabitch, well . . . that was Kadin's own damn business.

"Sure." Spazz looked up, giving Kadin his full attention. "What are you thinking?"

"Bugging their hotel."

"You might have to use local talent for that one. I don't see you passing as a chambermaid."

Kadin rolled his eyes. "I've got it covered."

He'd already spoken to the operative who ran the safe house.

Spazz went to get the bugs.

Kadin found Rachel alone, eating from a plate of fruit in the kitchen.

"How are you feeling?" he asked her.

She popped a piece of papaya into her mouth, chewed, and swallowed before answering. "I'd feel more like a human if I had something to wear besides scrubs."

The tan pants and top had no style and didn't show off her feminine curves at all, but she still looked cute in them. He didn't think she'd appreciate his saying so, however.

"You think you can restrain yourself from leaving the house if I get you real clothes?" he asked, only half kidding.

"You think my attire is what's holding me back right now?"

"Point taken."

She took another bite of fruit, pineapple this time, and the juice dribbled from the corner of her mouth. The dark pink tip of her tongue came out to lick it away.

And just like that, Kadin's dick was hard and aching.

Rachel's pale blue eyes narrowed as if she knew exactly what was happening to him and wasn't particularly happy about it. "Tell me."

He was so damned rattled by her that he nearly admitted his desire before his brain clicked in and he realized she was asking about his discussion with his men.

"Tell you what?" he taunted anyway.

Pushing Rachel's buttons to make that certain spark ignite in her eyes used to be one of his favorite things to do. Apparently old habits were harder to break than relationships.

Sure enough, annoyance made her nostrils flare and her too-kissable lips tighten. "You didn't hang back with your boys just to shoot the breeze. What's your plan?"

"Do *you* have one?" he asked with genuine curiosity, wondering how much of her insistence on staying was being driven by her emotion and how much was based on an idea she had for the outcome.

"Not one that isn't going to tank my career," Rachel admitted in a tone of frustration.

Which said two things. One: she did have a plan. And two: Rachel Gannon considered the Egyptian woman, Jamila Massri, more important than her own career.

"But you're going to do it anyway."

"I don't have a choice. I let Linny down; I won't be responsible for the same thing happening to Jamila."

"Linny was an adult."

"Barely." There was a wealth of pain in Rachel's voice. "She was just a kid, and I left her to fend for herself."

"She was in college."

"She'd dropped out, and I didn't even know it."

"That's not your fault."

"Isn't it? If I'd been a better sister, I would have known about something like that."

"Why didn't your grandmother tell you?"

Rachel laughed, the sound nothing like amused. "She didn't want responsibility for us after Mom and Dad died, but she gave us a home and kept us together anyway. She took a very hands-off approach after Linny turned eighteen, and I knew that. Linny acted like Grandmother's attitude didn't faze her, but she had to have felt abandoned by us both. I should have looked closer, paid better attention."

The pain hiding behind Rachel's tough-secret-agent exterior pricked at the heart Kadin had done his best to brick away for the past ten years.

"You were hurting, too." Rachel had been abandoned, first by her parents in death, then by Kadin, and then emotionally by her grandmother.

"No. Grandmother and I hadn't been close since Mom and Dad died. Her frequent trips and cruises didn't bother me."

"She and Linny were all you had left of your family. Her decision to leave you and your sister completely to your own lives had to have hurt."

"Maybe it would have hurt the girl you remember. I'm not her anymore." Rachel shrugged. "Besides, Grandmother had her own demons to deal with. Losing her child must have devastated her. She pushed me and Linny away to spare herself the pain of losing us, too."

It amazed him that Rachel could understand her grandmother's pain so well even while denying her own. "You were still that girl back then. You'd only been working for the DEA a couple of years when Linny killed herself."

Saying the words hurt him. How much more painful must they be to the sister who had loved Linny so deeply? Even after all this time?

"Twenty months. Since the month after Linny went off to college." Naked pain flashed briefly over Rachel's once-expressive features. "I tried to keep in touch as much as possible, but they sent me undercover within the first year. I showed aptitude."

Undercover for the DEA? Shit. "What was the case?"

She named a bust that had involved a drug ring and underage prostitution and had stretched across six states. The ring had been ripped apart at the seams by an impressive investigation that had included a series of undercover operatives a few years back.

He swore.

She shrugged. "I'm good at what I do."

"At what cost?" And he didn't mean Linny.

"Does it matter?" she asked, proving she wasn't talking about Linny, either.

Rachel was talking about herself as if she didn't count, and Kadin hated it. "It does to me."

"*Don't.* Don't lie to me. I'm an expert at reading people now, Kadin." She shook her head, her eyes narrow with disbelief and a tinge of anger.

"Then you know I'm telling the truth."

Pure fury twisted her beautiful face before the rage disappeared and nothing was left but her blank regard. "I don't know how you ended up being the one to extract me. I don't know why you're helping me with Jamila. And honestly? It just doesn't matter. The important thing, the only thing I care about right now, is that you are."

She took a deep breath and pushed the bowl of fruit away from her before standing up from the table. "But don't make the mistake of thinking I believe for one single, solitary second that it's because I *matter* to you. I never did. It just took me some time to figure that out."

"You mattered too much. That's why I left."

Chapter Ten

"**D**rop it." Rachel's tone was flat, no give in it.

He sighed, pushing the fruit back to her spot at the table and indicating with a nod that she should sit down again. "Spazz thinks there may be grounds for expanding the orders on your case."

"What are they?"

"He's not sure, but he's digging."

Rachel returned to her seat, and Kadin told her about Chuma's tension and the mention of the Treffert tank.

"TGP has eyes on the think tank and its output. I might be able to access our files on them if Spazz can get me a secure connection." She was eating the fruit by rote, as if she understood she needed nutrients to get back to full strength but had no other reason to eat it.

When he'd walked into the kitchen, she'd clearly been enjoying her snack, and it bothered him that the emotionless stranger had returned to inhabit Rachel's body.

"And in the meantime?"

"We're bugging the hotel here in Marrakech."

"And Jamila?"

"Cowboy and I will be running sit-rep surveillance on her."

"Thank you."

Kadin sighed. "No thanks needed. I let Linny down, too."

He wasn't even surprised when Rachel gave a short, affirmative jerk of her head. "Yes, you did. You abandoned us both. I may forgive you someday for breaking your promises to me, but I'll never forgive you for dumping her out of your life, too. She needed you, and you weren't there."

Rachel looked away, as if she could see something besides the stucco walls of the Moroccan safe house. "She lost too much, too many people, and I let that happen. Trying to get back my own happiness, I cost Linny hers. I'll never forgive myself, either."

"Rachel, she was going to college. The campus of *her* choice. What were you supposed to do, give up your job? Move to Oregon with her?"

Rachel surged to her feet again, spinning away from him and then back, her face reflecting long-held pain, the emotionless mask shattered to reveal the real woman. "If it could have saved her life, that's exactly what I should have done."

"She wouldn't have let you, Rach. Linny wasn't going to live with her big sister while she was going to college."

"Why not? I lived with her and Grandmother while I was at university."

"By *your* choice, right?"

"Yes. I'm not saying Grandmother would have been happy if I'd moved out and left her with a teenager to deal with on her own, but I wasn't going to leave Linny until I thought she was ready." Something in her tone said that had been a tough call to make for Rachel.

That surprised him, but he didn't have the luxury of dwelling on it now. He needed to open Rachel's mind to the idea that Linny's death was not her fault. Even if she didn't believe it immediately, there needed to be a spike set firmly into that train of thought.

"And she was ready when she left for Oregon," he pressed.

"We thought she was. We were wrong."

"No. She met the wrong man."

"I should have stopped it."

"You couldn't. Whatever her reasons, the need for a fresh start, wanting more independence . . . whatever they were, Rach, Linny wanted to move to Oregon to go to school. And she didn't want you moving with her."

The wince on Rachel's face said he'd guessed right on that last part.

"It doesn't matter. She's dead, and I'm not abandoning Jamila."

"No one's asking you to, sweetheart." Well, her boss was, but Andrew Whitney didn't count.

Not when it was Kadin's call how and when the Atrati team and Rachel left Morocco.

She nodded, her throat working, and he wanted to hold her, but every line of Rachel's body screamed to leave her the hell alone. He wanted to touch her so badly, his fingers were aching with the need, but he'd given up that right.

A small, wounded sound came from her throat.

Rights and nonverbal cues didn't matter in the face of that small sound.

He moved fast to wrap her up in his arms, and he didn't loosen his hold despite her immediate attempts to move away. "Relax, angel. Just give it a minute."

"What?" she asked, her hands still pressing against his chest as if she didn't know any other way now except to push people to a distance.

"Whatever you need." He didn't care if it made sense.

This woman was in so much pain, it was like a wall squeezing in around her. He wasn't going to let her shatter from it.

Not on his watch.

She might be right that he'd abandoned both her and Linny when they needed him, but he hadn't meant to. He'd meant to protect them both, just as he had his own family, from what he'd become.

But none of that was important right now. What was important was that Kadin wasn't going to do it again.

Even if Rachel was the one pushing him to leave.

"Everything okay?" Eva asked, coming into the kitchen.

Kadin reflexively tightened his hold, knowing Rachel would try to get away. "Give us a minute?"

"No." Rachel shoved against his stomach. Hard. "We're done here."

He just shook his head.

Eva cocked her head to one side. "It's just, I think Abdul's wife wants to make dinner. She's hovering out in the hallway, reluctant to interrupt whatever's going on in here."

Rachel punched him in the side. "Let go, Kadin. People need this room."

Shit. He might have listened if the punch hadn't felt more like a caress. She was trembling against him, for all her bravado, damn it. Rachel had forgotten how to lean on others, but Kadin was going to show her again.

At least while they were here in Morocco. Maybe later, too.

He'd missed her friendship as much as he'd missed her being his lover. And though he knew she'd never trust him enough again to give him her heart, he'd never met anyone who needed a true friend more.

And being friends was better than being enemies . . . or nothing at all.

"You're right."

She looked up at him, her pretty, pale eyes reflecting pain too big to hide. No matter how much she might want to. "So, let go?"

He just shook his head, not even smiling at the confusion sliding over her feminine features. His heart hurt in a way he'd been damn careful not to allow in ten years. He bent his knees and took her into his arms, lifting her high against his chest before she could get out the first yelp of outrage.

"We'll be upstairs," he told Eva.

The medic shook her head, her dark eyes narrowing. "I don't think that's what she meant, boss."

He didn't bother answering, just walked out of the kitchen, nodding at Abdul's wife as he passed her in the narrow hall. The cook-cum-housekeeper might well be a trained agent for all Kadin knew, since her husband was the one in charge of the safe house and who knew what else.

The Atrati operated in secret, even from each other sometimes.

The Moroccan woman said something in Arabic under her breath. It sounded like she was bemoaning crazy Americans, but he wasn't listening all that closely, so he couldn't be sure.

His focus was almost entirely on the rigid and now fuming woman in his arms.

"You can't just pick me up and carry me around," Rachel grumbled.

"Eva said you still need rest."

"She didn't mean I couldn't walk." The exasperation made Rachel's voice rise so that Cowboy poked his head out of the door of the room he and Neil were still in.

"You need any help there, Trigger?"

"Nope. I've got it."

"All-righty, then."

Cowboy disappeared, and Rachel made a frustrated noise.

"Problem, angel? You wanted him to come, too?"

"No." She huffed out another less-than-happy breath as he started up the stairs. "I don't want to go back to our . . . *my* room."

"I can be a reasonable man," he informed her, in case she'd forgotten.

Her snort said she didn't believe him.

Since her anger was an improvement on her bottomless hurt, he didn't complain. Bypassing the second floor, he continued up toward the roof.

"Where are we going?"

"The living room inside is narrow if long—typical for a Moroccan home but not so comfortable for men of my stature. The roof, on the other hand, is a nice, open space." Besides, the sunshine would do Rachel good.

She didn't reply, but when they reached his destination, her indrawn breath said Rachel found the roof as inviting as he and his team had.

Encompassing the entire length and breadth of the house that had been built sometime during the reign of the Almoravids in the Middle Ages, the rooftop garden was dotted with potted palm trees and an assortment of bright, blooming flowers that would make most horticulturists jealous.

Off to one side and under a cloth canopy was a long, rectangular, wrought iron table and chairs sufficient for eight to dine comfortably. The other side of the roof had two distinct conversation areas. One was comprised of a surprisingly modern and comfortable grouping of deep sofas and four matching armchairs.

The other, not under a shade structure, was made up of a couple of smaller sofas arranged kitty-corner to each other with a single oversized table arranged in the open *L* they made.

Kadin took Rachel to the uncovered area. She could use the direct exposure to sunlight for a bit, and this part of the roof would be in the shade in less than hour as the sun moved across the sky.

He set her down with care on one of the rattan couches. "There. Not our room."

See? He could be reasonable. Really.

She just sighed, letting her head fall back so the sun warmed her face.

A memory of her doing that when they were still kids assailed him. It was the first time he'd seen her as someone to desire. Before that, they'd been friends.

It was while watching her simply soak in the sunshine one day that he'd realized he loved her. She'd looked so beautiful, and he'd known he wanted her to be his.

Forever.

Life had gotten in the way of forever, but she'd never lost that beauty. Other people might think she was average, her hair too medium brown, her eyes too pale a blue to catch attention, her features just a little too normal for the cover of a magazine, but he'd never seen another woman he found even half as compelling.

He lowered himself onto the sofa by her feet, pulling them into his lap.

She didn't fight him, so he started massaging one foot.

"You're awfully good at that. Do they teach it in the Marines?" she asked in the voice he'd already figured out he didn't like.

It was the one that put everyone at a distance, the one that let Rachel's cynicism show through.

He laughed anyway, because the idea was so ridiculous. "No."

"Ah, one of your old girlfriends, then."

"I don't have old girlfriends." Except her, and she knew what she'd been to him. More than a girlfriend. His greatest joy and biggest sorrow.

Well, maybe she didn't know *that*.

Her eyes shot open at that. "Right."

He shrugged. "I don't do relationships."

"He's not lying," Eva said as she crossed the roof toward them. She carried a tray with a pitcher and glasses. "Mrs. Abdul thought you should have something to drink if you were going to be spending time on the roof in the sunshine."

"How did she know we came up here?" Kadin had to ask.

Eva shrugged. "Don't know, but I think the Atrati is wasting her talents as a housekeeper. She'd make a great spy."

"We aren't in the spy business. We're soldiers."

"Most of the time. Maybe TGP should recruit her," Eva said to Rachel.

Rachel shook her head. "We don't keep foreigners on the payroll."

"Sure. Right." Eva didn't sound as if she believed that.

Frankly, Kadin didn't, either. "Who says she isn't already on *ours* as more than just a housekeeper? Her husband has some pretty decent connections in this part of Africa, and they do run this safe house together."

Eva didn't bother to answer.

Rachel didn't seem to notice; she was too busy enjoying whatever type of juice Mrs. Abdul had sent up with the medic. The sound his former lover made as she sipped was damn near pornographic.

He switched his gaze to Eva to see if she noticed, but his medic appeared every bit as enamored with the drink as Rachel. Only the Puerto Rican's reaction didn't affect him the way Rachel's did.

Kadin had to adjust himself before his cock got strangled

by the placket in his fatigues. "Maybe we should get the recipe for that juice if it's going to put such a look of bliss on a person's face."

Rachel smiled. Just a little one, but it was there. "Maybe we should."

"So, Cowboy says you're running surveillance on Miss Massri." Eva was looking at him in question.

"We are."

She gave him a sarcastic grimace. "But we aren't spies?"

"We're what we need to be."

"Okay, then. What's my assignment?"

"You and Peace will be monitoring the listening devices while Rachel goes through what we've recorded so far for anything useful. After she gets Spazz into TGP's file on the Treffert tank."

"That could take forever, and there's no reason to believe I'll pick up something Neil or Cowboy missed," Rachel argued.

"Not really. Spazz's devices only record conversation, not dead air. There should only be a few hours' worth to wade through." Eva frowned. "What's the Treffert tank? I thought I was up on military-grade weaponry, but I've never heard of that one."

Kadin found himself explaining yet again what Spazz and Cowboy had heard Abasi Chuma talking about.

A few hours turned out to be sixteen, but Rachel wasn't complaining.

Only eight hours away from the deadline Whit had given her, she was tired and nearly comatose from not taking breaks, no matter what she'd claimed when Kadin called in to check on her. She still wasn't complaining.

Because listening to the sound recordings from Spazz's eavesdropping devices had proved to be more than a little illuminating.

In fact, it had turned her own conclusions right onto their head.

So far she'd not only heard references to the Treffert tank but also several mentions of Jamila as well.

Why?

Because the man who had come from Egypt with Abasi Chuma was Jamila's uncle. Couple that with the fact that her father had just arrived with her in Marrakech, and there could be little doubt the brothers were heavily involved in the criminal organization for which Chuma worked.

That was the biggest revelation. Being able to listen to Chuma and his cohorts interact without censoring themselves made her realize that, unlike what she'd first believed, Chuma was *not* the top dog.

Oh, he was high up in the organization. That was obvious from the way the men who had captured her deferred to him, but he and Jamila's uncle interacted like equals.

From a couple of comments the two men had made, she surmised they both worked for the same boss. They never named him, which told her two things.

The first, their subordinates didn't know who the head honcho was. The second, these men were good at and careful about keeping their secrets. It implied that knowledge of who that man was could be dangerous to the man himself.

Why would that be?

Someone important with a stellar reputation? Someone who had connections to government officials and other people of power?

Chuma might have fit those criteria. At first glance. Initially, Rachel had assumed he did. But now that she knew more about him, and now that a new way of thinking about his organization had opened up, it put other observations she'd made during her investigation in a different light.

There was a person in this mix who fit all the criteria—powerful, dangerous, but untouchable—a man Rachel herself had never even suspected as anyone other than someone turning a blind eye to his soon-to-be son-in-law's questionable activities.

Jamila Massri's father.

The man might be as innocent as he appeared, but Rachel didn't generally give men the benefit of the doubt.

Besides, she adhered to the tenet of Occam's razor: given multiple possible scenarios to explain an outcome, the simplest one was almost always the correct one.

Massri's future son by marriage and brother worked for the same man. A person they had to contact pretty frequently to do the things they did. Someone with connections who facilitated acquiring privileged information and then sold it to the highest bidder.

Who better than a well-respected doctor with a low-level government appointment that gave him access to those in the know without pointing to him as an obvious person of interest?

She'd been fooled, and it frustrated her.

She'd let herself be blinded by the unassuming-doctor persona Massri used as camouflage. Even his own daughter considered Abasi Chuma more of a "man's man" than her father.

This discovery, or, rather, deduction, which Rachel's gut told her was right on, was a huge step forward in TGP's investigation. Whit was going to be thrilled.

Chills ran straight down Rachel's spine at the thought. Once Whit found out that Dr. Massri was at the top of the food chain in the organization that her fellow agent Bennet Vincent had uncovered during his operation in Zimbabwe, Whit was going to want Jamila flipped for sure.

No way was Rachel letting that happen. Jamila was already at risk. Setting her to spy on the doctor would increase that risk at least tenfold.

A man who would give his daughter to a man like Abasi Chuma wouldn't hesitate to kill that same daughter if he discovered she'd betrayed him. Even unwittingly.

Feeling sick to her stomach, Rachel felt terror wash over her at the idea of Chuma discovering his fiancée's connection to a TGP operative.

Catching and imprisoning Dr. Massri wouldn't remove the threat to Jamila, either.

Even in prison, men like Massri still had allies on the outside. Allies who could take his revenge on Jamila.

The problem was bigger than just getting Jamila away from Chuma or even out of Africa, for that matter. Somehow, Rachel had to get the other woman to safety without making her a target for Dr. Massri and the unsavory people he worked with.

Rachel was about to turn off the verbal feed and go call Kadin when something Chuma said to Jamila's uncle caught her attention. Taking quick notes, she tried to understand what they were talking about and its significance.

Because the change in both men's tones indicated that whatever they were discussing was of some importance. That none of the other men was in the room at the time also pointed to its being of interest.

She highlighted the short discussion in the printout of the recording, correcting a few words the voice-to-text software had gotten wrong, just as she'd been doing all along.

This time felt more important than changing a *womb* to *woman,* though.

★   ★   ★

Planting the bugs in the hotel room went without a hitch; Abdul's operative reported back to Kadin with an all-clear not fifteen minutes after going into the building. Spazz had said he would wait to activate the listening devices remotely until thirty minutes after Dr. Massri and his daughter checked in to the hotel.

That way, if the rooms were swept for bugs upon the Massris' arrival, at either his or Chuma's order, the tiny devices would not register.

Kadin knew that Rachel wasn't entirely convinced of Dr. Massri's involvement in Chuma's criminal activities, but it didn't hurt to be prepared, regardless. And underestimating the caution of those they were gathering intel on wasn't something either he or his team made a habit of.

Jamila and her father checked in to the hotel, and not long after, Dr. Massri left her there. Cowboy followed the doctor to a large house outside the city, where he remained until nearly midnight.

Dr. Massri returned to the hotel long after his daughter had gone to bed, having eaten a solitary dinner in her room. Jamila had spent the evening online and then watching a documentary on the migration pattern of birds.

Exciting stuff.

When it became apparent that Dr. Massri had no plans further than going to bed himself, Kadin spoke to Cowboy through their communication earbuds. "Back to the safe house."

"Roger that."

It was a thirty-minute walk, and they arrived, from different directions, within a couple minutes of each other.

Kadin knew he should check in with his team first, but he made a beeline for the room he shared with Rachel. He needed to see her sleeping safely in the bed.

Of course, it was empty, and unless Rachel made the

bed with the same precise folds as did Abdul's wife, she hadn't so much as napped in it in the last sixteen hours.

A growl of frustration on his lips, Kadin double-timed it back downstairs and to Spazz's command center.

Chapter Eleven

Sure enough, Rachel was there, going over something with Spazz. Cowboy was watching them surreptitiously while he shot the shit with Peace.

"Where's Eva?" Kadin barked, because saying what he wanted would just send Rachel into one of her snits.

He wasn't prepared to deal with that just yet, no matter how much he usually enjoyed doing so.

"Sleeping, Trigger, like dat *wahine* should be doing." Peace indicated Rachel with a nod of his head, his attention split between them and the earbud feeding him information from Spazz's listening devices.

Kadin let out another growl, this time glaring at Rachel's back. She hadn't even bothered to turn around when he came in.

"She be one stubborn *wahine,* Trigger. Eva be dat pissed wid her."

Peace never hid his Hawaiian origins, but the accent got thicker when he was making a point.

"Rachel," Kadin barked, deciding he didn't have a choice but to deal with her snark.

The woman needed rest.

She turned then, her eyes wide, as if she had no idea what had him so irritated.

"Save it," he warned her. "You told me you were resting."

"I was resting."

He just glared.

"I took the extra laptop to the roof garden and relaxed on one of the big sofas while listening to the recordings."

"You were only supposed to listen for a couple of hours at a time."

Her snort just pissed him off more.

"You ignored Eva's medical advice," he accused.

Rachel shrugged. "You don't want to know how many times I've checked out of a hospital against medical advice."

Hell. He didn't want to know how many times her job had put her *into* the hospital, but he couldn't stop himself asking. "How many?"

This time her clear blue eyes widened in genuine surprise, as if she couldn't believe he'd asked. Neither could he, but he wanted an answer.

"That's really not important right now, is it?"

"Spazz?"

"Yeah, Trigger?"

"How many times?"

The sound coming out of Rachel was something between a shriek and a growl, muted by her still-tender voice box. "You are not seriously asking him to stop important research to hack into my medical file."

"I won't be. If you answer me."

"Well, now, maybe dat stubborn *wahine* met her match now," Peace said with satisfaction as he wrote something on the tablet computer in front of him.

Rachel's frown at the Hawaiian soldier was lost on him as his focus remained on what he was hearing. When she turned the expression to Kadin, it went sulfuric.

"Seriously, you're going to make an issue out of this now?"

"You brought it up."

"Not because I thought you'd actually care."

"I guess you don't know everything about me that you believe you do," he said with more force than current conversation warranted.

"Four, all right? Sheesh!" She turned away from him.

But he was not done with this.

"You were in the hospital four times?" he demanded in a voice he barely recognized as his own.

What the hell had she been doing to herself over the past ten years?

"Yes," she flipped over her shoulder. "You want details?"

Oh, the sarcasm was just dripping.

"I do." His tone was nothing but pure demand.

"Forget it."

"Spa—" Kadin didn't even get the other man's name out before Rachel was spinning around again, this time fire shooting from her pale eyes.

She crossed the distance between them in three quick strides and poked him right in the center of the chest. "You are being an ass. We have important stuff going on here."

"And you can get right back to it after you answer my question. You're just taking more time arguing with me," he pointed out reasonably.

"I had my appendix out the year after you dumped me. I got knifed on one of my first cases, but I made the damn collar." She ticked each incident off on her fingers. "I took a bullet to my right thigh on that case I told you about."

"Shit."

She smiled grimly. "Don't worry, there was no lasting damage. It was a through-and-through."

A serious thigh wound would have required physical therapy and a hell of a lot of recovery time. "That's three," he ground out.

"I ended up in the ER dehydrated with the flu last year."

"How the hell did that happen?"

"I collapsed in the canned-soup aisle at three in the morning, and they called an ambulance instead of waking me up." She sounded as if she thought the store clerk had overreacted.

"What were you doing in the grocery store at three in the frickin' morning?"

"Buying chicken noodle soup. What else?"

And then he understood. This woman he'd thought would grow up to be a nursery school teacher, surrounded by her own family and those of her pupils, was completely alone.

She had no friends close enough to take care of her when she was sick. No one to even notice she was too ill to be on her own. No man to give her the babies she'd wanted so much when they were together ten years ago. No family to care if she showed up for Sunday dinner.

"Where is your grandmother?"

"In a nursing home. She has Alzheimer's."

Kadin's heart broke to hear precisely how alone Rachel had been. "When was the last time you spoke to her?" he asked gently.

"At Linny's funeral. It was pretty much the last time she was able to make sense. I've visited her, but . . ."

"I'm sorry."

"You're sorry? After ten years? You even care? Get real."

"I am."

"Fine. You're sorry. Now get off your ass and help me save Jamila Massri."

"I am doing my best," he practically yelled. He'd just spent sixteen hours on surveillance detail.

"Do better!" There was no *almost* about the volume coming out of her throat.

"She's sleeping, like you should be."

"I'll sleep when she's safe."

Shit. He just knew Rachel was going to say something stupid like that. And, worse, mean it. "She's safe right now."

"For how long?"

That wasn't an answer Kadin had, and the look on Rachel's face said she knew it.

He took a deep breath, regrouping, and only then realized that everyone in the room was staring at him and Rachel with varying degrees of shock. Eva stood in the doorway, her hair sticking up at odd angles, revealing that she'd just gotten out of bed, her expression indicating she'd witnessed the argument between Rachel and Trigger.

Kadin ignored them all and asked Rachel, "What do you have?"

"The principle players and the name of the top dog. I think."

"Explain."

She did, and when she enumerated her reasons for suspecting Dr. Massri of being the boss rather than Chuma, Kadin couldn't disagree.

He said a word he'd always been careful not to use in front of this woman. Another habit he hadn't thought to break.

"We think we've figured out the connection to the Treffert tank, too," she said, indicating Spazz with a wave of her hand.

The blond computer geek nodded. "It's bad, Trigger."

"Nuclear-holocaust bad, or this is gonna be a-shitload-of-paperwork-for-Roman bad?" Kadin probed.

"Less than World War III but more than paperwork."
Spazz didn't even crack a joke with that one.

And that worried Kadin more than anything that had
been said in this room. "Sit-rep," he demanded, wanting
an immediate breakdown on the situation.

"The Treffert tank has made some breakthroughs in
acoustic levitation." Spazz's eyes glowed with admiration.
"It's amazing. The system's far from stable, or even usable
in its current form, but the idea is air transport using a
fraction of the energy currently necessary for thrust-based
technology."

"What good is it to Chuma's group if they can't use it?"
Kadin asked, not surprised he was a little confused.

He often was when talking to Spazz.

"They aren't thinking of using the technology to move
people or goods." Rachel's pretty oval face was set in
stressed lines. "What does this ring of criminals specialize
in?"

The Atrati's exposure to information on the ring that
had been operating in Africa was limited to their two operations, Roman's the year before and this one, so Kadin
went with what he knew these people sold. "Intel and
weapons technology?"

"Right."

Kadin still felt like he was double-timing it through a
dark forest. "But this levitation thing isn't a weapon."

"It could be." Spazz sounded more than serious; he
sounded worried.

"How?"

"*If* they can figure out how to harness it and keep it
more than marginally stable, the acoustic levitation system
might be misused to create a shock wave that could level
cities."

"You said it wasn't nuclear holocaust."

"It's not. Yet. Right now, it's these bastards making plans to kidnap the autistic savant who has made the biggest breakthroughs on it."

"They're going to try to force him to turn it into a weapon?" The thought of someone like his nephew being used that way filled Kadin with fury and fear.

Making his nephew do anything he didn't want to was a very iffy proposition because of the different way the boy related to the world around him. What methods Chuma and Massri might employ to try to force an autistic man to work for them didn't bear thinking about.

Not if he wanted to keep the contents of his stomach.

"I need to talk to Roman. That savant needs protection, now." Kadin grabbed his satphone and started dialing.

Rachel grabbed his hands, stilling his movements. "Wait."

"What?" he demanded, images spinning through his brain that he wasn't processing very well.

"I don't want Whit to know that Dr. Massri is the big boss yet."

No trouble figuring out why. "You don't want him giving orders to flip Jamila."

"I don't want him sending another TGP agent who will actually do it." Rachel's entire body was tense with stress, and that was the last damn thing she needed after what she'd been through.

"Whit's not a monster."

"No, but he's a man who puts duty and patriotism first, last, and always. Just ask his daughter, the TGP agent."

"Are you saying that's a bad thing?"

"One thing I learned working DEA? Collateral damage can be a heck of a lot worse than anyone anticipates, and I don't subscribe to the-ends-always-justify-the-means theory."

"I know that about you." He'd known it ten years ago.

It was one of the biggest reasons he knew he had to let her go. He never wanted to watch the light of love turn to disgust in Rachel Gannon's eyes when she looked at him.

"If you don't tell him about Massri, how do you plan to get approval to extract Jamila?"

"I don't."

"What do you intend to do, go rogue?"

"Take a leave of absence and figure out a way to do a voluntary extraction."

"If Massri decides his daughter has betrayed him, getting her away from him isn't going to keep her safe."

"I know."

"She's better off where she is, Rachel."

"Is she? There's still the problem of her marrying Chuma."

"The wedding isn't set to take place for three more months."

"That could change."

"Doubtful."

"You think Chuma's the type of man to wait for his wedding night if he decides he wants her before that?"

"Is there any indication he's not going to wait?" Kadin needed Rachel to take a rational step back, but she was wrapped up in her emotions right now.

It was a side of the woman he knew well and in another situation would be glad to see was still there under the cynical government-agent exterior; but it wasn't going to help her make the most practical choices right now. Or even the best ones for Jamila Massri.

"With a man like that, his intentions could change on a whim."

Kadin couldn't deny it. He'd known men like Abasi Chuma. He'd killed men like Chuma . . . because sometimes his government decided a dog just had to be put down before it bit more innocents, infecting them with its rabies.

He'd done less of that since joining the Atrati, but the ability to make the hard choices and act on them still resided inside Kadin.

"You are under direct orders not to be seen with Jamila in Marrakech," he reminded Rachel.

She gave an affirmative jerk of her head, but the stubborn tilt to her chin said that, orders or no orders, she was getting Jamila out of there.

"Listen. I'll tell Roman to keep the information about Massri's pay grade out of his briefing with Whit, but we need to act before this autistic genius gets himself kidnapped by the people you're so determined to save Jamila from."

"Are you sure he won't tell Whit?" Rachel asked.

"Yes."

"You trust him."

"More than you trust Whit."

She looked offended. "I would trust Whit with my life."

"But not Jamila's."

Rachel was silent for several seconds but then sighed and admitted, "Not when American secrets and lives are on the line, no."

"He doesn't have your save-the-whole-world mentality?"

"No." At least she didn't deny that part of herself. "He sees it as a side benefit of saving his own country."

"You don't."

"I'm not that tunnel-visioned. Or naïve."

Some things about Rachel had not changed, but her innocent view of the world? He had to agree. That had been blasted with the special C-4 of life.

And long before she'd been kidnapped and tortured by the people she was investigating.

★ ★ ★

Rachel called Whit while Kadin was talking to his chief.
"Rachel?"

"Yes, it's me." She swallowed, her throat suddenly dry.
"There's been a development."

"Go on," Whit said with more impatience than she was
used to hearing from him.

"Chuma and his cohorts have their sights set on someone else." She explained about the Treffert tank and the
roundabout connection Spazz had discovered between it
and Abasi Chuma.

"Explain that again," Whit ordered in a tone devoid of
emotion.

She did.

"You're leaving something out, Rachel."

"It's nothing, sir."

"The connection isn't Chuma. What you're describing
is tenuous and vague, but your tone tells me you're dead
certain of your conclusions. Which means you know exactly how the Treffert tank and this ring of intel and
weapons-technology dealers are connected. And it's not
through Chuma. That leads me to believe you've discovered he's not the top of the food chain in this organization."

"Oh, he's at the top, sir," she said with the first total
honesty she'd shared since she'd begun speaking to her superior.

"But not *the* top."

She wanted to lie, had already done so by omission, but
found she simply could not do it. "No, sir."

"Who is?"

"I'm not sure." She *wasn't* positive; she just had a very
good hunch.

"You think it's Massri."

"Sir?"

"I'm not an idiot, Rachel. I've been doing this job for a very long time."

"I'm sorry, sir."

"For believing I'm stupid, or for not trusting me with the truth?"

"I didn't think you were stupid." She just thought she was better at subterfuge. Darn it.

"You believe I'll insist on flipping Miss Massri."

"Yes, sir."

"I have a daughter, and though she may not believe it, I would give my life for her."

"Yes, sir."

"There is no doubt that Dr. Massri is not of the same mind."

"No, sir."

"He would sooner kill her than let her undermine him."

"Yes, sir." Rachel couldn't help the catch in her voice.

And suddenly Kadin was there, his hand on her shoulder. "I'll call you back," he said into the satphone in his hand and then severed the connection so fast, his chief couldn't have had enough time to respond.

Rachel stared at him, at a loss for words.

"Rachel?" Whit prompted in her ear.

"You okay?" Kadin asked.

"Yes," she replied to them both, not sure she meant it.

"I am not issuing orders to flip Miss Massri," Whit said, sounding tired.

"To me . . . or to *anyone?*" Rachel couldn't help asking.

"To anyone."

"Thank you, sir." Rachel felt her knees buckle, her relief was so great.

She didn't fall, though; she simply sagged into Kadin, who was somehow holding her, his strong arms supporting her weight.

"Unfortunately, that's all I can do for the young woman

right now," Whit continued in her ear, oblivious to her reaction.

"What do you mean, sir?"

"You cannot bring her in, for her own sake as well of
that of our investigation." Clearly Whit had processed the
risk to Jamila in the space of seconds. "As of this moment,
Jamila Massri is out of the investigation in any capacity."

"But sir, what about the Treffert tank angle?"

"We will put additional security on all the members of
the think tank immediately, but that has nothing to do
with Miss Massri."

"She's at risk here, sir."

"So are thousands of American lives if this network
isn't fully disbanded. We need the investigation to continue."

"Then let me be the one to continue it."

"That's not possible." Whit was silent, and she could
picture him rubbing his eyes as he did sometimes. "Your
cover has been compromised at the very least. Chuma and
Massri cannot see you."

"I can't leave her, sir."

"I can't sanction protective surveillance, Rachel."

"I'll take my vacation," she insisted again.

"All vacation requests are currently on hold."

So he'd said, but that didn't make any sense. "You're
saying you *can't* give me vacation leave? But why, sir?"

"I'm not at liberty to say. These things happen sometimes."

But not at TGP. It wasn't the usual government agency.

"I'm not com—"

"The best I can offer you right now," Whit said, cutting
across her insubordination before she could get a direct refusal of orders completely out, "is indefinite unpaid medical leave due to the traumatic nature of your assignment's

end, and transport home when you decide to return from Africa."

Rachel didn't worry about the financial consequences or what this might mean for her career; she just said, "Thank you, sir."

"Wrap this up, quickly, Rachel. The medical leave isn't just an excuse. You need psychological debriefing and support."

"I'll do my best, sir."

"I'll be sending in another agent to continue the work you started. Will you be available to brief her?"

"Yes, of course." She was surprised Whit was going to send in another female agent, but the man *had* been doing this for a long time.

He knew what he was doing, even if Rachel didn't understand it.

"Rachel?"

"Yes, sir?"

"Watch out for yourself. I don't want to lose a good agent to her need to protect someone else."

Rachel didn't have an answer that Whit would want to hear, so she simply told him good-bye.

"What's going on?" Kadin asked.

"He's not going to try to flip Jamila, but I'm off the case."

"And?"

"And I'm on unpaid medical leave." She repeated the rest of what Whit had said.

Kadin nodded, his expression giving nothing away of what he was thinking.

"Roman tells me he needs a medic on a team he's got in the Congo," he announced to the group.

The cold wind of abandonment blew over Rachel, making her shiver. "Okay."

She needed to get out of his arms, stand on her own two feet . . . like she'd been doing the last ten years. But she couldn't make those self-same independent, strong-willed feet move.

Chapter Twelve

Kadin shifted, though not away. If anything, she ended up plastered more securely to his side.

He addressed the others in the room. "Roman wants Eva in the Congo tomorrow."

The female medic nodded her understanding. "What are my travel plans?"

"Helicopter transport. You'll be meeting your helo at a small airfield two hours south of here."

Rachel wondered why they weren't using the main airport but then realized it was probably a matter of security. And secrecy.

"What about us, Trigger?" Cowboy asked.

"Peace is going with Eva. Roman wants her to have an escort. . . ." He stopped talking, as if he was waiting.

Eva, who had been on her way out of the room, stopped and turned slowly. "He said *what?*"

Kadin's grin was pure evil. "He wanted you to have an escort."

"And you recommended *me?* Thanks a lot, brudda." Peace didn't look even slightly like he was looking forward to the assignment.

"I don't need an escort, asshole," Eva said to Peace in a vicious tone.

"See what I mean?" Peace asked with a wink at Rachel.

And Rachel got it. Eva was pissed that her chief thought she needed protection. She clearly had no trouble taking that anger out on the closest target at hand.

"Roman said he wanted your skill set on the team in the Congo, too, Peace," Kadin said, his amusement at his own pot-stirring ringing in his voice.

"Right," Eva spat. "As if Roman Chernichenko would send a team to that region without a weapons specialist."

"He sent Colt. Who's now in Hôpital Pitié-Salpêtrière in Paris, on the critical list."

That took the wind out of Eva's sails. "I'm sorry to hear that. Colt's a good guy."

"I'm a good guy, too," Peace claimed, sounding hurt but looking like he had a bit of Kadin's devilment in his eyes, as well.

"You're an idiot. You'd better watch your ass, is what you'd better do, *asno*. No one on my team is ending up in some French hospital. You hear me?" Eva demanded before leaving the room, muttering to herself in Spanish.

"They don't need a computer expert?" Spazz asked.

Cowboy's body jerked, as though he didn't like the question.

"They've got that new guy on their team."

"Hansen?" Spazz asked.

"Yeah."

"He's good, but I'm better."

Kadin shrugged. "You're the best. That's why you're on my team."

"You hear that, Cowboy? I'm the best."

"I would have told you that. If you'd let me." The cowboy soldier's tone implied he meant more than his words said on the surface.

Neil ignored him, his attention fixed on Kadin. "What are our orders?"

"I didn't get them."

"What?" Cowboy asked, his eyebrows raised.

"I hung up on Chief."

"He's not going to like that."

Kadin shrugged. "He's used to it."

Neil laughed. "Are you kidding? There's only one guy who is normally more laid-back than you, and that's Peace."

"Normally," Cowboy drawled. "When your filly doesn't have you tied in more knots than a new roper's lariat."

Rachel was expecting Kadin to deny that she was *his,* but he just shook his head. "He'll get over it."

"Yeah, but will you when he assigns you to the next team dropping into Afghanistan?"

"But you aren't with the military anymore," Rachel protested, forgetting the rest of their conversation for the moment.

"I'm not."

"Then why go to Afghanistan?"

"We go where we're needed."

"Well, they don't need you there," she said before she had a chance to censor her words.

Kadin didn't laugh or tell her it wasn't up to her. He simply squeezed her tighter, and she let him. "Not right now, they don't."

"So?" Neil prompted.

"I'm staying in Africa with Rachel."

For the second time in less than half an hour, the relief coursing through Rachel would have taken her to the floor if her former lover hadn't been holding her up.

He looked down at her, his beautiful sherry brown gaze narrowed with determination. "You need someone at your back, angel. That someone is going to be me." The promise sounded so sure, so long-term.

She wouldn't let herself be tricked into believing she had someone to rely on for life, but he was here *now.* And she'd learned with Linny's death that sometimes the only way to keep going was to live in the present and let the future take care of itself.

"Okay, then, we've got our orders," Neil said, as if Kadin's words had made up his mind about something.

Cowboy nodded. "The Atrati don't leave their team leaders hanging. It's not the way we roll."

Neil smiled at Rachel. "Besides, I'm a sucker for a damsel in distress."

Rachel didn't ask if he meant Jamila or her; she wasn't sure she wanted the answer to that. She didn't consider herself one of the people needing rescue—and hadn't, until recently, for a very long time. But there was no denying that Kadin's team had done exactly that. And that brought her back to a place she didn't want to be.

Feeling less than invincible and maybe not as expendable as she'd believed since Linny's suicide.

"And Spazz needs someone riding herd on his crazy ass," Cowboy added with a smirk. "I'm just the man for the job."

Neil glared at the other man but didn't make a vehement denial, and Rachel wondered if his attitude toward his teammate was softening.

Kadin just shook his head as if the other two men were idiots, but the grateful expression on his warrior's face told the real story. He lifted the satphone again. "I need to talk to Roman."

The little black box beeped with an incoming call right then, as if it had been timed.

Kadin finished his call with Roman, acutely aware of the fact that Rachel had not tried to move out of his arms the entire time he had been talking to his superior.

She was just devious enough to have stayed close in order to be able to hear Roman's side of their conversation, but Kadin preferred to believe she was willing to accept his comfort. If only for the present.

"We're cleared to stay in Morocco for the time being," he said as he set the satphone down.

"How?" Rachel demanded, her tone wary, the tension in her frame increasing instead of lessening as he would have expected.

He looked down at her, trying to read the expression in her blue gaze. "Our mission is to extract you from Africa. You refuse to be extracted. Roman has approved additional time to help you see reason."

"You don't have to respect my wishes," Rachel said, as if she couldn't keep herself from pointing that fact out.

"I do." Whatever his team or Roman or even Rachel believed, there was no way in hell's half acre that Kadin was going to drug Rachel and dump her unwilling ass onto a plane.

"Thank you."

He knew the words had cost her.

It was there in the pinched lines of her pretty face.

He brushed his thumb over her brow, smoothing the worry lines, needing her to relax a little. "You're not alone."

"For now." But she didn't fight when he pulled her just that much closer.

"Now is all that matters."

In his line of business, agents didn't know if they'd be alive the next day, much less the next year. Oh, the Atrati were the best at what they did, but there was no way to ignore the fact that it was a damn dangerous job.

They all learned to live in the moment. It was one of the reasons he'd been able to stay away from this woman for a decade. Living in the now left the past and the future off-limits.

"I've learned that lesson, too. It's the only way to get

through the day sometimes." Her words reflected his thoughts so closely, it was uncanny.

The last thing he'd wanted for Rachel was for her to become too comfortable in his world. That was one of the reasons he'd left hers.

But for some reason the sweet young woman he'd left behind had rejected that gift and gone looking for the harsher side of life herself.

Damn it all to hell.

All he could say now was, "Then we're in agreement."

"We watch Chuma, Massri, and Jamila."

"You think like a government agent, even when you're on unpaid medical leave," he teased her.

"What do you mean?"

"It's not your case any longer, but you want to keep your eyes on the players anyway."

Telltale pink seeped into Rachel's cheeks, but she said, "Keeping Jamila safe requires knowing what those men are up to."

"Maybe. We could just throw her ass onto a plane, your director's orders be damned."

"Chuma and Massri are going down soon. She can't disappear right before the authorities move in. Not if she doesn't want to spend the rest of her life looking over her shoulder for one of her father's *friends* bent on revenge."

Kadin nodded. The suggestion had been worth a try, but he'd known what Rachel's response would be before she made it.

"When does your other TGP agent arrive?" he asked her.

"As soon as she can get here."

"*She?*" Spazz prompted, sounding as unimpressed by the idea as Kadin felt. "Your director thinks sending another woman in is a good idea?"

Call them sexists, but having just rescued one woman

from being tortured, he and his men weren't eager to hear about another in the same predicament. Eva would hand them their asses for even thinking like that, but then, the medic thought she was titanium plated.

"Whit knows what he's doing." Rachel rubbed between her eyes, showing by her gesture if not her words that she was worried, too. "My guess is, she'll be a very different type of agent from me."

"Ah . . . someone to appeal to Chuma or Massri's baser natures." Spazz didn't look too happy at that option.

Kadin wasn't, either. Chuma's *baser nature* was pretty sick, and even a supremely trained agent could find herself in a world of hurt with a man like that.

Kadin was just really glad that wasn't the type of undercover Rachel specialized in.

"We need to catch sleep while we can. Our principles are tucked up in their beds; it's time we found ours," Kadin said in his command tone.

Spazz opened his mouth to argue, but Cowboy put his hand right over the other man's lips and promised Kadin, "We'll go up."

Spazz said something that was too muffled by Cowboy's hand to be understood.

Kadin's fellow former MARSOC soldier looked down at the glaring man sitting at the computer. "Whatever you want to look into will wait for morning. That big brain of yours needs rest. Your body needs sleep. Now, get your ass up those stairs and into your rack before I decide you need a bed buddy to make sure you stay there."

Kadin wanted to laugh, but he kept it in. Rachel looked so out of it, she wasn't even taking in the interplay.

Spazz knocked the other man's hand away. "If you get into my bed, it won't be to sleep."

"Well, now, sugar, that's up to you, isn't it?"

The two men left the room, bickering, the sexual tension so thick between them, Kadin wouldn't give odds for more than one rack being used.

"That just leaves us," Rachel said quietly, making no effort to move.

"That it does, angel. That it does." He picked her up high against his chest and headed out of the room.

Kadin didn't even try to hide his smile of triumph when Rachel tucked her arms around his neck and rested her head on his shoulder. She couldn't see his lips from that angle, anyway.

She sighed, her breath brushing over his neck and sending sexual sparks exploding through him. "You've got to stop carrying me around like this."

Yeah, that was a sincere complaint.

"Why?"

"You've spent the last sixteen hours on surveillance. You must be tired, too."

Maybe he should be, but the energy of sexual desire was zinging through him. Despite learning to sleep anytime, anywhere in the Marines, Kadin sincerely doubted he was going to get a whole lot of rest tonight.

Not with Rachel's delectable body in the same house, much less the same bed.

"I'm not too tired to carry you." He started up the narrow stairway. "You should have been in bed hours ago."

"I sleep better with you in the room."

Her admission shocked him, and he stopped halfway up the stairs, meeting her gaze. Her eyes remained a mystery in the muted glow cast by the night-light in the wall that served as the only illumination between the lower and upper halls.

But her expression was tinged with an unmistakable vulnerability he was sure she'd rather he couldn't see.

"You need to debrief." He hadn't meant to say that, but it was true all the same.

This woman needed to unload at least the most recent demons riding her.

"I will, when I get Stateside." But her promise rang hollow.

He couldn't help thinking of the number of times she'd checked out of a hospital AMA. Every single time she'd been in one. That didn't bode well for her taking her mental health seriously.

"You'll debrief with me here."

"Or what?"

Smart girl. She knew he wouldn't make a demand without backing it up.

"Or my team is going to do what it does best."

"What does that mean?"

"We do extractions, Rachel, and we do them without prejudice." She didn't need to know he was bluffing.

"I'll just be on the next flight back."

"We'll take Jamila with us."

"Kadin, that's not an option, and you damn well know it."

"Neither is you refusing to debrief."

She looked away, as if meeting his gaze even in this dim light was too much. "It's not necessary."

"I disagree."

"Kadin . . ."

"Rachel, *I'm* here for *you.* If not me, who? Who are you going to tell what they did to you in that house in the mountains?"

"And if I said anyone *but* you?"

"I wouldn't believe you." He would have, even yesterday.

But not today.

"Why?"

"Because you may hate my guts for walking away from you ten years ago, but you still trust me. And even though it has been ten years, I know you better than anyone else alive. Who better to hear the words that need saying?"

Her face contorted with a flash of grief, but she didn't deny his words as she would have even twenty-four hours ago.

"Maybe they don't need saying. Maybe I don't need to talk about it. You got me out. That's all that matters." She sounded like she was trying to convince herself.

Maybe she was doing a better job with that than convincing him, because he didn't buy it for a second.

"No."

She gave him a naked look of such pained helplessness, he wanted to kiss her, to promise her that everything was going to be okay.

But that wasn't what she really needed right now. "You want to keep Jamila safe? You need my help. You debrief."

She didn't say anything, but he wasn't a fool. He knew this discussion wasn't over.

He continued up to their room, pushing the door shut behind them with his hip once they were inside.

He didn't release her immediately. She felt too good in his arms, and he wasn't entirely sure of his control if they went to bed right that second.

"Kadin?"

"Uh-huh?"

"You need to put me down."

"Do I?"

"Yes." It was the smile in her voice that made him do it.

He wanted to see that expression. He released her legs, carefully lowering her into a standing position beside the bed. A small curve still lingered on her lips, and it was all he could do not to bend down and claim it for his own.

He stepped away, digging deep for his control as he stripped down to his shorts in preparation for sleeping. Maybe he should have left his fatigues on, but damn if a pair of pants was going to do what his willpower couldn't.

Either he mastered himself, or he didn't.

And not controlling his need simply wasn't an option.

She stood, unmoving and staring at the bed, the entire time he got rid of his boots, fatigues, and weapons. As if she didn't hear him taking off his clothes right behind her. She would probably sleep in her scrubs, the way she had last night, but then, why didn't she get under the covers?

He was starting to worry about that silent stillness. Was something wrong?

He moved toward her, intent on finding out what was going on in that beautiful head of hers.

"You're saying you won't help me with Jamila if I don't debrief with you," she said just before his hand landed on her shoulder.

He aborted his movement and considered how to answer. "I won't help the way you think I should."

"You'll kidnap us both and take us out of Africa."

"Yes." And maybe he would, too, if she refused to take care of herself.

She spun to face him, her expression troubled and confused in a way that he hated seeing. "We're on the same side here, Kadin."

"No. You're all about Jamila. I'm all about you."

"Don't say that."

Fine. He would put it in terms Rachel could accept. "My mission is to get you safely out of Africa. Your long-term safety is reliant on you debriefing after what you went through at the hands of those bastards in the mountains."

"They tortured me with a car battery. They weren't even inventive with it."

He nodded, not saying anything. It was her turn to talk.

"What difference does it make if I talk to you about it or wait until we get Stateside and talk to someone else?"

"You know the answer to that question."

"Spell it out for me, anyway," she demanded.

Fine. Maybe she needed reminding of what she'd been taught during training for her job. "The longer you wait, the more you will internalize what happened to you, making it a deeper part of your psyche."

He wasn't going to let that happen.

"Who taught you that? Or did you read it on the side of a cereal box?" The words were snide, but the expression in her pale eyes was nothing but wounded vulnerability.

"I've got a lot of experience." And the Atrati were much bigger sticklers than the modern military for debriefing and psychological coaching.

"Who do you talk to?"

"My team."

"They're your family now."

"No." Damn it. *No.*

He cared about the men and women of the Atrati, and he would die for any member of his team, but he hadn't given up his family.

Just pushed them to a necessary distance.

"So, what are they?"

"My friends."

"I don't have friends."

He'd already figured that out. "You push people away."

"If you let them in, they'll leave eventually. Everyone does."

She had more reason to believe that than most. Even so . . . "That's a lonely way to live."

She shrugged. "I have my job."

A job that had gotten her stabbed, shot, and so run down, she'd ended up in the hospital with the flu.

"You need more."

She nodded, surprising him. And her next move almost paralyzed him with shock. Rachel shoved her scrubs down her legs and then pulled the top off over her head, leaving her completely naked.

And unlike when he'd given her the massage, this time she'd bared herself for him, giving him tacit permission to look his fill. And look he did.

"Rachel?" His voice cracked like a randy teenager's, but, damn, if that wasn't the way she wanted him to feel, she shouldn't be standing there bare-assed naked in front of him.

"You said it yourself. I need more."

"Uh-huh." He didn't have a clue what she meant, but agreeing with her seemed like a good idea.

The woman was standing there with her fists planted on her smooth, entirely revealed hips. And no matter how many other female bodies he'd seen over the years, there wasn't a single one that had ever done it for Kadin like this woman's.

She was five-feet-five-inches of pure, feminine sex appeal. His fingers spasmed with the need to touch breasts that would fit perfectly in his hands. Tipped with raspberry pink nipples hardened to morsels that made his mouth water, they were as real and genuine as the woman they belonged to.

Her body was more toned than it had been ten years ago, the curve of her ass just as tempting, her features more mature, her lips even more kissable, but her pale blue gaze was a lot less innocent.

And, holy hell, she was still the one and only woman he had wanted to spend the rest of his life with. The one woman who made all others forgettable in comparison.

She cocked her head to the side, studying him. "I remember that look in your eyes."

"What look?" he asked, the words barely making it past his dry throat.

"The one that means you want sex."

"I want *you*."

She nodded, her eyes going heavy-lidded just like that. "Good. I want it, too."

He noticed how she'd changed the desire from personal to generic, from his need for *her* to the craving for sex itself. Ten years ago, he would have called her on it.

Ten years ago, he would have had the right.

He didn't anymore.

Besides, his cock was too damn hard with all the blood from his brain for him to think clearly enough to do much more than agree.

To whatever she wanted.

Thankfully, that was him right now.

Chapter Thirteen

Then a thought came to him. "You're not getting out of debriefing by having sex."

"Tonight I am."

He opened his mouth to argue, but she shook her head. "Tonight, I want to forget. The pain, the terror, the certainty that death was my only way out."

Shit. "Whatever you need, angel."

"I want to remember, too," she said, as if she hadn't heard him. "I want to remember that touch can bring pleasure bigger than the pain could ever be."

"I'm not sure—"

"Shut up, Kadin," she ordered. "With you, the pleasure is that big."

Ten years ago, it had been, but that still hadn't been enough to keep him by her side. Not when he'd felt the call to protect his country with his life and abilities. And he'd known it wouldn't be enough to keep her with him once she discovered what he'd become.

She brushed her hair back over her shoulders before tweaking her own nipples. "I'll make a deal with you."

It about brought him to his knees. "Yeah?"

"Words for sex."

"What?" He knew his head wasn't working the way it should, but that didn't make any sense.

"I'll talk about it all with you, but you give me sex." She brushed her hands down her body.

He couldn't tell if she was pleasuring herself or teasing him by drawing attention to what she was offering. It didn't matter. He wanted it. Wanted her, with an ache that had lived inside his gut for more than a decade and he was damn sure by now would always be with him.

"Not just tonight?" he clarified, praying it wasn't just for that night.

Once he touched Rachel intimately, he didn't think he was going to be able to give that up again anytime soon. If ever.

She shook her head slowly, the movement deliberate, her expression intent. "As often as I want it."

He didn't grin with triumph only because he wasn't going to do anything to mess this up. If she wanted sex for talking, hell, that was all good as far as he was concerned.

"Okay."

She put her hand out. "Your word?"

"My word." He took her hand in his own but didn't shake it.

This wasn't a business deal, however she wanted to look at it. This was Rachel offering and asking for sexual intimacy.

His mind wasn't so sure it was a good idea, but he was smart enough to accept that sex between them was inevitable if she wanted it. His body, on the other hand, was all about what a great idea it was, his cock so hard, it pressed the knit of his boxers out in an obscene lump.

He used his hold on her hand to pull her toward him, and she came without hesitation, her breathing turning shallow in the space between one heartbeat and the next.

He cupped her face, just that touch sending his libido into the stratosphere. "You are so beautiful."

"You're the only one who has ever thought so." She

gave a strangled sound of amusement, her own desire burning bright in the pale orbs of her eyes. "I'm average, and that works for me in my job."

"There's nothing average about you." Not one damn thing.

From the heart that wanted to save the world and shattered at her inability to save her own sister to the character that pushed Rachel onward when a lot of people would have given up, this woman was extraordinary.

And he didn't want to hear her arguments to the contrary.

He wanted to kiss her. So he did.

Feminine lips, soft with desire, moved against his in a way that was familiar and yet wholly different.

He'd left the girl Rachel was a decade ago; the woman he held in his arms was both stronger and more defenseless than ever. For one thing, she never would have made this sex deal back in the day; she was more sexually open, but she was as closed off emotionally as she could make herself.

She was still too damn perfect for the man he had become, as well.

Pushing thoughts that had no place in the present aside, he yanked her closer, fitting their bodies together from chest to pelvis.

He groaned, a shudder working its way through his entire frame. The sound she made and the way she clung to him, pressing closer, her free hand squeezing reflexively against his shoulder, told him better than words that she was just as affected by the contact as he was.

He let go of her hand so he had both of his own free to explore all the silken, feminine flesh she'd exposed to him.

Again, this was different from when he'd massaged her. He'd tried so hard to keep his thoughts above the waist then, but right now? All he could do was think about how good his sex was going to feel inside her, surrounded by slick and swollen female flesh.

But not just any woman's. Rachel's.

He couldn't have held back the thrust against her body those thoughts brought if he'd wanted to. And hell if he did.

She wrapped her arms around his neck, undulating against him in a way guaranteed to drive him insane.

He groaned, the pleasure so intense, he was afraid he would come in his shorts for the first time since being a horny adolescent. She'd made him do it back then, by allowing him the simple pleasure of touching her breasts.

She'd been his first in so many things.

Her leg hooked around his hips, and she climbed his body so her naked sex rubbed against the head of his cloth-covered erection.

Oh, shit. That was good.

It would be even better when he got his boxers off.

He shoved at the shorts, keeping her close with one hand while the other did its best to get the offending material out of the way. The waistband got caught on his cock, and he let out a growl of frustration, the pain barely registering in the face of his need.

She laughed breathlessly as their kiss broke from the jerking around.

He groaned, yanking at the stupid band trying to make his cock bend in entirely the wrong direction. "You think it's funny?"

Making no effort to let him go or make it any easier on him, she nodded, her gaze glittering with mischief and heat.

Oh, damn, that heat.

He finally managed to get the boxers off and kicked them away with a more vicious movement than was warranted, but he was on the verge of vowing to go commando for the rest of his life.

Or at least as long as he had access to this woman's body.

Rachel used her hold on his neck to pull herself back up his torso, wrapping both her legs around him and undulating up his body with devastating effect to his libido. She completely trusted him to hold her up, and he'd be damned if he dropped her.

This time when she stopped with their sexes in alignment, her moist nether lips kissed the tip of his hard cock. She shimmied a little against him, causing his brain to short out and his body to go rigid with the need to climax.

Just that damn fast.

This woman was dangerous.

"Want it," she moaned.

"Need it." He grabbed her ass, pulling her more tightly against him, the tip of his engorged penis sliding into the mouth of her honeyed depths.

He'd had sex in the last decade, but damned if this wasn't the first time in those years he felt the sense of completeness just connecting this much. The feel of her wet heat against his naked cock was a single breath away from being too damn much.

So much more intense than with anyone else. Ever.

And then realization struck why that was. Or at least why he wanted to believe it was.

"Shit," he ground out. "Condom."

"I'm clean," she promised, sliding downward, taking him further inside.

"I am, too, but Rach—"

"No," she said fiercely, holding on to him with her arms and legs in an iron grip. "No condoms between us."

"You don't know . . ."

"I know I can trust you, darn it. You know you can trust me." She stopped and stared at him, her eyes filled with that wounded vulnerability he so desperately wanted to dispel. "You do trust me, don't you?"

"I do."

"Then no condom."

"Pregnancy?"

"Mirena."

"Who?" Who the hell was Marina, and why was Rachel bringing her up now?

"It's an insert. No pregnancy, almost no period. Good for an agent." Rachel undulated again, this time causing his sex to sink more deeply into hers. "We're covered. No babies."

He stopped himself from saying, *Maybe someday.* Shit, what was he thinking? They didn't have that relationship anymore.

For good reasons that he just couldn't think of right then.

"Just make-you-scream sex," he whispered into her ear before biting gently into her earlobe.

"If you think you're up to it," she taunted, though her tone was more breathless than challenging.

"Oh, I'm up to it all right, angel."

"Prove it."

"My pleasure." He carried her to the bed and laid her down. "And yours, too."

She nodded, making no attempt to deny it.

That was so damn arousing, her sexual honesty. She'd always been like that, even when they were younger and she was a lot shyer about her desires. He'd never known another woman as willing to admit how he made her feel as Rachel.

He'd never cared how much he affected a woman as he did Rachel, either.

"Do it," she ordered.

He wasn't about to say no. He surged into her in one long, inexorable thrust, eternally grateful she was as wet as she was, because it was one hell of a tight fit.

"Don't do this often?" he panted as he stilled above her, trying to regain a measure of control and surprised how intensely he needed an answer to that question.

"Intimacy requires trust."

"Sex isn't always intimate." He'd had enough experience with the other kind to know what he was talking about.

"For me, it is."

For some reason, that made him want to beat bloody every man she'd been with since Kadin had been forced to walk away from her, a confused and hurting twenty-year-old kid.

"Hey, Trigger . . . don't leave."

Since he hadn't moved, he knew she was talking about his mental tangent.

"Don't call me that."

"I will if I want to."

Something cold gripped his insides. "Don't."

"Stop talking, *Kadin*. Start moving."

"Forgot the foreplay," he ground out as he did what she wanted, moving their bodies together, sinking deeper into her with every thrust of his hips.

"Don't care."

"I'll still make you scream."

"Yes." She wanted it, wanted the oblivion of sex with a primal need he understood only too well.

He sat up, sliding his forearms under her legs and shifting her so he went deep with every thrust.

She looked up at him, her expression filled with carnal need and emotion she'd deny was there. But he knew what he saw.

"You're good at this," she praised.

"With you, I'm the best."

"Don't say that."

"Why not?"

"It's not about it being you and me. It's just sex."

He shook his head, laughing inside at her naïveté. It was all about who they were and had been to each other, but if she needed to tell herself different, he'd let her.

"Stop looking so smug, and pound me into the mattress, Mr. Atrati-man."

"You always were pushy in bed." Once she got past her initial shyness.

Rachel had always known what she wanted and let him know, even if half the time he was sure she couldn't handle it.

"And you always wanted to treat me like I'm breakable."

"You're a hell of a lot more fragile than me."

"Don't you believe it." She tilted her pelvis, forcing him to go deeper. "Let go of my legs."

He laid them across his thighs, happy to have his hands free to touch her.

With a look of concentration he'd seen in battle but rarely the bedroom, Rachel dug her feet into the bed on either side of his legs, meeting him thrust for thrust, enhancing the push-pull of their coupling with passionate intensity.

He reached down and cupped her breasts, loving the way they fit his big hands so perfectly. "No one else fits me like you do."

"Remember that, when you walk away the next time."

"Damn it, I—" But he couldn't promise not to leave again.

And she knew it.

"Don't," she ordered. "Just make me scream. That's the only promise you have to keep to me anymore."

It was the one he knew he *could* keep. He pinched her nipples, playing with them until they were red and swollen and she was making small broken sounds of want.

If he reveled in affecting her this way, he could damn well be forgiven. Rachel made him feel like a god in bed, and somehow he'd forgotten that.

Hell, he'd forgotten on purpose, but remembering and experiencing it were one hell of a rush.

Letting one hand slide down her flat stomach, he brushed his thumb over her close-cropped pubic hair. "You trim down here now. I like it."

"Me, too."

The hair was soft and short enough, there was no guessing when he let his thumb dip between her labia and find the swollen nub of her clitoris.

She jolted at the first touch, her body going rigid and then picking up pace as she slammed toward him on each downward thrust.

"You're the most responsive woman I've ever touched."

"And your cock's the biggest one that's ever screwed me."

Fury washed through him, increasing his sexual need to dominate and prove that he was not just the biggest cock she'd ever had but the best lover.

He grabbed her hands and pulled them above her head, looming over her as he ground their hips together, taking control of their movements almost completely.

She didn't seem even slightly intimidated, just moving against him as much as she could, giving and receiving pleasure without apology or mercy.

"Don't like the comparison?" she taunted.

And finally, he understood. "No."

"Remember that, too."

"I will."

"Let go."

"I like this." He always had, but she was the only woman he'd ever wanted to hold down during sex.

"Me, too, but right now I want to touch."

He released her wrists, glad to notice they weren't even red from his hold.

She shook her head, as if she knew what he was looking for. "I'm not breakable."

"You're too damn sexy, is what you are."

"Glad you think so." She reached up and flicked his male nipples with her short fingernails. "You're pretty hot yourself."

Damn, that felt good, electric jolts of pleasure going straight to his dick. She was the only woman who ever took time to find erogenous zones on him besides the obvious one.

And he had to admit, she was pretty good at it.

They touched and moved together with one powerful thrust after another, their jolting rhythm unbroken even as the pleasure built toward an explosion. He was so close to coming, he knew he had seconds to bring her off before he lost it.

Leaning forward again, he trapped his hand between their bodies as he took her mouth like the warrior he was.

This was one battle he was determined to win. She would climax before he let himself go.

He thrust his tongue into her mouth, and she met his aggression with pure, white-hot desire. Her hands came up to lock behind his neck, her legs wrapping firmly around his hips.

He broke the kiss to move down her neck and bite at the spot that used to drive her crazy.

She detonated with the scream he'd promised her, her

inner channel clasping his penis like a lubricated fist. And he was toppling over, too, filling her with his ejaculate, experiencing a fierce satisfaction at the thought of leaving something of himself behind in her body.

And an inexplicable sadness that this could not result in pregnancy—in the child they'd always promised each other.

He'd never admit that, though, even to himself, so he concentrated on the pleasure, the amazing way it felt to be connected to this woman in such intimacy.

She had been right. For her and *with* her, sex was not just a physical act. It couldn't be.

Not when his whole being, body and soul, was melded with hers so completely that for a moment in time there was no distinguishing between them.

Even if she wanted to pretend that the physical act of sex was all they shared.

He lowered his body down onto hers fully, holding his weight with his forearms but craving the closeness of touching her everywhere possible.

"So good," she slurred against his neck.

He smiled, his cock throbbing with an aftershock from the best sex he'd had in a decade. "Mmm, good, but it gets better."

"Not possible."

He grinned. Now, that was a challenge, even if she didn't realize it. "Oh, yeah, angel . . . remember?"

"What?" she asked, sounding replete but not exhausted. Just where he wanted her.

"Foreplay, angel, foreplay . . ." And he set about reminding her just how good at that he could be, too.

The next morning, Eva and Peace were gone before Rachel woke up.

That wasn't what had put her in a less-than-happy mood, however. It wasn't even the fact that she'd woken up alone.

No, what had her ready to snap off the head of the first person who spoke to her funny was the fact that she'd *cared* she was the only body in the bed that morning.

It made sense that Kadin would rise early to see his team members on their way. There was no reason he should have stayed in bed with Rachel or woken her to tell her he'd be downstairs.

Or wherever he actually was, because he *hadn't* been downstairs, and Mrs. Abdul informed Rachel that Kadin had gone out. Not where, naturally.

Kadin would have to have left instructions for Mrs. Abdul to divulge that information. And he hadn't. Which wasn't a problem. Really.

He and Rachel had indulged in sex the night before— at her instigation—not renewed their epic love story.

She *knew* that. She did.

And she wouldn't want it any other way. Couldn't let herself go there, even if she wanted to.

Rachel just wasn't that woman anymore.

So, no way should it have even caused a blip on her radar to be by herself when she woke up. Only it had.

And that had her scowling as she tore a piece of flatbread off and dipped it into the tzatziki-like mixture Mrs. Abdul had put onto Rachel's plate, along with fruit, bread, and what smelled like roasted pork, shredded and mixed with mango chutney. Rachel would reserve proper identification for when she ate it.

"What did that bread ever do to you?" Kadin's voice came across the rooftop garden.

Rachel's head jerked up, and she let her frown fall on him. "Nothing. What are you talking about?"

"You look a little angry there, angel. Something wrong?"

"No," she denied, even less willing to share her reason for her cranky mood with him than to face it in her own head.

"I see you decided to go shopping in my duffel." He was referring to the fact that she'd opted to wear one of his black T-shirts rather than the scrubs top.

It was way too big for her, but she didn't care. "It's real clothes. I would have worn your pants, too, but they just fell off."

It had nothing to do with the fact that the shirt smelled like him.

Kadin smiled, looking way too easy in his own skin for the morning—make that almost *afternoon*—after. Another thing that pissed her off . . . how much sleep she'd apparently needed. She hadn't woken until hours past dawn.

"You're still healing both mentally and physically," he said, as if reading her mind.

She repaid that comment with a frown. He could stay out of her head, thank you very much.

Only she'd committed to letting him inside, hadn't she? Reminding herself of that truth was bound to make her bad mood worse.

But, darn it, he'd been right about one thing. Telling a stranger about what she had gone through was not an option for her.

"You do look out of sorts today, angel." He settled on the couch beside her, leaning toward her so his words whispered intimately across her face. "I know it's not the sex. That was amazing. Are you *that* tired of wearing scrubs?"

"You told me you would get me real clothes," she accused, glomming on to something she could admit to being annoyed over, fighting urges to both move away and close the distance between them.

"I did."

"So, when are you going to?"

"I told you, I did."

"What?" She was in no mood for verbal games this morning.

"Finish your breakfast, and then you can come downstairs to our room and see if you approve of my purchases."

"You went shopping for me?" Already that morning?

He smiled, the warm expression coming too easily to him. "I don't make it a habit to break my promises, Rach."

"Only the important ones."

Chapter Fourteen

W*ell, crap*, Rachel thought. *Where had that come from?* The past was in the past and was going to stay there if she had anything to say about it.

Kadin winced, but he didn't call her on it. He just indicated her food with a wave of his hand. "Eat."

Wanting to talk about the past not at all, for once Rachel did as she was instructed without arguing. She ate.

Kadin remained beside her, his body fully into her personal space and way too close for comfort. Only she liked it. A lot.

Darn. Darn. Darn.

This man was the only living person who could still break through to her emotions. She needed to get away from him before all of her defenses crumbled.

He sipped at a large mug of coffee she hadn't noticed him carrying, the aroma tantalizing.

She reached toward it. "Let me have some."

"Mrs. Abdul didn't give you any with your breakfast."

"She gave me juice."

"Which you practically had an orgasm over yesterday."

"It's good." But Rachel wanted some coffee.

"Eva left orders to keep you away from caffeine."

"What? Why?" Darn doctors. They were all the same.

"She said it would be hard enough for you to establish healthy sleep patterns after what you went through without stimulants to keep you awake."

"I slept just fine last night."

"Yes, you did. I didn't even get a mumble out of you when I tried to wake you and tell you where I was going."

He'd tried to wake her? Rachel's mood improved immeasurably upon hearing that.

Which annoyed her all over again.

"Uh-oh. Your smile just turned upside down."

"Stop."

He grinned, making no effort to hide how much he enjoyed being in her company. "I'll give you a sip of coffee for a good morning kiss."

"You're an ass."

"I'm an astute bargainer."

She kissed him, getting lost for a little while in his taste and the sensation of peace she had when she was this close to Kadin.

They drew back at the same time, his gaze heated. Her own face was devoid of the frown that had stuck there earlier.

"Now my coffee," she demanded in a voice too husky for her own liking.

"Just a sip."

She shook her head. Medics and overprotective mercenaries. What could she do?

The coffee was delicious, and she ended up drinking half the mug before giving it back.

Kadin just laughed. "I think I should have asked for more kisses."

"You suck at negotiating. I would have given you the kisses without the coffee." She was, after all, the one who had prompted the return to sexual intimacy between them.

Maybe not for reasons he could understand or even approve of, but they worked for her.

She'd had sex in the last ten years, but very little of it. She'd been telling him the truth that sex for her meant intimacy, and she didn't trust easily.

Which meant the men she'd been willing to allow near her were few and far between.

At first, she'd been waiting for Kadin to come back, certain he would realize he needed her just as much as she needed him. But he hadn't, and over time, she'd tried dating other men, even if her plan to get Kadin back had always played in the back of her mind.

Nothing had ever stuck, however, and no sex had even come close to what she'd shared with Kadin ten years ago or the night before.

In the last few years, Rachel had been unwilling to allow anyone close enough for sex to become an even remotely possible option.

"That's good to know," Kadin said, bringing her back to the present.

"You think?"

"Oh, yeah." And he went for another kiss, this one just shy of mind-melting.

When he pulled away, she couldn't hold back the sound of protest inside.

"I want more, too, angel, but we've got surveillance to do today and, if Whit is as organized now as he always has been in the past, an agent to bring up to speed at some point."

She knew Kadin was right, but that didn't make it any easier. It was probably a good thing this man was the only one who got her engine revving like this.

Sex like they enjoyed together could be a major distraction. And any distractions were a problem for an agent who specialized in deep cover.

"Okay. So, new clothes?"

"Yep. I would have taken you shopping with me, but it's not safe for you to be seen on the streets of Marrakech right now."

"Agreed." There was a good possibility that Abasi Chuma had connections in the city; the choice to have her brought to Morocco hadn't been on a whim, she was sure.

Being seen in a public venue like the marketplace would put Rachel at high risk of discovery, which would only up the danger of her connection to Jamila being discovered.

"Any word from the guys on the mountain or Dr. Massri?"

"Chuma's coming into Marrakech, and Massri is livid that they haven't been able to find you."

"Any talk of Jamila?"

"Not between them. She didn't come up even casually."

"Typical. She's flown all the way from Egypt to be with Chuma, and both her father and fiancé ignore her existence."

"In this case, I'm thinking that's a good thing."

"It is." But it still angered her on Jamila's behalf. "I just want her out of there."

"It'll happen, Rachel. Trust your people to bring Massri and Chuma down."

"I do. It's the timing I'm worried about."

The clothes Kadin had purchased for Rachel proved two things. One, he was every bit as observant today as he had been a decade ago. They all fit. And two, he didn't expect her to leave Morocco in the next couple of days.

There was a week's worth of clothing, which was more than he had with him in *his* duffel. He'd bought a couple of things that would allow her to blend into the colorful culture of Marrakech as a native. Traditional clothing for

a woman in this part of the world that would hide everything but her eyes.

He'd also bought Rachel casual clothing similar to
things she had in her own closet at home. It was uncanny . . . and a little unnerving to think he really knew
her that well.

Even after all this time.

Had she not changed as much as she thought? Or had
the woman she'd become always resided inside the idealistic girl?

Either way, Rachel really appreciated his covering both
bases, giving his nonverbal support to whatever she
needed to do to protect Jamila.

He'd remembered sandals, too, but she left those off before making her way down to the computer room and
Neil Kennedy.

Kadin and Cowboy were out on another visual recon-
naissance of the hotel and the house Dr. Massri had gone
to the day before.

If Rachel missed Kadin's presence, she wasn't about to
admit it to herself, much less anyone else.

Neil was muttering at the computer when Rachel came
into the room.

"Is it talking back yet?" she asked.

He looked up, his blue eyes narrowed with frustration.
"You think that's a joke, but the AI I installed gets almost
as mouthy as some of my other teammates."

That made her laugh, the sound real and unfettered by
anything else for the first time in years.

Neil's frown turned to a smile. "Somebody got some
last night."

She could feel herself blushing but didn't deny it.

"Oh, ho! I was right. Not that I doubted it, but it's nice
to get the confirmation."

"I didn't say anything."

"Exactly."

She frowned but couldn't muster much heat. "Shut it."

"Oh, it had to be *good* for you to be in this mellow a mood."

"I'm not *mellow*," she denied, only to realize that was exactly how she felt.

Despite everything, Rachel was more relaxed than she'd been since taking her first agency job at the DEA.

"Good sex will do that for you."

"Amazing sex."

Neil gave her an exaggerated grimace, putting his hands up as if to ward her off. "Spare me the details of squicky hetero sex with my teammate."

"Sex isn't any fun if it doesn't get a little squicky."

He broke up at that, nodding. "Now, ain't that the truth?"

"Speaking of . . ."

"Uh-uh. No way. We are not going there. My relationship with Cowboy is off-limits even if you want to dish the dirt on Trigger and his mighty tool."

"It *is* mighty." She gave a not-so-faked sigh of remembered pleasure.

Neil covered his ears and yelled, "Too much information!"

"You're the one who mentioned *tools*."

"Not because I wanted details." The horrified expression on the mercenary's face was too funny. "I'm perfectly happy remaining so far in the dark about Trigger's prowess that you could grow mushrooms in my mind—you feel me?"

Grinning, she hopped up to sit on the table Spazz had turned into his desk. "So, Cowboy? You admit it's a relationship."

"That's what he says he wants."

"But you don't?" She didn't believe it. Not the way Neil looked at the other man.

"He hurt me. A lot."

She nodded, understanding better than a lot of people would. "But he wants you back."

"After throwing me away."

"He was in the closet." It was a guess, but not a very risky one.

"It's complicated. . . ."

"Family, then."

"Yeah. Family's always complicated."

"Even when they aren't around anymore."

"Yep. You're smart. For a girl."

She smacked him on the arm. Hard.

"*Ow.* Damn. You don't *hit* like one."

"Remember that, and I won't have to pour syrup over your keyboard while you're sleeping."

He threw his body over his laptop protectively. "You leave my baby alone."

"Does Cowboy know he has that kind of competition for your affections?"

"He knows." Neil sighed, his expression going serious. "He knows me better than anyone else."

"And he still hurt you. It's hard to forgive that." She should know; she'd never managed to forgive Kadin.

Maybe she would have, if she'd understood. Or if the cost of trying to prove to him that she did fit into his world hadn't been so high.

Neil nodded. "I would have said *impossible.*" He didn't sound like he was sure he still believed that.

"Me, too."

"But maybe not?"

"Maybe if you knew why?" Something she'd never gotten from Kadin.

"Wyatt didn't want to lose his family. They're close, really there for each other, you know? All he ever wanted to do was grow up and run the family ranch with his dad and brothers."

"Instead, he became a mercenary?"

"He started off in the Marines. Serving our country is a tradition in his family. His oldest brother was in the Army, and the youngest is a National Guardsman. Both saw time overseas."

"Cowboy did, too."

"He and Trigger were in the same unit. They came to the Atrati at the same time, too."

"Why didn't Cowboy go home to the family ranch?"

"To hear him tell it, he was just playing a little, taking a detour on the road to his dream."

"A pretty dangerous detour."

"Yeah. I've always believed he needed to get away, to live as himself, but he never saw it that way."

"He held on to the dream."

"Tighter than he held on to me."

"Because admitting he loved you would have cost him his family?" she asked, not understanding that kind of conditional family love.

Rachel had lost too many people to take for granted the gift of family. You didn't just let your family go for being something different than you expected or maybe even wanted.

She'd been let go of and knew just how much it hurt. She'd lost her parents by accidental death, her sister by suicide, and her grandmother by subtle rejection and then dementia.

"Yeah."

"And did it?"

Neil stared at her, his expression filled with surprise. "How did you know he told them he loved me?"

"I'm assuming that for *you* to love *him,* Cowboy has to

be at least smart enough to know there would be no chance at a relationship with you if he was still lying about himself to the other most important people in his life."

"*Other* most important people. You think I'm that significant to him?"

"He came out so he could be with you, didn't he?"

"I hope he came out for himself."

"I'm sure that was part of it, but come on. The timing is because he loved a man who wasn't going to be his dirty little secret ever again. Right?"

"Shit, you ever consider being a therapist or something?"

"I've already got a career."

"And a man who is willing to tank his for your sake." The sober truth in Neil Kennedy's gaze touched a chord in Rachel.

"Talk about complicated. Nothing between Kadin and me is that simple."

"Yeah, I get that."

"So . . . ?" she asked, glancing pointedly at the computer.

"So, Chuma and Massri went back to the house Dr. Massri was at yesterday." And just like that, the heart-to-heart was over.

Rachel didn't mind. She was no more eager to explore her feelings for Kadin than Neil was to figure out what, exactly, was happening between him and Wyatt. She understood that. Sometimes, ignorance was more than bliss . . . it was necessary for self-preservation.

"What about Jamila?"

"She's been at the hotel all morning. That girl spends a lot of time online."

"I know. She has friends from all over the world on Facebook."

"Does her daddy know that?"

"No. She admitted to me that she keeps a separate account that he and Chuma know nothing about. It's what gives me hope that she's strong enough to move on from these men."

"Because she likes to play Words With Friends with strangers?"

"Because she chafes at having every aspect of her life monitored and controlled, even though she doesn't realize that's what she's doing."

"Well, she'll be getting off the computer later. She's supposed to go shopping this afternoon and then to dinner with Chuma and her family. It sounded like some other friends might be there, as well. Interesting that Chuma and Massri have friends in Morocco."

"But considering Dr. Massri's role in medicine and politics, not completely surprising."

"Nope. It's a damn good cover he's got."

"It is. And there's no way of knowing which people in his life are cohorts and which are simply innocent acquaintances."

"Like you thought Massri was with Chuma."

"Yes." It still bugged Rachel that she hadn't read the man's place in the organization right. "Where are they going to dinner?"

"They didn't talk details. I get the feeling neither Massri nor Chuma thinks Jamila needs to know much more than when to show up, dressed and presentable."

"Show up where?"

"Well, they're picking her up from the hotel."

"But they're letting her shop alone?" Even back in Egypt, Jamila's time on her own was pretty limited.

Their coffee dates had been another one of Jamila's small rebellions. She'd eked out time to meet Rachel at the same shop each day between her morning family obligations and afternoon classes at the university.

Rachel found it difficult to believe that Dr. Massri

would let Jamila wander the market stalls of Marrakech on her own.

"No." Neil typed something into his computer. "I don't get the impression that that young woman gets to do much on her own at all."

"She doesn't."

Neil nodded, though his attention was caught by something on his screen. "Her aunt flew in this morning. They'll be shopping together before the dinner."

"So it can all look like a family vacation." It made sense.

One of the reasons Dr. Massri had flown under the radar so well was because he made his travels appear so legitimate. Taking family with him was a good tactic to alleviate suspicion.

Especially in this part of the world, having his daughter and brother as well as the man's wife with him would make Dr. Massri's trip seem completely innocent.

Once again, Mr. Abdul provided someone local to follow Jamila and her aunt covertly while they did their shopping in the marketplace. The operative had little to report, except that both women showed a fondness for knock-off designer handbags.

Until he also noticed that someone *else* was trailing the two women and doing a poor job of hiding it.

Still, if it were a bodyguard, the women would be aware of the man dogging their every step. As it was, he made no attempt to approach them, nor did they appear to acknowledge him in any way.

That worried Rachel. A lot. Why would Dr. Massri suddenly feel the need to put covert surveillance on his daughter twenty-four/seven?

And if not he, who?

In no scenario could Rachel read this development as a good thing.

Kadin called in while the two women were still out shopping to say that Dr. Massri and Abasi Chuma were back at the house on the outskirts of town.

"There's something going on here," he told Rachel and Neil over the comm-link.

Neil had fitted her with her own earbud earlier.

"What do you mean?" Rachel asked, her worry ratcheting up at the quality of Kadin's tone.

"Spazz's toys aren't working."

Rachel gave Neil a questioning look. He hadn't mentioned any of his listening devices malfunctioning.

"I gave Trig and Cowboy a directional sound amplifier," Neil said to her with a frown. "It's not my best. I wasn't expecting to be doing this kind of surveillance on an extraction."

Rachel couldn't help being impressed at the array of equipment Neil had brought to aid in getting her out of Africa.

"But the parabolic microphone system he's using can pick up a conversation clearly from three hundred feet. Massri's friend's house is in a very low-population area outside the city. Accessing their discussions should be a piece of cake for that little baby."

Kadin said, "Unless they're operating a jammer."

"Are you receiving static?" Neil asked.

"A hell of a lot more than you can account for by natural circumstances."

"Well, damn. That's not good."

No, it really wasn't, but it wasn't all bad, either, Rachel didn't think. "So, we learned one thing," she pointed out.

"What's that, angel?" Kadin asked, his tone when he spoke directly to her changing to something she refused to recognize.

"That house is every bit as important as we suspected it might be." Which made it all the more imperative for them to get some kind of eyes or ears inside the place. "Dr. Massri isn't just visiting a political ally."

Kadin made a thoughtful sound. "Or the politician is a paranoid sonofabitch."

"Maybe." Neil didn't sound convinced. "Politicians have a lot of reason to have their homes jammed, but few do. It puts them on the bubble for hiding secrets. Even in Morocco. Besides, he'd have to be using pretty sophisticated equipment for you to be getting nothing but fuzz through my receiver."

"So?"

"So, even paranoid politicians don't usually employ military-grade anti-surveillance technology. You'd be getting at least a word here and there with your average jammer purchased through regular retail outlets."

"Right," Rachel agreed.

Though she was not the technology guru that Neil was, she had a feeling about that house. And it wasn't a good one.

Kadin went silent for a minute. Then he came back to the link. "I tried again, and you're right. We're not even getting the occasional stray word. Neil, do you have information on who lives in that house?"

"I would have had it last night if Cowboy didn't make me go to bed," Neil grumbled without answering.

"Ah, baby, ain't no way a simple man like me could *make* you do anything you don't want." Cowboy's soft Texas drawl came over the comm-link, showing he'd been listening all along.

"The name?" Kadin prompted, sounding a lot less impatient than Rachel would have expected.

Neil pulled up a document on his screen. "On the surface, it looks like the house belongs to a French-run import/export consortium based in Marrakech."

"And under the surface?"

"Take a guess."

Rachel didn't give Kadin the chance, jumping in with the name herself. The French SympaMed board member who had been identified in Bennet Vincent's investigation in Zimbabwe the year before.

"But he's dead."

"His partners aren't," Rachel replied. "They're obviously not all behind bars, either."

Chapter Fifteen

It had taken a few months—and moving in on the co-horts Ibeamaka had given up in exchange for a lighter sentence—for TGP to realize that the organization was more far-reaching than the corrupt Zimbabwean official had known about.

When intel taken from one of the seized hard drives had pointed to Abasi Chuma's company, TGP had sent Rachel to Egypt to investigate further.

"You knew that, though. Or you wouldn't have been in Africa," Neil pointed out.

"True, but no one expected the espionage ring we thought we'd mostly disbanded to span the continent and still have active members from European countries, as well."

Kadin said sarcastically, "Whitney is going to love finding that out."

"Right." Her boss was going to go nuts.

He was a man who liked things tied up and taken care of. Finding out the wasps they'd taken out were only scouts for the nest was going to put him in a bad mood for a week.

"Speaking of Whitney, any word on when your replacement agent is supposed to arrive for her situation report?" Kadin asked.

"No. Whit has been oddly silent since our phone call yesterday. Something is going on in DC, and he's in the center of it."

"He sure as hell is," Neil said under his breath.

Rachel gave him a look. The computer geek knew more than he was saying, and once Kadin was done with this communique, she was going to push for some answers.

"We're coming in," Kadin said.

"You don't want to wait and see what happens?" Rachel asked.

"We can't see shit," Cowboy said, frustration lacing his tone. "Or hear it, for that matter."

She couldn't argue with that.

"Don't blame the equipment," Spazz piped up.

"Don't worry, baby. I've never doubted your toys were the best."

"Damn it, Cowboy, stop calling me *baby*."

"Stop calling me *Cowboy*." The Texan's tone held a lot more plea and real frustration than Neil's had.

Some kind of deep emotion spasmed across Neil's face. He yanked the headset off and flung it down beside the computer. "Shit."

"Tell Spazz I want to know who is actually living in that house, because somebody is." Kadin's words indicated he knew what his communications and technology specialist had done.

"How'd you know . . ." Rachel let her voice trail off.

"I know my men." Kadin sounded tired. "Cowboy is sitting here glaring into the sun, his earbud so tight in his fist, I think it's going to need repairs when we get back."

"You don't sound angry."

"I'm not."

"Most commanders would be at least mildly annoyed by two of their team members pitching drama like this."

"I understand where both men are coming from."

"Do you?"

"Yes," Kadin barked.

Rachel didn't know why he sounded mad now, when he hadn't before, but she had a feeling finding out wouldn't do her own equilibrium any good.

Static filled her ear, and she realized Kadin had turned off his comm-link, so hers was getting only feedback. Neil must have switched off the command center's link, as well. She pulled her earbud out, clicking it off. "Kadin wants you to figure out who is living in that house now."

"I'm working on it," Spazz said without looking up from the computer.

"I don't think he's going to give up on you."

"Of course not. He knows I'll get him his information."

"I wasn't talking about Kadin. I'm talking about Cowboy."

"Why not? He did last time."

"And?" She wondered if Neil would admit it.

"And he realized he screwed up."

"He's trying to fix it."

"I know." Neil typed furiously on the computer.

"Can I help?"

"Get me some coffee?" he asked, before grimacing. "Shit. Never mind. I can get my own coffee."

She smiled. "Relax. I don't suddenly think you're relegating me to the 1950s secretarial pool, okay? Besides, if I get you coffee, I might be able to sneak some for myself."

"Eva got you on a no-caffeine diet?"

"She may have left instructions to that effect."

"Yeah. She's always trying to cut my caffeine intake. Says it makes me impulsive."

"How's that working out for her?" Rachel asked, as if she didn't know the answer.

"About as well as her instructions for you are going to."

They shared a commiserating smile of caffeine addiction, and Rachel left to get some of Mrs. Abdul's coffee, which could have doubled easily as ambrosia for the gods. She wondered if she could smuggle some of the freshly roasted Moroccan coffee beans home in her suitcase.

Rachel had just walked into the command center with the coffee tray (having snuck an additional cup onto it when Mrs. Abdul wasn't looking) when she heard faint sounds of commotion coming from the back of the house.

Cowboy and Kadin must have come back before they'd told her and Neil they were going to.

"I think the guys are back," she said to Neil as she leaned over to place the tray on the table opposite the one with his computer.

"Really?" Neil asked, his eyebrows drawn into a questioning frown.

"I heard them coming in the back of the house."

"Huh." Neil shook his head as if it still didn't make sense, but he didn't gainsay her.

She was handing him his cup, sweetened with three sugars (no wonder the man got a bit spazzed at times), when she heard a wholly unexpected voice coming from the doorway.

"That smells good. I could sure use a cup," said Beth Crane née Whitney.

Shocked, Rachel almost dropped Neil's coffee in her hurry to turn and face Beth.

But Rachel found it nearly impossible to believe that Whit would send his own daughter in, especially after what had happened to Rachel. Not to mention, she had always been under the impression that Beth and her husband were inseparable as one of the agency's rare partner pairings.

Neil saved the coffee with only a small expletive, his blue eyes wide with curiosity.

Rachel barely noticed as her shock grew when she took in the two other people crowding the doorway. Beth's husband, Ethan, had his hand resting protectively on the other TGP agent's shoulder.

Ethan's presence made sense, but only because Beth was there. Whit hadn't mentioned sending a team, though.

Even harder to believe was the presence of the other agent standing as tall as Ethan's six-feet-three-inches in her four-inch spiked heels.

"Jayne . . ."

The beautiful woman, who maintained constant deep cover as a premier and *very* exclusive exotic dancer, smiled.

Though the expression didn't quite reach her eyes. Hard and green as emeralds, they had long since seen the last of whatever innocence they might once have held. "Hello, girlfriend. I hear you've got a nice, juicy case to hand over to me."

Rachel nodded; she had no inclination whatsoever to argue for the right to stay on the case. Right now, Jamila's safety was her biggest priority.

Besides, Whit could not have sent an agent who would inspire more confidence in Rachel that her former assignment was in good hands.

"But what are Ethan and Beth doing here?"

"I'll tell you everything you want to know if you give me some of that delicious-smelling coffee," Beth offered.

Ethan growled, "No coffee."

Instead of handing her husband his head for that bit of bossiness, Beth just pouted. "But it smells so good."

"You know what the OB said: keep caffeine to a minimum."

"*OB*. As in obstetrician," Jayne reminded Beth, her expression turning dangerous. "No way in hell would your father have let you come along if he was aware of your condition."

"And he doesn't need to be—not until we get back." Beth gave Jayne a fierce look that Rachel wouldn't have tried with the woman *she* secretly deemed SuperAgent.

"Now, this is interesting," Neil said as he unhooked his laptop from the extra monitor and printer on the table.

"What are you doing?" Rachel asked him.

"You don't think I'm going to miss this explanation, do you?"

"But you're supposed to be researching the resident of that house."

"Don't you see me bringing my computer?" he asked in the same way he might have inquired if she'd been dropped on her head as a baby.

Before Rachel could ask Neil *where* he was bringing his laptop, Beth smiled up at Ethan. "He's funny. Can we keep him *and* his coffee?"

"Stop flirting." The TGP agent glared down at his wife. "And forget the coffee."

The woman pouted again, and Rachel watched with amusement as her husband made another sound of frustration—before kissing her as if he couldn't wait one more second to do so.

Jayne rolled her eyes. "They've been like that the whole trip."

"They're always like that," Rachel replied.

If there was one person she could call *friend,* it would be Beth Crane. Rachel had kept the other woman at a distance for a while, just as she did everyone, but Beth had kept pushing and had gained enough traction in Rachel's life for her to be sincerely worried by the possibility of the woman being pregnant and possibly in danger.

They weren't mercenaries dropping by black parachutes at night into a war-ravaged area, but their work wasn't toast and coffee in the staff room, either.

Jayne picked up the tray with the coffee cups. "Where am I taking this?" she demanded.

Rachel gathered the presence of mind to ask, "Who said we're going anywhere?"

"Your friend and his disconnected computer."

"Come on, this is most definitely a discussion we need fresh air for," Neil cajoled. "Let's go up to the roof."

Rachel nodded grudgingly. They could have talked in the computer command center, but maybe some fresh air would do Beth and everyone else good.

And the rooftop garden was one of the nicest things about being at a safe house in Morocco. "I'll get some juice for Beth."

"Don't let her trick you into thinking she's being thoughtful." Neil waggled his eyebrows. "The woman is addicted to Mrs. Abdul's fruit juice. I swear, she makes more orgasmic noises when she's drinking it than my last partner did having sex."

Beth laughed. Ethan was watching Neil suspiciously, and Jayne's expression was simply one of waiting. Not patient. Not impatient. Just waiting.

If Rachel thought *she* was closed off, then this woman was an emotional vault.

Kadin and Wyatt arrived while Rachel was waiting in the kitchen for Mrs. Abdul to prepare a tray of juice and refreshments.

She told them that they had guests.

"He sent three agents?" Kadin asked, sounding as poleaxed as Rachel had felt when the trio arrived.

"Beth said something about being on vacation. Or leave. Or something." Which didn't make much sense. Not with what Whit had told her on the phone the last time they spoke. "And she's pregnant."

Kadin's brown gaze narrowed. "You're shitting me."

"I'm not."

"No." He didn't add anything to the single-word denial.

He didn't need to. Rachel was just as unhappy at the idea of a pregnant woman coming into the situation here as the mercenary was. She was glad Whit hadn't left her to dangle in the wind, but to send his pregnant daughter as unofficial backup? Even if he didn't know she was pregnant, it all seemed so not okay.

"It sounds like we need to find out what is going on," Kadin mused aloud, his eyes filled with concern she had an awful feeling was directed at her.

She was not that fragile.

Silent, Wyatt was looking toward the ceiling with bad-tempered longing, as if he could sense Neil's presence through the two stories of the house.

Despite his clear preoccupation, he showed his well-trained Texas roots when he grabbed the tray before Rachel had a chance to do so. Not that Kadin would have allowed her to carry it.

He still treated her as if she was delicate, even though she was a fully trained, highly experienced government agent. But Cowboy had been faster.

They arrived on the roof to find Ethan and Neil laughing together over something, the TGP's agent's suspicious attitude apparently gone. At least temporarily.

Rachel couldn't help noting that Ethan had placed himself on the end of settee he shared with his wife, though, putting himself between her and the Atrati. Jayne sat alone in an armchair, leaving the sofa open and the other small settee occupied by Neil.

Cowboy practically slammed the tray down onto the table next to the one with the addictively aromatic coffee before folding his muscular frame into the space beside Neil.

"Hey, baby." Cowboy slid his hand onto the back of Neil's neck, leaning forward to kiss the corner of the other man's lips.

As statements of possession went, it wasn't a bad one. As openly gay behavior, it was pretty darn impressive, as well.

For the first time since meeting him, Rachel saw Neil totally flummoxed.

"Wyatt." Neil stared at Wyatt, his laughter suspended, his cheeks darkening.

Though Rachel thought it was from pleasure, not embarrassment.

"You making new friends, sweetheart?" Wyatt asked in his slow Texas drawl.

Wow. Two publicly executed endearments in less than a minute. Cowboy was staking his claim with prejudice.

"They want to keep me," Neil said, sounding as dazed as he looked.

"They can't have you."

"We can't?" Beth teased.

"No." Cowboy didn't look away from Neil. "He's mine."

"For how long?" Neil asked, the vulnerability on his face almost painful to see.

"A lifetime."

Neil swallowed, not answering, but Rachel was sure the two men had a lot of talking to do later.

"Okay, then." Kadin looked satisfied and something else, maybe even envious. "Glad that's finally settled."

Neil opened his mouth to say something.

Before he could argue with Kadin's assessment of the situation, Rachel interrupted with introductions.

"The Atrati allows romantic relationships between team members?" Jayne asked with clinical interest.

Kadin shrugged. "We don't have a policy against it."

"*Gay* relationships?" Jayne pressed.

"Even the American military repealed DADT."

"Even without Don't Ask, Don't Tell, there's still a lot of bigotry out there."

"Not on this team," Kadin said with absolute certainty.

Rachel couldn't help herself. She reached up and kissed the underside of his chin in approval before sitting down on the sofa, toward the center, the invitation clear.

Kadin took it, sitting next to her and making no effort to hide the growing intimacy between them. Her brain told her this was a bad idea, but her heart gloried in the move.

Jayne shook her head at them all. "Emotional entanglements make for poor decisions."

"I'm not driven by my emotions," Rachel claimed, though for the first time since Linny's death, she was not entirely certain she spoke the truth.

Jayne poured herself a glass of juice, confidence spilling from the elegant TGP agent. "Jamila Massri." She didn't say anything else, just settled back to sip her juice.

"She needs protecting," Rachel said.

Surprisingly, Jayne nodded. "From what Whit has told me, I would have to agree." Then Jayne fixed Rachel with green eyes tipped just enough to indicate Asian ancestry somewhere distant in the redhead's family tree. "Your decision to put your job on the line in order to be the one to give it was without a doubt fully motivated by emotion."

"Don't let Jayne fool you," Beth said with more warmth for the other woman than Rachel would have expected. "She would have found a way to protect Jamila Massri, too. It's to her benefit that she doesn't have to work that aspect of the assignment."

Jayne simply shrugged, her shrewd gaze giving nothing away.

"If Jayne's the agent on assignment, what are you and Ethan doing here?" Kadin asked of Beth.

Beth grimaced. "You know about the congressional audit of the State Department that's going on right now?"

They all nodded.

"Well, some Tea Party congressman got wind of The Goddard Project. He's grandstanding on it, calling *the agency that should have been closed after World War II* a gross waste of taxpayer money. He's saying TGP is another example of our government's abuse of the people's trust."

"But what we do is necessary." Rachel hated politics.

"Yes, it is, but because our agency is under the State Department and directly under the presidential umbrella, it's a prime target for the Tea Party's opposition."

"Have they gone public?"

"Oh, yeah. We may perform black ops, but we are no longer a dark agency. Dad is going nuts. And you don't even want to know what happened when Mom finally found out exactly what my father and I *really* do for a living."

"Poor Whit." Rachel didn't envy her boss his situation. "That explains why he sounded so out of sorts the last time I talked to him on the phone."

Beth grimaced. "I know, right? He's, like, a *religious* Democrat, and he's having nightmares of Sarah Palin showing up in his office to chase him out."

"But she's not—"

"Doesn't matter," Ethan interrupted, looking a little too gleeful. "That's why they're called *nightmares*. The Old Man is scared of the Alaskan bogeyman."

Beth poked her husband. "You are enjoying my dad's distress way too much. Have you forgotten that not only is he your boss, but he's soon to be the grandfather of your child?"

"Come on, sweetheart, you've got to admit it's kind of funny to see the unflappable Andrew Whitney running around looking positively unhinged."

"I do not find it funny at all."

Ethan's expression finally registered what a pile of poo he'd stepped in. Voluntarily. "Now, Beth, you know I care about the man."

"You love him. Not as much as you love me, but don't pretend he's not important to you. You even call him *Dad* away from the office."

"He'll be fine," Ethan tried again, clearly uncomfortable with Beth's revelations in front of the other agents.

She smiled slightly, as if maybe she'd aimed for just that reaction, to pay him back for the crack about her dad. Beth had an ornery streak.

"I have to concur," Neil said. "My sources indicate TGP will remain a viable agency when all is said and done."

"What sources?" Jayne asked.

Neil just shook his head. "A man has to have his little secrets."

Cowboy settled back against the small couch, pulling the other man closer. "And this one has more than most."

"I swear he has a line tapped in the Oval Office," Kadin grumbled beside her.

The way Neil didn't automatically deny it made Rachel wonder.

"What kind of device wouldn't get picked up by the scans?" Beth asked.

Neil grinned, his expression full of caffeine-stimulated glee that Rachel envied hugely. "There's prototype technology that might do it."

She wasn't getting near the coffee tray now that Kadin was back. But sneaking sips from his mug might be on the agenda.

"That still doesn't explain what *you* are doing here," Rachel prompted Beth when it seemed that she was about to get sidetracked by Neil's subterfuges.

"Dad's over a barrel right now, but he takes care of his agents." Beth shrugged. "Ethan and I are not here on official TGP business, but we *are* here to make sure you come home in one piece, both physically and emotionally."

Why was everyone acting as if she was going to have a nervous breakdown, or something? So, she'd been tortured. It happened. In her line of work more frequently than getting hit by lightning.

She'd survived. Kadin and his team had gotten her out. That's what mattered. Why couldn't anyone but her see that?

"I thought all vacation requests were on hold," she said, redirecting the conversation away from a path she had no intention of going down.

"They are, but we're a federal agency, and that means both Ethan and I have ironclad access to either maternity or medical leave."

"Your father is unaware that you *are* actually pregnant, is he not?" Jayne pointed out again, her disapproval of the situation clear in her tone.

"You shouldn't be here," Rachel emphasized.

Beth waved away their concerns with a flutter of her hand. "I'm, like, a minute pregnant. There's nothing to worry about."

Ethan didn't look so sanguine, but he did look resigned. Rachel would have liked to have a listening device for the private conversation they must have had leading up to this trip. Whatever ammunition Beth had brought to the fight, it had been sufficient to push her overprotective husband into taking, effectively, a "vacation" in Marrakech.

"You're four months pregnant, and your dad is so going

to have your ass when we get home and he finds out," Ethan said. "But don't worry," he added, looking to Rachel. "I'm not letting Beth do anything that puts her at risk."

Four months? That was past the first trimester and well past being a "minute pregnant," as Beth claimed. But it also explained why she looked so energetic, no pregnancy-related nausea in sight.

"I can always tell him it was your idea," Beth threatened.

"I recorded our conversation." Ethan looked proud of his forethought.

"I erased the recording and wiped the drive it was on."

Neil burst out laughing. "I like her. Can we keep her?" he asked, repeating her earlier words, this time directed at Kadin. "The Atrati could use another techno-geek."

"How did you know I was a techie? It's a relatively new thing for me."

Neil just gave Beth a *duh* look.

She nodded at his laptop. "What are you looking for right now?"

Neil told her, and pretty soon they were lost in tech-speak, throwing ideas at each other on how best to find the information Kadin had asked for. Finally, Cowboy herded them both back down to the computer command center so Beth could use her own computer, Ethan following protectively.

Jayne uncrossed her legs and pulled a tablet PC out of the bag at her feet. "Are you up to going over the case with me?"

"Why wouldn't I be?" Rachel asked, confused. Did she look tired, or something?

She was actually feeling pretty good.

Instead of answering, Jayne gave Kadin a look of censure. "She hasn't been debriefed, has she?"

That again? Rachel was ready to scream, but she held back just because it would probably feed into everyone's idea that she was on some sort of emotional edge.

"We're going a little bit at a time." Kadin pulled Rachel closer in a sweetly telling gesture.

She might not like his assumption that she was vulnerable and weak, but she did like the feeling that he was protective of her. Even if she didn't need it.

"*You're* debriefing her?"

"Yes."

Jayne just shook her head. "Okay, let's go over what you learned in Egypt. Then we'll move on to the intel you've gained since coming to Morocco."

Jayne was really good at interrogation, and she pulled information out of Rachel that she had no idea she'd stored in her memory banks. But by the time the other TGP agent pronounced herself satisfied with the information Rachel had provided and left to organize her notes, Rachel was full-on exhausted.

Chapter Sixteen

"Angel, you look like you could use a nap," Kadin said as he offered her another glass of juice.

She took it, needing the wetness in her throat after all that talking. "I'll go if you go with me."

"If I come, you won't be napping."

"There's more than one way to recharge a woman's batteries," Rachel informed him.

Kadin shook his head. "You are one dangerous woman—do you know that?"

"Not like Jayne. She's the real deal."

"And what are you? A pretend agent?"

"No, but Jayne . . . she's something. I'd pity Chuma and Massri if I didn't despise them so much."

"Then it sounds like Whit sent exactly the right agent for the job."

They were back in their room before Rachel answered. "I thought he'd sent the right agent when he sent me."

Kadin turned her to face him, his gorgeous features set in stern lines. "He sent the best, but you got caught. It happens. Why do you think we get paid so much to do what we do?"

"No one should have been back there. I'd been watching for days, and they never varied their routine."

"Maybe there was an alarm you triggered that you didn't know about."

"Maybe. And maybe I just had really bad luck."

"Yeah, luck isn't always on the side of the angels."

"Why do you still call me that?" she asked, needing to understand that, at least.

"You're still the angel I knew ten years ago, under that tough secret-agent exterior that can stand up to hours of torture without breaking your cover. You're still sweet, kind, and gentle."

"I'm not." With understanding came the realization that he was living in some kind of time warp about her. "I'm not *her* anymore, Kadin."

"Oh, angel . . ." He shook his head. "I can't help the way I see you any more than you can help wanting to save the world."

"Sometimes, I think the world can go hang."

"Yeah, but then you get up and go to work the next day."

"You're not hearing me."

"I hear you just fine. You've never seen yourself the way I see you; why, after all this time, should that change?"

She reached up to touch his lips, wondering how all the right words could fall from them so easily. And still not make her feel like they were on the same plane.

"You called my name, when they were hurting you." The expression in his sherry brown gaze said he wasn't sure that was a good thing.

"I went back to the place I last felt safe."

"Tell me."

"Now? I thought you wanted me to sleep." And she'd wanted something entirely different.

"You will, after. Now, tell me."

She did, sitting cross-legged on the bed, her back to the

wall and Kadin sitting across from her. She told him how frightening it had been to wake up tied to the chair; how her mind had latched on to her training the first time they shocked her. How it had felt to piss herself, to know her vocal cords had been damaged, because the pain in her throat rivaled the hurt in the rest of her body.

How, finally, all her training hadn't been for shit, and she'd had to go inside herself and find a place where she could protect Jamila and the assignment.

That place had been Kadin and their past together. A place where Rachel had last been truly safe, believing that, despite the pain of losing her parents and living with a grandmother who wanted anything but responsibility for her granddaughters, her future was golden.

How she'd made an exit plan when she felt her grasp on reality wavering.

He made a sound like a wounded animal then.

"I had to protect the assignment. I had to protect Jamila as my unwitting informant."

"Never again."

She didn't have an answer for that. She couldn't promise she'd never be in that situation again, no matter how unlikely. Because that was the nature of her job. And her job was all she had left after losing everything else.

"Our future wasn't golden, though, was it?" She might play mind games with herself and go back to the time she'd thought it would be, but that's all they were. Games. "Why, Kadin? Why did you dump me? We were forever, and then . . . we weren't."

Rachel finally voiced the question she'd wanted so desperately to ask ten years ago but had been afraid she already knew the answer to.

She hadn't been enough for him anymore, not after he joined the Marines and saw some of the world, leaving their Sacramento lives behind.

"I walked away to protect you," Kadin said.

There was no doubting the sincerity in his tone, but it made no sense.

"From what? You abandoned me!" And unlike her parents, he'd had a choice.

But then, so had Linny.

"From what I'd become."

"A killer?" she asked bluntly, no desire to soften it.

"A trained assassin. For the Marines. I killed for my country."

"So does every other soldier who stands on the front line in war."

"I killed men and women who would never have a chance to look into my eyes. I killed without knowing why they had to die, but I wasn't stupid. I knew not every target was a military threat."

"So? Do you think I expected you to join the Marines while our country was at war and you weren't going to kill anyone?"

"Surely you don't believe the ends justify the means."

"Sometimes." She really wasn't that girl he still remembered.

Wasn't sure she ever had been.

"Sometimes, I was pretty sure they *didn't,* but I pulled the trigger, anyway."

"And that made you walk away from me."

"Can you honestly say you would have wanted me to stay if I'd told you the truth?"

"Yes, back then, yes." And now? She was an agency-trained sniper, too. She'd never had to assassinate a target, but she'd surely at least maimed or incapacitated her share of human beings while she'd covered her fellow agents on raids. "You were an idiot, but then, maybe it was just an excuse. You didn't want the encumbrance of your high school sweetheart hanging around your neck."

"Are you kidding me? I never let you *go,* Rachel. There's never been another woman for me. Not in that way. In ten years, I haven't had a single woman in my life who would call herself my girlfriend, much less get me to call her that. I've never told another woman I love her. I never will."

Right. That was so easy to say, but he'd been gone ten years. He claimed he'd never let her go, but he hadn't given her that luxury. "You left me."

"No. Maybe . . . physically, but damn it, what's left of my belief in the good of humanity is still wrapped up in dreams of an innocent girl who wanted to spend her adulthood raising babies and teaching other people's kids. You've gotten me through the worst that war has to rain down on a man."

Not her. The girl she'd been. The woman she'd given up to prove something to him, something he didn't want to know. She couldn't stop the gallows laugh that came out of her.

"What?" he asked, his brow furrowed.

"I became this." She swept her hand down, indicating her twenty-eight-year-old, agency-trained body. "To prove to you that you didn't have to leave me behind. That I could fit into the bigger world you'd discovered in the Marines."

"What are you saying?"

"I thought I had become too boring for you, and that's why you left. You said we didn't fit anymore—do you re-member?"

He nodded, a dawning look of horror coming over his features.

"I made a plan; I was going to become someone inter-esting, someone you would want again. I went to college with the intention of getting into federal law enforcement.

What could be sexier than a secret agent?" she asked self-deprecatingly.

Oh, man, had she been naïve back then. There wasn't any glamour in doing what she did.

"You joined the DEA to . . ."

"Get you back? Yes. I couldn't give up. I believed our love was too big to let go of. I was an idiot."

"But I didn't want *you* to change."

"You didn't want me at all. Not the real me, the woman who could have handled being married to a MARSOC Marine. I'm not sure you ever saw the real me at all." She shook her head. "And I lost Linny because I was still trying to be that sexy, intriguing woman. I thought . . ."

It was hard to go on, but she had to get this out. "I thought I'd see you again someday, when you were in town visiting your family or something, and you'd realize how perfect I was for you."

"You were perfect the way you were."

Oh, she'd been perfect, all right. A perfect fantasy, and she'd never even known. "I thought that, of all the people in my life, you knew me best, and now I realize, ten years too late, you barely knew me at all."

He looked stricken. "That's not true."

"It is true. And *damn* it." She scrambled off the bed, spinning away from the sight of him.

She slammed her hand against the wall, the pain pouring out of her heart bigger than anything physical could be. She stood there, panting, leaning against the wall. "I was so busy trying to become the woman I thought you wanted, I let Linny go. I let her down trying to save a relationship that was always doomed."

If she'd only known that ten years ago. Would it have made a difference in her life?

In all honesty, Rachel could never regret going into law

enforcement. Her one true regret was that in her effort to shine at her new job, she must have neglected signs of how troubled her little sister was becoming.

Even looking back had never revealed those signs, though. No matter how many times she replayed phone conversations and e-mails in her head. Rachel never saw the descent into dangerous depression her sister had taken.

Linny would have made a great undercover agent herself.

Amid the pain, that thought almost brought a smile to Rachel's heart. If not her face.

She could hear Kadin moving and then felt his big hand on the center of her back. "Linny made the decision to hide what was going on from you. She loved Arthur Prescott, and that had horrible consequences for her, but she never told you any of it. She chose to take her own life. If anyone is responsible, it's him."

Kadin was right, but he was wrong, too. Just as he had been about Rachel. Yes, she'd wanted to raise their babies and had at one time wanted to be a teacher, but she wasn't the pure innocent he believed her to be.

She never had been.

Overcoming the grief of her parents' deaths had made her stronger than he would ever understand.

"I'm going to take that nap now."

His other hand slid down her arm. "Rach . . ."

She threw his hands off, stepping away from him. "Don't."

"Rachel, damn it. I didn't know."

He hadn't known anything. She whipped around to face him. "You knew leaving would hurt me. That it would hurt us both, but you chose to do it anyway."

Because a fantasy wasn't enough to hold on to for a man who lived with the reality of war.

"I'm sorry." He reached toward her again but didn't

touch her, his hand hanging in the air between them. "I was a coward, and I walked away before you could reject me. There's no good way to look at that, but I swear I didn't mean to hurt you as much as I did."

"If you had, you really would be the bastard I've called you so many times in my head."

He winced in acknowledgment of that statement. "I should have stuck around, but I didn't feel that I had the right. You deserved so much better."

"I needed someone to *be* there. So did Linny. That was it. No Superman required."

"You don't think I understand that *now,* Rach? But ten years ago, I was a kid, too, and my pride was bigger than my brain. Or my heart, I guess."

"Your pride."

"Yes. There's no way to make you understand how *disgusted* I believed you would be with me."

Understanding came like a lightning bolt. "Maybe you were disgusted with yourself."

"Maybe I was. Pulling the trigger was too damn easy, and I should have felt something more when I killed a man."

"What? Pity? Remorse for killing the enemy?"

"Who never even got to face me!"

"You killed him so he wouldn't have the chance to face and kill many others."

"Ideally, that would be true. Was probably true most of the time."

"How do you know it wasn't?"

"Because I know how men in power use their militaries."

He'd been living with the guilt of what he *might* have done for a decade? That was just so . . . so *Kadin.*

"And sometimes what they ask is right."

"But not always."

"So, what? You should hate yourself because you did your best to serve your country?"

"Of course not. And, damn it, when did this debriefing become about me?"

"When you started spouting idiocy."

"Twenty-year-olds can be supreme idiots."

"Yes, they can, but it seems to me like you still harbor some of those thoughts."

"Maybe, not a lot, but some. Maybe," he said again, clearly not sure.

She shook her head. "You think too much." He always had.

He sighed, his expression pained. "I used to overthink myself out of the right answer on tests."

She remembered. It used to frustrate him so much, but he kept doing it. "And you thought yourself out of us."

"I . . ."

There wasn't anything to say to that. Knowing he'd had this idealized view of her back then, a view he still clung to today despite what he could see with his own eyes, told her more than anything else could that they had no future.

But they had the present. And in the present, they were going to save Jamila Massri. Somehow. Some way.

"We have a job to do."

"We'll do it. Jamila Massri won't die because she got entangled with the wrong man."

It was a promise Rachel hoped he could keep. Hoped *she* could keep for Jamila.

"But right now, you need to lie down." Kadin reached for Rachel again.

She allowed the touch to land, the big hand to caress her back.

"Maybe you need something else, too."

"Payment for my debriefing?" she asked, not sure if making love again was the smartest move for her.

Not sure if she had a choice, the way she was feeling.

She desperately needed the connection after opening up and reliving pain from so recently and so long ago. She thought he did, too. And she still cared enough about him for that to matter.

She didn't know how many days she had left of Kadin's presence in her life, but she would take advantage of them while and when she could.

His brown eyes turned dark with desire so fast, she could have no doubts about how much Kadin Marks wanted her.

Fantasy woman or not.

"It's not exactly payment if it doesn't cost me anything I don't want to give," he pointed out.

"Opening up about what happened costs enough for both of us."

Rachel couldn't and wouldn't even try to say it hadn't cost him, too, emotionally. It was clear that it had.

Kadin nodded, his demeanor so serious, so intent. "Maybe it does, at that."

He stepped away from her. Removing his clothing with quick, economic movements, he didn't take his time stripping. But her body responded as if he was putting on a show worthy of a professional.

Only no stranger dancing on a stage, no matter how perfectly honed his body or handsome his face, could turn her on the way the smallest glimpse of Kadin Marks did.

At the sight of his naked body coming into view, Rachel felt a familiar tightening in her lower belly, while her nipples drew into tight buds inside the lacy bra he had bought her. He had muscles on top of his muscles, legs as thick as her waist.

Having that body next to her in bed made her feel safe, feminine, and hot. Really, really hot.

She'd wanted him from the moment she woke in his tent in the forest.

His sex was already well on the way to rock hard, and her vaginal walls contracted in response, sending shivers of sensation through her.

Her lungs struggled to get enough air as her entire body flushed with heat.

He looked at her, his expression turning feral as he took in her reaction to him, none of which did she make the least effort to hide.

This between them, at least, was as real as it got. No fantasy needed.

They were so hot together, they could melt the glacier cap on Mount Everest.

He made a primitive sound as he crossed the distance between them to yank her fully clothed body against his naked one. "You drive me bat-shit crazy when you look at me like that. You always have."

"Like what?" she taunted, making free with her hands all over his exposed skin.

"Like you can't wait for me to be inside you."

"I can't."

That sound, almost a whimper, mostly a growl, came out of his throat again.

He had scars that showed he hadn't spent his entire career at the end of a sniper's rifle. She traced them now with her fingers.

As she touched one on his chest, he said. "Extraction in South America."

She nodded, leaning forward to kiss the scar. Then she licked over it, tasting his salty male skin, bringing back visceral memories she had thought were buried so deep, even *she* couldn't find them again.

That first weekend of leave he'd had from the Marines that he *hadn't* told his family about. Only Rachel.

She hadn't told anyone else, either, except Linny.

Rachel hadn't had to lie to her grandmother about staying over with a friend. Because Grandmother simply hadn't asked. Or cared.

A freshman in high school, Linny had thought it wildly romantic that Kadin wanted to spend the time alone with Rachel and encouraged Rachel to go.

Kadin had rented a hotel room downtown, spoiling Rachel with an in-room whirlpool bath (which they'd made delicious use of several times over the weekend) and a romantic steak dinner delivered by room service.

They'd eaten naked, feeling grown-up and naughty, no clue what the future held for them both.

That weekend, they'd shared the kind of intimacy that wasn't supposed to be possible when you were young and naïve.

At one point, Rachel had been determined to taste every inch of his body. Kadin had let her, but it had pushed him to the limits of his control.

When he'd finally snapped, he'd made love to her with near-violent passion. And she'd met him thrust for thrust, hungry kiss for hungry kiss, until they'd both collapsed into sleep so deep, they hadn't heard their wakeup call the next morning.

She'd been so certain that weekend that this man would be hers for a lifetime.

Instead, they'd only seen each other twice more before he'd been sent to the Middle East. When he returned a year later after increasingly sporadic letters and e-mails, he broke it off with her, telling her that she just didn't fit his life anymore.

No wonder. He'd seen her as an idealized version of herself she could never hope to be.

He, on the other hand, really had been her ideal man. Probably still was, if she let herself think about it, scars and all. His only important flaw? The fact that he didn't love her and never really had.

But love and happily-ever-after were for other people. Hadn't Rachel realized that finally after learning of Linny's suicide?

She only had *now,* and she was set on taking advantage of it.

Her fingertips found another scar on his back, and she outlined it with a barely-there touch.

He grumbled, "Afghanistan."

"It feels like a gunshot wound." She should know. There was a distinctive pattern to the puckering of her own flesh where she'd been shot.

"It is."

"There's no exit wound."

"The medic had to dig it out. I was out of commission for a while, but they got me back into the field. And I got my target before I passed out from the pain."

"A Marine's too tough to stop fighting because of something so little," she mocked, hiding the fact that she was more impressed than she wanted to be.

He really was a hero.

He kissed along her hairline, teasing her ear with his tongue. "*I* didn't check myself out of the hospital against medical advice."

No, that had been her, but she hated hospitals with a deep, abiding passion. She could never shake the memories of that time in the hospital after her parents' accident. Her dad had been pronounced dead on arrival, but by a cruel twist of fate, Rachel had been there, dropping off another girl who worked with her at the chain pancake house.

The other girl had cut herself after dropping a tray of

glasses. She'd gotten four stitches and gone home. Rachel's life had been changed forever by that trip to the ER, though.

She'd stood on the sidewalk, horrified as she watched the paramedics roll the first stretcher into the ER. She'd seen the blood and the broken, lifeless body and had no idea it was her dad. The second ambulance arrived, and another stretcher was rolled out, and Rachel had seen it was her mom.

Then she'd known.

The next hours were spent in a haze as she waited for her mom to wake up, agonized over knowing she'd have to tell Mom that Dad was dead. The doctors were so hopeful that, despite the extensive injuries and coma, Mom would rally and get out of the ICU.

They'd been wrong, and Rachel had never had to deliver the devastating news. To Mom. She'd had to tell Linny and their grandmother.

"Good to know," Rachel said, pushing the old trauma away. "You still have a practical streak."

"You still don't."

"You'd be surprised at how practical I can be now."

He tugged her top off. "Maybe I'm more interested in your wanton streak."

Chapter Seventeen

"It's still here." But only with him. Only for him.

He followed the line of lace along the top of her bra cup with his fingertip. "I knew this would look hot on you."

"I couldn't help noticing that all the undergarments you bought me are on the sexy side."

"A man has to take his pleasures where he can."

She shook her head, smiling. "So, you're saying that you're an opportunist?"

"Can I help it that it excites me to think of you looking so damn sexy where no one else gets to see?"

She looked down at his impressive erection and shook her head. "I guess not."

"Would you want me to?"

"No."

As he undressed her, Rachel went back to touching the marks on his skin that hadn't been there ten years ago. He continued telling her where each one was from, and she would touch, kiss or lick them . . . sometimes all three.

He was shaking with need, his sex engorged and leaking steady drops of pre-come when she gave a biting kiss to the last scar on his left thigh. (That had been a knife wound like one of her own.)

She knelt before him, completely naked now, her fingers gliding over the firm contours of his thighs. "It's hard to believe the knife could pierce your muscle—it's like granite."

His gaze shifted to a knife scar that marred her right side. "They're damn effective weapons, knives."

"Not effective enough." She was still alive, and so was he.

"It was too damn close."

"Was it?" she asked, surprised, because the scar on his thigh wasn't very big and nowhere near an artery.

"Not that. Yours." His erection hadn't flagged, but his mind was clearly going places she didn't want it to right this minute.

"Stop. I healed. I'm fine."

"Show me."

She smiled up at him, knowing he didn't mean what she was about to do, but that just made it better. He expected her to stand, to let him do some touching, too.

Instead, she opened her mouth and took the head of his cock inside. The sweet, only slightly salty, flavor of his pre-ejaculate exploded over her palate as the scent she would never forget filled her nostrils.

His own unique fragrance, strongest right at the base of his penis. It was a clean scent that drove her crazy with need.

She'd read about pheromones, but he was the only man whose scent caused her body to prepare for his.

He gave a harsh groan, tilting his pelvis toward her. "So good, Rachel."

She knew. He loved this. She hadn't done it for anyone else. Ever. Didn't know if it was easier with a smaller penis. Didn't care.

She liked the way her jaw stretched around him, the way only the head fit comfortably in her mouth. She always pushed farther, but he'd never pressed her to go so far that she gagged.

And he never made her feel like it wasn't enough. She wrapped her hand around the long, thick shaft, stroking him in time with the movements of her head. He reached down and enclosed her hand in his, helping. Exciting her so much, she could feel the wetness between her legs.

"Shit, angel . . . that's too good." He sounded like a man in pain, but she knew it was the opposite.

She would have laughed if her mouth wasn't too busy.

"I'm going to come, Rach," he groaned out.

She didn't let up on her suction, or the movements of her hand.

He didn't pull his hand away, either, showing what he wanted to happen, even if he was giving her the out.

She reached up with her spare hand and tugged gently on his balls, something else she remembered he loved. Kadin shouted as he came, his salty essence shooting down the back of her throat.

She always forgot how strong the flavor was—so different from pre-come. Or maybe it had been the intervening years, but she swallowed quickly, feeling a primeval joy in taking him inside her this way.

It didn't have to make sense. Even he didn't need to understand.

She only knew she liked it.

Still half hard, he pulled back. The satiated pleasure in his gaze in no way diminished the desire there. "Your turn, angel."

"I . . ." She hadn't let anyone go down on her, either. Not in a decade.

The sex she had had was accomplished with rubbers and efficiency, at her instigation. And maybe that was one reason it had never come close to comparing to this.

It didn't matter.

Kadin never let her pull back. He would give her pleasure until she screamed from it. And she would revel in the sensations only he could wring from her.

He lifted her to her feet and then swung her into his arms and carried her to the bed.

"I never realized what a caveman streak you've got going," she teased.

"You bring it out in me."

She believed him but had no breath to say so as he started touching her in ways guaranteed to bring her to the brink before his mouth ever closed over her sex.

He played her body with the confidence and expertise of a master. The master of her pleasure.

By the time he pushed her legs wide and up, she was shivering with unsatisfied desire. He smiled as he took in her sex. "Still so pretty down here, all dark pink and swollen, shiny with wetness."

"It's just skin."

"Shaped into kissable lips and a tasty morsel I like sucking." His words alone sent electric bolts of sensation zinging through her.

He dropped down until his mouth hovered over her mound and inhaled deeply. "Mmmm . . . you smell so good, too, so sweet."

"I smell like sex."

"Yeah." That one word was laced with enough satisfaction for a soliloquy.

His tongue darted out, flicking her clitoris with unerring accuracy before he licked the highly sensitive flesh, tasting her as only he had ever been allowed to do. He played with her clitoris, alternating between using the tip and flat of his tongue, enhancing her pleasure with every tiny movement but never pushing her over to orgasm.

"Kadin . . . *please,*" she groaned.

He lifted his head, their gazes meeting, his lips slick with her wetness. "Please what, angel?"

"You know."

"Why don't you tell me, anyway?"

"Make me come!" The demand would have been more forceful if it hadn't sounded so much like a plea.

He smiled, and a thick finger slid inside her. She contracted around it, whimpering and squirming, needing more.

"You are the most beautiful women alive when you are like this."

Back in the day, she might have teased him about thinking she wasn't beautiful *all* the time. Instead, she whispered, "I'm glad you think so."

He nodded, his brown eyes so dark with passion, they were almost black. Then he lowered his head again, and it wasn't his tongue that scraped against her swollen bud. It was his teeth. Oh, so gently, with exactly enough pressure, his teeth worried her clitoris with devastating effect.

She nearly came off the bed, her body bowing in intense pleasure. "Kadin!"

His only answer was to slide his other hand up her body until he could reach one of her nipples. He tweaked and played, alternating between plumping her breasts and teasing the oversensitive buds at their tips.

Her climax came roaring out of nowhere, the scream that accompanied it a pure release of passion so primal, she didn't care about the twinge it gave her throat.

She was still shaking with aftershocks when he surged up over her, sliding between her legs with his newly engorged sex. He stopped with the head pressing against her entrance.

"Okay?" he asked, his skin flushed, his muscles rigid with the effort it took to control himself.

She nodded, knowing it should be too much, but somehow it wasn't. His possession stretched her swollen, tender flesh to a point just short of pain.

This feeling that she knew no other man could ever give her had less to do with climaxing than the sensation of completeness during coitus.

He pressed forward so their bodies touched from the juncture of her thighs up to the point where her breasts pressed against his hairy chest. Covered in a fine sheen of sweat, they slid against each other, the extra load of sensations of that simple movement impacting her sensitized body with tsunami-like power and making her postorgasmic aftershocks into mini-cataclysms all their own.

His big, soldier's body shuddered as her vaginal walls contracted around him over and over again. "Oh, yeah, angel . . . just like that."

She smiled, feminine power surging through her, and repeated the involuntary movement voluntarily, squeezing so tightly, she gave herself another mini-climax.

"Shit . . ." His voice trailed off as he thrust deep inside her. "Nothing else like this ever."

And there wouldn't be. For either of them. Because this kind of sex? It was like worship, and it only happened once in a lifetime. She was sure of it.

"We fit here," she said on gasping breaths as he moved against her, his big body covering her and filling her with sensual delight and that ephemeral sense of safety she knew better than to ever take for granted again.

"Yes, angel. I never should have walked away."

Sex confessions didn't count. They weren't real. Everybody knew that, but her heart still liked hearing him admit the mistake. Even if he wouldn't feel the same when his dick wasn't buried as deeply inside her as it could possibly go.

"I loved you, Rachel."

"Yes." For a long time, she'd convinced herself it had all been a lie, but life wasn't that black-and-white.

And she knew it now.

"You loved me, too."

"I did." Enough not to have cared that he'd become the kind of man who did things he thought her idealistic self couldn't have handled.

But there was no point in saying that now.

"You're all I wanted in a woman," he said against her neck, the words achingly sweet and sad at the same time.

She turned her head, brushing his lips with her own. "Shh . . . no more talking."

No more lies, even if he thought he meant them.

He kissed her, saying things with his mobile lips and surging body she couldn't believe any more than the words he'd spoken out loud.

They'd both climaxed once already, so the pleasure built slowly, and Rachel let herself get lost in the slide of their bodies, the devouring of their lips. The urgency increased so subtly from one moment to the next that, once again, she was on the edge without realizing it.

But he wasn't ready to let her go over. He wanted more. She remembered him in this mood, and she let him have his way.

He pulled out, maneuvering her onto her stomach and then up onto her hands and knees before slamming back into her with one long, powerful thrust.

Mewling sounds fell from her lips, and she felt no shame in that. "You feel even bigger this way."

He went deeper, bumping her cervix, completely claiming her body with each tilt of his pelvis.

He reached around, pressing his middle finger into her slickened folds, caressing her clitoris and heightening her pleasure until her second, mind-shattering climax exploded through her.

She cried out, the aftershocks so intense, it was like a string of orgasms devastating her body and rocking the very foundation of her world.

"Yes, Rachel, my angel!" he shouted as he came inside her, coating her channel with his seed.

Hot moisture tracked down her face to drop below her onto the bed. She would never have let anyone else see those tears, but when he turned her head to the side to kiss her, she made no effort to hide her reaction to what they'd just done.

His dark eyes filled with an emotion she would never trust again but that warmed her all the same. "It's almost too much, isn't it?"

He understood. Someone else might have thought she was crying with regret or pain, but not him.

He understood that it was part of a release so intense, her body needed more than a scream to acknowledge it. It needed tears.

Kadin brushed his hand down Rachel's cheek. She was so beautiful in sleep, peaceful in a way she never could be awake. She'd fallen into slumber almost before he'd pulled out of her earlier but had snuggled right into him as he tucked them both under the light blankets.

Her tears after climax had nearly unmanned him. Damned if he hadn't felt moisture burning in his own eyes, as well. The sex had been *that* good.

Powerful. Miraculous, even.

He didn't know how he was going to live the rest of his life without it, but one thing had become very clear when they talked before making love. Rachel blamed him as much as she blamed herself for Linny's death.

Maybe even more.

She might have been able to forgive his stupidity as a twenty-year-old kid thinking she was better off without him. She might even have forgiven his weakness in walking away rather than facing her rejection. But she could never let go of the resentment she felt for the loss of her baby sister.

How could she? Linny was gone, just like Rachel's parents, leaving her alone in a world that had taken so much more from her than it had ever given.

And he'd been part of that loss, making everything worse when he'd convinced himself he was protecting her, giving her a chance at a normal life.

He'd been twenty and, yes, an idiot.

He was older and wiser now, but his window for happiness with Rachel was closed, and he was the one who'd pushed it shut.

Regret rode him harder than a Humvee trip through the mountains of Afghanistan, and there was nothing he could do to alleviate it, either.

No magical mix of words that would make it all better. Not when his weakness had cost Rachel the one person she'd always wanted to protect above all others.

Rachel stirred beside him. He forced the sadness from his expression, giving her a smile as her pretty pale eyes fluttered open.

She didn't return it, further emphasizing the yawning gap between them.

"What time is it?"

"Time for dinner." Spazz had knocked on the door a few minutes earlier.

Rachel nodded, moving to get up.

He pulled her back to him. "Hey."

"What?"

"This."

He kissed her. It wasn't all-out passion. They didn't have time for that. Spazz had found information on who lived in the house they were investigating and said Roman had sent a troubling e-mail.

Whatever that meant, it precluded more hours of pleasure in bed with Rachel.

Forcing himself to remember that, Kadin pulled back from the kiss.

"As things to wake up to go, that's pretty much in the top five," Rachel said, sounding happier than she'd looked upon waking.

He didn't ask what her number one would be, since he wasn't sure he wanted to know. "Works for me, too."

She nodded, squirming to get out of the bed. "We need to get a move-on."

That was usually his line, so it made him smile to hear her use it.

She grabbed one of his T-shirts and yanked it on with quick movements before picking up her clothes from earlier and heading to the door. "I need a shower."

"Rachel?"

She stopped at the door and looked back at him. "What?"

"You okay?" He didn't come right out and ask if she wished they hadn't made love.

That would just be too damn touchy-feely for him, not to mention that, if the answer was *yes,* he really would rather not hear it. But he didn't like the preoccupied expression in her eyes.

"Not really."

His gut tightened. "What's wrong?"

"I don't know. I just woke up with this feeling of foreboding. I've had them before, and it never means anything good."

He remembered that. "Like when your parents died."

Rachel had called him from work telling him about her

feeling that day. Then she'd texted him later to say she thought it must have been about her friend cutting herself on a broken glass. She was taking the other girl to the ER.

The rest of that day and night and the one that followed it had been the stuff nightmares were made of.

And even after seeing how she reacted to losing her parents, how much she'd hurt, though she hid her pain from everyone but him, he'd walked away. He hadn't just been an idiot at twenty; Kadin had been incredibly selfish and was only now realizing it.

How stupid did that make him as a thirty-year-old man?

"Yes." She grabbed the door handle, her grip white-knuckled. "Is everything okay with Jamila?"

"As far as we know. Her family and Chuma left the hotel for dinner a few minutes ago."

"Do we still have someone tailing them?"

"Cowboy's on it with Abdul's man."

She nodded, looking no less tense. "That's good."

"There's no reason to believe she's not okay," Kadin tried to point out. "She's been engaged to the spawn of satan for nearly a year and not gotten caught in the grinder yet."

"I know. I just . . . I feel worried."

He jumped out of the bed, grabbing his own clothes, except a T-shirt. He'd wear the one she had on after their shower. Smelling Rachel on him would never be a bad thing.

"Let's get showered, and then we'll do a situation report over dinner, okay?"

"Okay." She blew out a breath, as if she was trying to relieve the tension, but it obviously didn't work.

Her entire demeanor was one of a woman on edge. And he remembered from past experience that feeling wasn't going to leave her alone until she found out what was coming.

"Did you have this feeling before Linny?" he asked and then wished he hadn't.

She stopped dead in the hallway on the way to the bathroom. "No. If I had, I might have been able to save her."

He couldn't argue that, but Rachel's *premonitions,* for lack of a better word, were beyond his comprehension. He didn't understand how they happened, why they occurred sometimes and not others.

All he did know was that they cost her emotionally, and she was a woman who couldn't afford to pay more in that way.

"You are one of the strongest people I've ever known," he said as they entered the bathroom.

She laughed at that, the sound more bitter than amused. "I don't think so."

"I do. You were stronger than me." Stronger than he'd ever given her credit for. "Still are." She was going to be able to walk away from him and survive.

He wasn't so sure about himself.

Suddenly Spazz's taunt-fate-and-be-damned attitude of the last year made a hell of a lot more sense to Kadin.

And only as he realized that did he also acknowledge that, in the back of his head for the last ten years, he'd had the hope that someday he and Rachel would find their way back to each other.

They ate their dinner on the rooftop, everyone there except Cowboy.

"So, the man living in the house Chuma's been visiting is one Terne Lavigne," Neil said, giving the name its proper French pronunciation. "He is a former corporate employee of SympaMed, living far beyond the means of someone with his background and without visible signs of income."

"His name came up in TGP's research," Jayne offered.

"But we dropped that line of inquiry because we could not locate him."

Rachel remembered reading that in the file as well but said nothing.

Neil nodded to Jayne, giving Rachel a searching look before adding, "When I dug deeply enough, I found out that Lavigne is also listed as a contributor to two of Dr. Massri's pet political projects."

"What else did you find when you started snooping in files you're not supposed to have access to?" Kadin asked.

Beth jumped in with enthusiasm, showing how much she enjoyed the technical side of espionage. "He's a silent partner in a weapons factory as well as primary shareholder in several African mines supplying raw materials to the factory."

The rest of the table discussed the significance of these discoveries, but Rachel didn't add much to the conversation.

Her sense of foreboding was too acute to be ignored. It didn't help to find out that Jamila, her family, and Chuma had ended up at Lavigne's house for dinner.

"Do you think he's the player we've been looking for?" Jayne asked.

"The one at the very top of the entire organization?" Beth asked. She then had some kind of silent communication-between-geeks with Neil. "I think it's possible."

Ethan smiled at them both tolerantly, clearly proud of his wife's accomplishments of the afternoon.

Rachel pushed her plate away, feeling sick. "And Jamila's in that house." A house they couldn't get eyes or ears into.

Jayne's cell phone went off at that moment, the ring tone bringing the first lightening of spirit Rachel had had since waking. It was the 1980s hit "Who Can It Be Now?" by Men at Work.

Rachel just knew Jayne had made that Whit's ring tone. Considering how anal the man was about secrecy—or had been before this congressional audit—it was pretty apropos.

Jayne's conversation was brief and not a happy one. She hung up and turned to the others. "Ralph Giroux is missing."

"Who is Ralph Giroux?" Beth asked.

"One of the autistic savants participating in the 'Treffert' think tank," Rachel guessed, her sense of unease growing even stronger.

Both Jayne and Neil nodded.

Chapter Eighteen

Neil added, "He's a highly functioning autistic Frenchman with absolute brilliance in the area of mathematics and applied physics. He's our acoustic-levitation genius."

"Missing, how?" Kadin asked.

Jayne was typing into her phone. "He didn't show up for his job today, and the la Sûreté agent assigned to guard him hasn't been able to locate him."

"*Agent*? As in, a single Moroccan police officer?" Kadin asked, his tone showing what he thought of that situation. "When TGP learned of Abasi Chuma's communications about grabbing up a Treffert tank member, each country's government was given a heads-up to the danger their savant or savants might be in. Most have acted accordingly."

"Yes, but only a single officer was assigned to Mr. Giroux's protection." Jayne's mouth twisted in a moue of disapproval.

Rachel understood the reaction. The National Police of France, formerly *la Sûreté Nationale,* might be Morocco's top federal law enforcement, but even the FBI usually worked in teams in cases like this.

"Because he's autistic, he didn't rate adequate protection," Kadin said with some bitterness.

Rachel thought he must be thinking of his nephew. Despite being wrapped up in her own growing sense of anxiety, she put her hand on his arm and squeezed in an attempt to comfort him. The look he gave her said he appreciated it.

But Rachel didn't understand one thing. "Why didn't your chief send Atrati to watch over these people?"

"The Atrati weren't given the contract. Each government was to take responsibility," Kadin replied. "The think tank participants are located all over the world, doing most of their work online."

"Putting their results at risk for hacking by any Tom, Dickwad, or Harry," Neil inserted with disgust. "The Atrati wouldn't have let Giroux be taken," he grumbled.

Ethan shook his head in clear disgust. *"Politics."*

A mix of emotions swirled through Rachel.

Jayne getting the call from Whit on *her* case brought home the fact that Rachel was no longer the agent of record in any of these matters. In fact, she was officially on voluntary unpaid leave.

Right this moment, Rachel didn't *have* a job, and she couldn't be sure she'd have a career to return to when she got back to DC.

Since Linny's death, Rachel had lived for her job. She didn't have anything else. And now that was in jeopardy, and *her* assignment was unequivocally in someone else's hands.

She'd thought she wouldn't mind. That it didn't matter. But she'd been wrong.

The emptiness that spread through her at the realization she was no longer officially working the case fed an undercurrent of malaise Rachel had been doing her best to ignore since getting out of that cell in the mountains.

Added to that, her connection to Kadin seemed to be loosening by the moment. The Atrati had not been given the contract to protect the presumed members of Chuma and Massri's think tank. He had not chosen to share that information with her.

She shouldn't have been surprised. She really shouldn't. It wasn't her case, and there was nothing she could do about it, but she'd thought maybe their . . . *friendship* at least went beyond official roles and job titles. That it extended to communicating about things.

She'd been wrong.

She felt the extinguishing of that tiny flicker in the vicinity of her heart that she could only describe as hope.

She'd defined the parameters of their relationship. Sex and help protecting Jamila Massri.

Only now, as Rachel realized how sharply defined those parameters were in Kadin's mind, did she understand that the tiny place inside her heart had wanted more. A lot more.

Bile rose in her throat as her own self-perpetuating blindness rose to mock her. Once again she'd made the wrong choice for her own happiness.

It didn't surprise her. She seemed to be a professional in that regard.

Her gut cramped, and she wanted nothing more than to make a beeline for the bathroom to empty the contents of her stomach. But she'd shown all the weakness on this assignment that she was going to.

Swallowing down the bitter taste in her throat, she concentrated on breathing, doing her best to track the conversation around her.

"Are you okay?" Beth asked, her expression and tone indicating her worry.

Rachel did something she seldom allowed herself to do, unless it was for the sake of the job. She lied. "I'm fine."

She was unable to inflect her tone with any level of animation, but that could not be helped. She felt dead inside.

But Jamila Massri was still alive, and Rachel was determined to keep her that way.

She leaned forward toward Neil, getting his attention with a touch to his knee.

He stopped talking to Jayne and looked at Rachel. "Do you have an idea?"

Not about the missing Frenchman. He wasn't her assignment. She didn't *have* an assignment, just a commitment to a young woman who deserved better than the future in store for her.

"We can't get sound in Lavigne's house, but can you get heat readings?" Rachel asked Neil.

He stared at her. "I might happen to have something with me that can do that. Thermal imaging comes in handy when planning an extraction. You think they've brought Ralph Giroux to the house here in Marrakech? That would be a pretty bold move, considering."

She hadn't been thinking of Ralph Giroux, but she didn't say that. If it got her what she wanted, heat readings placing the people inside the house, she'd go with it. "It's possible."

"There's no way of interpreting the heat signatures as belonging to any particular person," Jayne pointed out, her tone dismissive. "We don't know how many servants and guards Lavigne keeps in his employ."

"The location of those readings could tell us something, though. If there's a person in an isolated area of the house while the rest of the household is at dinner, that might indicate a prisoner," Rachel disagreed.

Heat signatures could also indicate if Jamila was in a room away from the others. Rachel's sense of impending doom was the only thing competing with the malaise growing inside her.

She might be wrong, and it could have everything to do with Ralph Giroux and nothing to do with Jamila Massri, but either way, sitting around and doing nothing was not an option.

Jayne thought it over for a few seconds before giving Rachel a look of approval and nodding. "That's possible," she said to no one in particular. "Although he is a French citizen, TGP has deemed the data he was working with potentially harmful to the U.S., so locating Mr. Giroux is now officially part of my assignment."

Rachel expected a shard of pain at this reminder that the assignment was no longer hers, but she felt nothing. She was going numb inside, her focus narrowing down to Jamila Massri and keeping the young woman safe.

"How close do we have to be to get an accurate heat reading on the house?" Kadin asked.

"Closer than I'd like. Fifty feet. Twenty-five to thirty would be ideal" Jayne responded.

Kadin nodded. "We have to wait for it to get dark, then, or at least dusk. There's too little cover around there."

"No." Through the numbness, Rachel's inner alarm was increasing in volume, not decreasing. "That could be too late."

The sun didn't set for another hour.

"It's not likely they're going to torture Giroux for information while they've got other people in the house."

"You mean Jamila and her aunt?" Ethan asked, having been quiet to this point, though his keen senses had taken everything in. "You think having the women there will inhibit them pushing their agenda with Giroux tonight?"

"Yes." Kadin sounded so certain.

But Rachel knew he was wrong. Oh, not about Giroux. Chances were, the autistic man was safe, at least for the night. Criminals as astute as these men had proven to be would have researched their quarry enough to try positive forms of persuasion first.

But Kadin was wrong in thinking that the women's

presence would prevent something bad from happening. Rachel was almost sure that Jamila's being there meant exactly the opposite. That something bad was going to happen *to her.*

Rachel stood up. "I'm feeling a little tired. I think I'll lie down for a while."

Her lack of animation gave credence to the lie, and she could see the acceptance of it as truth in the eyes of the others around the table. They'd been thinking of her as fragile all along; her withdrawal just fed that belief.

Kadin made to stand, but she shook her head. "Stay here. You've got planning to do."

His eyes narrowed.

"For Jamila's sake," she added for good measure.

He frowned, looking really unhappy about sending her off to bed alone, but in the end, he nodded.

Rachel ignored the continuing look of concern Beth shot her and the slight pity that flickered briefly in Jayne's eyes. Neither woman would understand what drove Rachel right now. How could they?

She went directly to the room she shared with Kadin and made quick work of donning the loose-fitting djellaba he'd bought her over her clothes, then adding the brightly colored *khimar,* similar to a large head scarf, over her hair, pulling one side up to cover her face like a veil.

She found Kadin's backup KA-BAR in his duffel where she'd noticed it when looking for the T-shirt she'd worn earlier. She strapped the combat knife around her calf, adjusting the sheath to fit her smaller frame. He didn't have a backup handgun in the duffel, but she was betting she knew someone who would.

Rachel went looking for Jayne's room. She found the other agent's things in the room Eva had vacated only that morning.

A quick search revealed a small stash of colored contacts

like the ones Rachel herself often carried on assignment. She chose a pair that would change her eyes to hazel, not the dark brown she'd worn as part of her cover in Egypt.

Different enough to be unrecognizable with her body covered by the loose folds of the djellaba and the rest of her features hidden behind the *khimar*.

She also found Jayne's gun and a silencer. Rachel took them both, along with extra clips of ammunition. She loaded the gun and screwed the silencer into place before tucking the gun into her waistband under the robe and the extra clips into the side pocket of her Bermuda-length cargo shorts.

The djellaba was better at concealing weapons than a standard-issue FBI suit. No telltale bump showed either at her waist or where the KA-BAR knife was strapped to her calf.

Rachel removed her shoes for the trip down the stairs to the first floor, careful to be soundless as she made her way to Neil's command center.

It didn't take her long to find the small handheld thermal-imaging camera. She'd been trained on one similar in her job at the DEA. Learning the use of thermal imaging was standard procedure for drug enforcement agents.

Though growers were getting more sophisticated at hiding the heat signatures from their grow lights, it was still one of the top ways to identify an indoor cannabis farm.

She also discovered a pretty nice lock-picking kit and some locks on a table near Neil's computers. Someone had been practicing his skills and left his tools to come back to later. Maybe Ethan? It didn't really matter who.

Rachel grabbed the picks, rolled them neatly into their case, and slid the bundle into the remaining empty side pocket of her cargo shorts.

Now it was just a matter of transportation. Finding the

keys to the Land Rover took precious minutes, but luckily Cowboy had left them in the command center.

Which made them easily accessible if Kadin or Neil— or, in this case, Rachel—had needed to take the Australian-made SUV.

She found Lavigne's house using the GPS memory on the Land Rover, driving by the entrance to the property rather than stopping when she came to it. She noted the trees lining the long drive and thought, unlike Kadin, that they would make adequate cover for approaching the house.

They'd have to.

She parked the vehicle behind a stand of trees on the other side of a small hill less than a quarter mile from the house. It was a risk, but Rachel knew that while parking farther away would lessen her chances of being discovered, it would also make escape less likely if she and Jamila were on the run.

She didn't even pretend she was only there to make sure everything was okay. She knew in her gut it wasn't. She was there to find Jamila and get her out.

As she went to close the door after climbing out of the Land Rover, Rachel spied a communication earbud in the center console. Cowboy must have left it.

Rachel put it into her ear, turning it on and receiving no buzz to indicate that the others on this frequency weren't active. Neil must have left the command center's receiver on.

She left the earbud on and in her ear. Once her disappearance was discovered, Neil might think to come on to the comm-link. At that point, she and Jamila would very likely need the others' help.

Rachel made her way from tree to tree, stopping at the last oversized oak nearest the front of the mansion. The house was surrounded by a six-foot stucco wall, but the iron gate stood open. Not exactly the kind of tight security she expected, considering the jammer in use and the possibility they had a kidnapped savant on the premises somewhere.

Which probably meant there was video surveillance. Sure enough, there was a camera in evidence, and it was pointed at the entrance to the mansion's grounds. However, unless there was a camera she couldn't see, there were no eyes on the area around the wall.

Interesting. Overconfidence? Arrogance? Most likely.

And the false sense of security created by living in such an isolated area.

She used Neil's thermal-imaging camera to determine that, inside the house, a group of people congregated in one room. Even accounting for servants, the head count and size of each signature seemed to indicate that Jamila and the others were all there, including Lavigne. In addition there was a signature that would indicate by size it was a woman who moved around the room.

Probably serving dinner.

Jamila was okay. For now.

The relief Rachel felt didn't even dent her sense of impending doom. She skirted the house, staying out of the line of sight of the fixed cameras on the walls. She verified her findings with Neil's camera from the back side of the compound.

She also discovered that there was indeed the heat signature of a person in an outbuilding behind the house. Another man stood outside the structure, no doubt the guard.

After Rachel made her way back to her watching position in the front of the house, she monitored the movement of the heat signatures as dusk settled over the landscape. It was just going dark when three of the diners rose and left the room.

Rachel tucked in closer to the tree and was unsurprised when Jamila's aunt and uncle exited the house a few minutes later. The fact that Dr. Massri was with them gave Rachel pause, increasing her sense of dread.

Perhaps even he did not want to be in the house when Chuma did whatever it was he planned to do.

And Rachel's gut was sure Chuma had plans.

The three remaining inside the house, presumably Jamila, Chuma, and Lavigne, rose and headed out of the dining room. The signatures were so close, Rachel was sure at least one of the men had a hold on Jamila.

As their signatures began to elevate, Rachel realized they were heading upstairs. A cold stone landed in the bottom of Rachel's stomach.

There was no good reason for an unmarried woman to be taken to the second level of this man's home. Not in this culture or the one Jamilla came from in Egypt.

"Rachel." Kadin's voice barked in her ear.

"Yes."

A sound suspiciously like a sigh of relief came over the comm-link. "Get your ass back to the safe house."

She didn't bother to say no. He had to realize Rachel wasn't going anywhere without Jamila. "I believe Mr. Giroux is in an outbuilding on the back side of Lavigne's estate. There is one guard at the door."

"If you extract Jamila, you'll compromise TGP's investigation." Kadin's words showed he knew exactly where Rachel was and what her priority was.

"If I don't, Chuma will destroy her."

"Not at dinner."

"They're not eating anymore."

"Massri's car just passed my checkpoint." Cowboy's laconic tone came over the comm-link. "Three passengers in it."

"Why didn't you contact me when you saw Rachel go by?" Kadin demanded.

"I didn't see her. I was scouting the surrounding area for a good approach. I saw the Land Rover from a distance. I assumed it was you going in for surveillance early."

Why were they talking about stuff that didn't matter?

"Rachel." There was a quality to Kadin's tone she couldn't quite read.

He sounded almost desperate.

But he wasn't the one with something to worry about here. Jamila was, and she didn't even know it. The three figures had reached the top of the stairs and were walking along what had to be the upper hallway.

"What?" she asked, not really listening for a response.

She was too focused on the small screen of the thermal-imaging camera.

"You're flushing your career down the latrine here, angel."

What difference did it make to him? "That's my problem."

"Come back, angel. We'll figure this out. Make a plan."

"I've got a plan." She was getting Jamila out of there, and if Abasi Chuma had to die in the process . . .

Rachel didn't plan to lose any sleep over it.

"Wait for us to get there. We're your backup, Rachel."

"There's no time." The images had stopped in a room on the second floor. "They've taken her upstairs."

The heat signatures separated, one man taking a position by what was probably the door, the other closer to the smaller heat signature that had to be Jamila. He wasn't touching her. Yet.

"Listen to me, Rachel. I need you to wait for us. Do you hear me?"

Of course she heard him. Neil's toys were impeccable. "Angel?"

"Rachel, you crafty bitch, you stole my equipment." Neil's voice came over the communications link.

"I needed it. I'm sorry."

"Nothing to apologize for, unless you don't wait for us to get there to move in. You know better than to go into a hostile environment alone."

The heat signatures remained static, as if they were talking. Rachel willed them to stay that way.

"I won't let her down." Not like Linny.

"You can't help her if you're dead," Kadin said, the sound of another Land Rover starting up.

"Where are you, Rachel?" Cowboy asked, his Texas twang unmistakable. "Exactly."

She told him, seeing no reason to withhold the information.

"I'll be there in five minutes. Wait for me."

"You're not that close. If you were on surveillance, the Land Rover wouldn't have been in the alleyway behind the safe house. Your comm-link wouldn't have been in it."

"I'm with Abdul's man."

"The earbud?"

"Was left in the Land Rover on purpose," Kadin said, a strange quality in his voice. Almost like fear.

But Kadin Marks didn't fear anything, did he?

"That seems sloppy."

"Yeah, well, I thought you might go off the reservation. You used to be impulsive."

She had been. "I'm not anymore."

The snort of laughter in her ear wasn't Kadin's. Neil's, maybe?

"I'd hoped you had enough training to take precautions when they were offered," Kadin growled.

"That was kind of you." He'd been watching out for her.

Even if he saw her as nothing but an old obligation, he'd taken that obligation seriously.

Kadin cursed creatively. "I wasn't trying to be *kind*. I wanted to make sure you didn't fry your own ass, Rach."

She didn't answer, her attention caught by what was happening on the small screen of the thermal-imaging camera. The two heat signatures were reading as one, which had to mean they were very close together.

Suddenly, the smaller heat signature went flying across the room, stopping against a wall. It slowly righted itself, the other form looming over it by the time Jamila was standing with her back to the wall.

Rachel's heart stalled and then sped up, her breathing going shallow as she dropped into that ultra-calm, no-matter-the-circumstances place she had to be in to do her job sometimes. "I'm going in."

"No, damn it, Rach. Wait for Cowboy."

She ignored Kadin's order and the ranting that came after. She ignored Cowboy's promise that he was almost there, his voice breathless, as if he was running full tilt.

She did a scan of the house again, verifying where possible guards or servants were.

Lavigne had to be pretty confident that the house was secure, because there were only four other people in the house, and two of them were moving around what had to be the kitchen because of the heat signature the oven was giving off.

Probably diligent servants baking bread for the next day.

The other two were nowhere near each other. One was on the ground floor, in the same position he had had been in the first time she'd done the scan. The other man-sized heat signature was also stationary, but in a room off the kitchen.

They weren't expecting trouble, then.

That worked for her.

"I'm leaving the camera in my current location," she told Neil over the comm-link. "You'll want to retrieve it."

"Rachel, just wait one damned minute more."

She shook her head, knowing they couldn't see the gesture. But it didn't matter.

Whatever was happening to Jamila couldn't be allowed to continue. "He threw her across the room. He's too close to her now."

Jamila was an innocent, not a government agent trained to cope with pain during interrogation.

Rachel could not allow her to go through anything like the horror she had experienced.

Rachel placed the camera on the ground and then approached the entrance as if she had a reason to be there. She went through the open front gate with her head down, the traditional Moroccan female attire her only camouflage.

Chapter Nineteen

Rachel's only hope for success was that the guard watching the video monitors would mistake her for a local woman come to visit one of the servants working in the kitchen.

Rachel didn't allow herself to feel relief when she reached the back door unmolested. There was still a locked door, two floors, and the men inside this house between her and Jamila's safety.

Making use of the lock-picking kit she'd found in Neil's command center, Rachel had the back door unlocked within seconds. She eased it open quietly, not wanting to alert the two workers in the kitchen or the man currently reclining (maybe even sleeping) in the room off of it.

She couldn't be sure of how the surveillance was set up and wouldn't bank on her illegal entry going unnoticed. Though the back door hadn't looked alarmed, that didn't make it so.

She rushed through the mansion, following where her instincts led based on the pattern of movements she'd seen the people inside making earlier. She reached the stairs and ran up them on silent feet, her focus split between her surroundings and reaching the room she knew held Jamila.

Rushing down the hall, she ignored the possibility that interior cameras were feeding her location to the guard on the first floor. She couldn't do anything about that right now.

Before she'd worked out in her head which door was the most likely to be her target, Jamila's scream came from the room directly to Rachel's right.

Rachel yanked the gun from her waistband and took off the safety.

Remembering the man standing either against or near the door as indicated by his heat signature, Rachel took aim and shot a starburst pattern right through the door. The silencer did its job, the bullets piercing the wooden door louder than the shots had been.

A man's shout of pain from the other side said she'd hit her target but hadn't killed him. But no hue and cry came from the first floor, the mansion's size working in Rachel's favor.

She shoved the door open.

It wasn't even locked. These men knew that none of the staff in this household would be coming to a screaming woman's rescue.

Abasi Chuma was scrambling in a drawer beside the bed when Rachel got inside the room. His hands closed over something before he spun to face her.

The Jordan-made Viper was black and deadly and pointed directly at her. She didn't pause, didn't give warning. She just shot him. Another starburst, this time in a man's chest.

Blood sprayed. Chuma fell back on the bed, his trousers around his hips, his sex grotesquely hard.

It would set in rigor that way, because he was dead. He would not be getting up again or hurting another woman as he'd hurt so many already.

Rachel scanned the room for Jamila and Lavigne.

The other woman was lying on the floor, her clothes torn mostly off of her, bright red marks showing livid against her olive skin in several places, blood smeared down her chin and on her thighs.

Rachel didn't let herself react to the proof of what Chuma had been doing. How fast he had acted in the space of time it had taken Rachel to get inside the house and up the stairs.

She simply turned to assess the threat of the other man.

He was awake but moaning in pain, his bloody hands pressed over a wound in his chest. "Help me! You must help me," he coughed out.

"Like you helped her?" Rachel asked, no inflection in her tone.

Yeah. That was going to happen. In another lifetime, maybe.

She bent over the man, and he looked relieved, as if he really believed she'd do anything to save the likes of him. Using a technique she'd learned after joining TGP, she applied pressure to the vulnerable spot on his neck that had him passing out within a couple of seconds.

With any luck, he wouldn't waken for several minutes to call for help.

Rachel rushed over to Jamila, pulling the other woman to her feet. "Come on. We have to go."

"Who are you?" Jamila asked, tears streaming down her cheeks.

Rachel yanked down the veil that covered her features. "We have to leave, Jamila. Now."

"Tanya? But you . . . you disappeared."

"I'll tell you about it later."

Jamila looked down at herself. "I can't. I'm . . . He . . ."

Rachel scanned the room and took in Chuma's suit jacket, which had been tossed negligently to the floor. She grabbed it. "Put this on."

"It's his." Jamila shrank from it.

"Not anymore."

Jamila's features hardened, and she nodded. "Give it to me."

Jamila pulled on the jacket, covering her nudity before turning to spit on the dead man on the bed. "This is what you deserve."

Rachel would rather hear the vicious anger in the other woman's voice than defeat.

"Come on," she said, though. They didn't have time for more closure than this.

Jamila didn't reply, and Rachel grabbed her arm, yanking her from the room. They'd deal with the trauma later. First they had to get out of there.

The silencer on the gun had done its job, and the hallway was empty. Rachel pulled Jamila along the hall and down the stairs. Their luck ran out at the bottom. A man came out of a room filled with monitors off the bottom of the stairs.

His eyes widened comically at the sight of the djellaba-clad Rachel dragging Jamila behind her. His hand darted toward his shoulder holster.

Rachel didn't hesitate. She simply took aim and fired, winging him.

He spun back from the force of the hit, but he'd been trained well by somebody, maybe military, because he came back around with the gun in his hand. Rachel jumped in front of Jamila, her gun still pointing at him.

He got a shot off before she did. She felt the heat and pain of the bullet grazing her skull.

Rachel dove for the floor, yanking Jamila down, too, before rolling onto her stomach and taking aim again. She squeezed off a shot that went wide, but another shot sounded, and crimson bloomed on the guard's chest before he fell to the ground. This time he did not move again.

"He wasn't a professional," Cowboy drawled as he offered a hand to Rachel to help her up. "A professional would have known to shoot for the torso. The kill shot can come after you've incapacitated your opponent."

"Right," she agreed.

Abasi Chuma was dead, and she felt no remorse about that fact. It had been him or her—she'd seen that in his eyes. And he'd already hurt Jamila.

There hadn't been a choice.

Rachel spun to help Jamila. "Come on, we have to go. There's another guard off the kitchen."

"Not anymore, there isn't, but the one outside with the prisoner will have heard the shots. Why didn't I hear yours?"

"Jayne carries a silencer for her gun."

"She's gonna be more pissed than a rattler caught in a hoedown when she finds out you stole her sidearm."

"I needed a weapon."

"Yeah, Calamity Jane, you sure did."

"What's happening?" Jamila demanded, pulling against Rachel's hold on her arm. "Who is this man? How did you come to be here? You were a tourist . . . in Helwan, lamenting the lack of good coffee."

"I'll explain everything later, I promise, but we've got to go. We don't know what kind of contingency plans Lavigne has in place for when his home gets breached and whether that guard set off the alarm or not."

"Right." Cowboy led them to the front door, not the back. "Kadin and Neil will be here with the other Land Rover."

Kadin was already rushing in through the door when they reached the front of the house. He took in Rachel and the woman beside her before scanning the entry for anyone else. "Sit-rep," he barked at Cowboy.

"Two tied up in the kitchen. One incapacitated. One dead."

"Two dead," Rachel corrected. "Lavigne is also shot, but he was still alive when I left him unconscious upstairs."

Neither man asked why she hadn't killed him, and she was glad. She could hardly claim that she *couldn't* kill. She'd proven that she could, but she wasn't a murderer.

And that's what she would have been if she'd assassinated a man who was already incapacitated.

"Ralph Giroux is secured," Neil said over the comm-link. "The guard won't be locking up other autistic men for a long damn time."

"Where's the Land Rover you came in?" Kadin demanded of Rachel.

"Over there." She pointed toward where she'd left the SUV parked.

"We'll take it and Miss Massri back to the safe house. Spazz and Cowboy will take Ralph Giroux."

"Spazz, I'll need a secure line to Roman as soon as we get to the house," Kadin said over the comm-link.

Neil replied, "You got it, Trig."

"You're arranging transport back to the States?" Rachel asked, sure she knew the answer.

"After."

"After what?"

"Egypt."

"Why are we going to Egypt?" she asked, startled by his reply. "We can't just dump Jamila and go."

Jamila said nothing, and Kadin just shook his head. "Of course not."

"Then why Egypt?"

"Dr. Massri is going to find out sooner rather than later what happened here tonight, and he'll give orders for anything incriminating in Chuma's and Lavigne's possession to be destroyed. He may even decide to go underground himself."

Jamila looked stunned. "My . . . my father? If by *under-*

ground you mean living without all the luxuries life has to offer, that would never be acceptable to my father. But why would he do such a thing?"

Rachel had to let that go, too intent on the implications of what Kadin had said. "We have to beat him to it."

But why was Kadin acting as if this was still Rachel's case? One that he had every intention of helping her close?

"*Incriminating?* My father? Abasi, too, is a . . . wanted criminal?" Jamila asked, as if the full import of Kadin's words had just hit her as well.

"He *was,*" Rachel emphasized. "He's dead, Jamila."

"You shot him."

"Yes." And an agency shrink would probably talk her into claiming regret so she could go back to work, but deep inside, Rachel didn't think she was sorry.

Or ever would be.

She valued human life, but she wasn't at all sure men like Abasi Chuma were anything but monsters under the façade of human skin.

Jamila's eyes burned bright with anger. "Thank you for shooting Abasi."

This woman might have been victimized, but she was no victim.

"So, Abasi . . . and my father . . . were wanted criminals?" Jamila asked again as they reached the Land Rover.

Rachel handed Kadin the keys. He took them, his brown eyes making promises that poked at the numb bubble where her emotions were.

"Yes, Miss Massri," Kadin said, turning from Rachel but somehow making her feel that his attention was still fully on her. "Abasi Chuma was a criminal guilty of crimes against many countries. As is your father."

"Abasi did not live to face trial, but I cannot be sorry." Jamila climbed into the backseat.

Rachel followed, wanting to be close if the other woman started to break down. And who wouldn't, after going through what she just had?

"Tell me what's going on," Jayne's voice demanded over the comm-link.

Rachel pulled the earbud from her ear. When they got back to the safe house would be soon enough to deal with the other TGP agent.

Kadin was talking in the front seat as he drove away from Lavigne's house. Rachel did her best to tune him out.

"I know where my father keeps his important files." Jamila spoke quietly, as if to herself.

But Rachel replied, anyway. "Why are you telling me this?"

"You said Abasi and my father were criminals," she said fiercely. "Abasi deceived me into believing he was a different kind of man. And so did my father. He and my father were great friends. But your man . . . he implied that my father is dangerous now."

Rachel was going to deny that Kadin was *her man,* but somehow the words wouldn't come. "Yes. I'm sorry, Jamila."

"You have nothing to be sorry for, unless it is becoming my friend under false pretenses, as I think you must have. But then, you must have had very good reason to do so."

"The security of a nation." Rachel wasn't grandstanding.

It's what the agents of TGP did. They kept America secure.

Or did their very best to, anyway.

Jamila nodded. "You will want my father's private files. The ones no one else is supposed to know about."

Rachel was sure Jamila was right. "Where are they?"

"In our home, but you won't be able to get to them without me." She paused, her expression lighting with satisfaction. "It is tricky, but I figured it out."

"Jamila, you need to stay here at the safe house where no more harm can come to you." Even as Rachel made the claim, she didn't know if she could keep the promise it implied.

She didn't know if Whit would bring Jamila in now or if he would wash his hands of his impulsive agent and the woman she was trying so hard to protect. The safe house was Atrati property, anyway. She couldn't make commitments to its use.

But Jamila had to stay safe.

Jamila's dusky jaw hardened, bringing a developing bruise there into stark relief. "No, I want to help take my father and Abasi down."

"Abasi's dead."

"His reputation isn't. My father is alive . . . he was very much alive when he left me alone in that house with full knowledge of what type of man Abasi was." Jamila's tone was filled with anger and betrayal so deep, it was clear her father had broken the familial bond of love and duty between them.

"I'm sorry," Rachel said inadequately.

"You have nothing to be sorry for. You stopped him." The vulnerability of the newly traumatized showed on Jamila's face for a brief moment. "I thought Abasi was a better man than my father. I thought he was my future."

"He did a good job of hiding his true nature from you."

"Yes, he did." Jamila's harsh laugh had Kadin's head jerking in attention. "But he was even worse than my father. At least, I think he was. Maybe my father is just as bad, and I only saw some of what makes him the man he is."

Rachel didn't know what Jamila meant by that, but she

was starting to suspect that the other woman's protected and cosseted upbringing was as much a subterfuge as Chuma's supposedly caring nature had been. "What happened tonight?" she asked.

"You saw what happened."

"Were they trying to get information out of you?" Rachel asked, desperate to know if her connection to Jamila had brought this on the other woman.

"They showed me a picture on Abasi's phone. It was attached to a text message someone else had sent him. The words made no sense. *This is her.*"

It made sense to Rachel. Her captors had sent a picture to Chuma, proving he hadn't seen her before ordering her taken to Morocco where she could be tortured for information.

Jamila continued. "It was of you, but you were tied to a chair, with marks on your face. Your eyes were darker, like I remember them from Helwan. You looked bad. They wanted to know if I'd ever seen you before."

"You told them about the coffeehouse."

"No." Jamila shuddered. "I was scared. I didn't understand why Abasi had taken me into a bedroom with Mr. Lavigne. They were looking at me in a way that made me uneasy. It was . . . what is that American expression? *Something was off.*"

"Tonight?"

"Yes, but before that, too. The way Abasi had been acting since I arrived in Marrakech. He wasn't even at the hotel when we arrived. The way my father had been behaving. He was on edge, violence just under the surface. I had seen him this way before, and it did not bode well for me."

Later Rachel would ask the other woman to explain that further, but Jamila needed to get this out, and she wasn't about to interrupt her.

"For the first time, when I was with Abasi, he frightened me. Badly." Jamila looked at Rachel, an unexpected and almost unbelievable sparkle of mischief in her espresso brown eyes. "Besides, I learned long ago that I got more freedom with subterfuge than honesty."

"So, you told them you'd never seen me before?"

"Yes."

"But why did he hurt you?"

"Because he wanted to, and Mr. Lavigne wanted to watch. I could tell he liked hurting me. It excited him." Jamila's voice dripped with revulsion. "Abasi told Mr. Lavigne that he knew I was ignorant, but he had no intention of losing this opportunity."

Jamila went silent for several seconds, her thoughts her own. When she spoke again, her tone was devoid of emotion. "Apparently, my father had been putting him off about being alone with me. Before now."

Rachel didn't understand. "He was going to let you marry the man."

"I know." Jamila's voice shook with betrayal and hatred. "My father is not the civilized man he seems to the world and insists I pretend he is to others."

"What do you mean?"

"He beat my mother to death and told me she deserved it, had driven him to it. He used to beat me, but I learned to be obedient and quiet."

Rachel had never suspected such a dark past in the innocent woman's behavior.

She thought maybe she was seeing the true Jamila Massri for the first time. It made Rachel question her own judgment. Had she seen what she wanted because of the similarities between Linny and Jamila?

She had to approach a subject she knew was going to be difficult. "You need to see a doctor."

"No."

"Please, Jamila."

"No one else is going to touch me."

"You need clothes and a shower," Kadin said from the front seat. "You'll get those at the safe house."

"She needs a doctor," Rachel said fiercely. Kadin needed to back her up on this.

"Mrs. Abdul." That was all Kadin said, but Rachel had to trust him that it meant what she needed it to.

"Okay."

"It will take Roman a little time to get transport to Helwan in place. Jamila will have time to collect herself."

The young Egyptian woman needed more than time, but Rachel wasn't going to say so and risk having Jamila believe Rachel saw her as damaged.

"Okay," she repeated, the only answer she could give.

"You saved me," Jamila said, the hollow quality in her voice worrying Rachel. "You came for me."

"You didn't deserve to be in that place."

"But now the evidence you so clearly seek is in jeopardy." Jamila had grasped the situation quickly, proving she was much smarter than her father or Chuma had ever given her credit for.

"That's not your fault."

"No, clearly it is yours . . . because you came after me."

Rachel just stared at the other woman, not sure what to say.

"You believe in the right and the good. I noticed that when we chatted over coffee every day."

"I . . ." Did she? Still? After everything?

"You did the right thing. I do not know how you knew what was happening to me, but you came in and stopped it." Jamila's eyes took on a glazed quality. "You shot them, as if you had all the power."

"You had power, too. You could have lost it when I told you we had to go, but you didn't. You ran with me, made it possible for me to protect you."

"It's not enough." Jamila held Rachel's gaze. "Who *are* you?"

Chapter Twenty

"Rachel Gannon. I'm an agent of the United States government."

"CIA?"

"I'm sorry, but that's not something I can divulge."

"So, tell me what you can . . . Rachel."

Rachel did, asking questions of her own now that Jamila was aware her father was involved in criminal activity.

Jamila spoke a name.

"What?" Rachel asked. "What does he have to do with this?"

"I do not know, but he is the one man who makes my father turn pale and sweat when he calls."

The idea was a startling one. "But he's a politician."

Not a small-time politician like Dr. Massri, but a man high in Egypt's new government who had made the impossible transfer from the old one. A big man. Constantly in the public eye.

Not the right profile for someone involved in this organization, much less higher still in the food chain.

"It's not his political leanings that make my father so keen to please him." Jamila tugged the suit jacket she wore tighter around her. "You wait and see, when you start go-

ing through my father's files, you'll find a connection to
this man."

"Your father will go to prison—you understand that,
right?"

"Not if the people he works for find out he's been exposed as a liability." Jamila's absolute certainty that Dr.
Massri worked for others blew their theory that he, or
even Lavigne, was the man in charge.

"What do you mean?" Rachel asked.

"I watch shows, online. . . . I'm not supposed to. Especially American and British programming, but I do. I
know how these things work. The people above my father
aren't going to let him turn state's evidence."

Jamila claimed to have gotten her information from
watching television, but Rachel wondered if there wasn't
more to it. She didn't have a simplified view of crime and
punishment, as so many people did.

"Do they have that kind of system in Egypt?" Rachel
asked, rather than digging deeper right then.

"He won't be taken to the United States?"

Rachel shook her head. "That's not the way my agency
works. It's more expedient if he's tried in his own country."

"You assume he's breaking Egyptian law."

"An organization like the one he's part of doesn't make
distinctions on where they get the intelligence and technology they sell."

Jamila nodded. "My father wouldn't care, either. He
spouts all that political patriotism, but he didn't care who
won in the latest conflict. He would have worked with either side. He only cares about his own power, but mostly
about money. My father loves being rich and derives great
satisfaction from flaunting his wealth.

"He claims that is how he courted my mother, showering her with gifts. He convinced her to leave England and return to her family's ancestral homeland as his wife. That did not work out so well for her. My father does not take care of anyone. He puts more value on his possessions than people. He would never dream of breaking one of his objets d'art the way he broke my mother."

"Your home is filled with nice things?" Rachel probed, remembering comments Jamila had made that had alluded to such.

"Nicer things than even a doctor can afford in our country."

Finally, Rachel understood how Jamila had so quickly accepted that Abasi Chuma had been a criminal and why her mind had automatically processed that her father was one, as well. "You already suspected he wasn't only a doctor."

"Why would a man like him get involved in politics? He does not wish to become a servant of the people. He enjoys the accolades he receives for what he does, but they are not enough. It's all about money for him. He has probably taken some bribes in his day. I never understood why he did not seek office. Surely the bribes would have been lucrative were he to wield more power, but now I . . . think I understand."

"He is involved in something that makes him a lot more money than political bribery."

"You wondered why my father arranged the marriage to Abasi."

Rachel nodded.

"I wondered, too, believing that Abasi and perhaps my father loved me after all. Now, I think Abasi must have offered something my father valued more than he did me."

Rachel had no answer for that. Both men were monsters.

"The people who are supposed to value you, they don't always," Kadin said into the silence of the car. "That doesn't mean you don't deserve to be."

"You do not think so?" Jamila asked.

"I know it. You are so important, Miss Massri, that Rachel risked her life and her career to get you out tonight."

"Is this true?" Jamila asked.

Rachel could only nod. She didn't want Jamila feeling bad, but she understood why Kadin had said what he did. He cared, like Rachel did, how Jamila saw herself. Kadin wanted the young Egyptian woman to know she was worth someone else taking a risk on her behalf.

"But why? You barely know me."

"I know you deserve a better future than a man like Abasi Chuma would give you. You are a lovely, kind person, Jamila. You deserve so much better than what happened tonight, than the way your father has treated you your whole life, it sounds like."

Jamila just stared, and then finally she said, "I think, someday, I would like to be what you are."

"You're smart enough and strong enough to be the best." Rachel made no attempt to dissuade her.

"I graduate from university in only two years. Perhaps I could finish those years elsewhere. I have money, left me by my mother. And dual citizenship from her legacy, as well. She never renounced her citizenship in the United Kingdom, so I was born both an Egyptian and British citizen. I do not have to stay in Egypt."

This time, Rachel let the relief flow through her. She hadn't known what to do about Jamila's future, but, unlike Linny, the young Egyptian woman had a plan. And the means to make it happen.

Jamila had been assaulted not an hour ago, and here she was, making a plan . . . to take back her power.

"You are amazing," Rachel said with feeling.

"I believe you are, as well, Agent Rachel Gannon, but I think I would like to see your true eye color."

Rachel laughed as this incredible young woman had meant her to, her smile lingering as Kadin pulled the Land Rover to a stop in the alley behind the safe house.

Mrs. Abdul ushered Jamila toward the back of the house, speaking in low tones to her. The Egyptian woman waved off Rachel's offer to go with her.

Something about the Moroccan woman inspired confidence and security in Jamila. Rachel wasn't about to insist.

Kadin took her to their room and pulled her into his arms, just holding her in a fierce embrace for several minutes. "Tell me what happened."

She told him, feeling safe in his strong arms. When she was done, he pulled away and looked down at her. "She's not dead."

"Not like Linny."

"She's going to survive all this and come out stronger on the other side."

"She's strong already." A lot stronger than Rachel had even begun to realize.

"Yes."

Neil and Wyatt hadn't arrived yet, and she asked Kadin about it.

"They're transporting Ralph Giroux and Terne Lavigne. It was decided Giroux should not be brought here to the safe house."

"Lavigne?"

"He's alive, and Jayne wanted him brought in for questioning. But he needed medical care, so my team is taking him to a secure facility."

"Where are they taking Mr. Giroux?"

"To the airport. The sooner he is returned to a familiar environment, the better for him."

Rachel nodded. "Neil and Wyatt will be escorting him?" she asked, feeling abandoned, though she knew her emotions were not rational.

Maybe there was more trauma left over from her time in the mountains than she wanted to admit, because the thought of the Atrati men leaving filled her with a panic she could barely hide.

"No." Kadin reached out and placed a calming hand on her cheek, showing he saw even what she tried to cover up. "Ethan and Beth are meeting them at the airport and will stay with Ralph Giroux until his caregiver arrives. Spazz and Cowboy will be back in plenty of time to go with us to Egypt."

"Whit isn't going to approve that."

"Of course he is. The case is blown right open. He needs agents in there gathering evidence before Dr. Massri has a chance to destroy it."

"But—"

"Shh, angel. Just go with it. Okay?"

She nodded, but inside she was filled with confusion. She felt prick after prick against the bubble of numbness until her emotions threatened to spill out and take her over.

Jayne found Rachel on the rooftop, where Kadin had left her to get her some fruit juice and make a phone call to his chief.

The other TGP agent was surprisingly placid about Rachel stealing her gun, but she was livid about the possible compromise to her investigation.

She ended her rant with, *"What were you thinking?"*

That, at least, Rachel had an answer for. "I was thinking Jamila Massri wasn't going to be collateral damage."

"Chuma hadn't targeted her because of you. She was in his sights all along. That doesn't make her collateral damage," Jayne said in a flat tone.

"He still hurt her."

"But not because of you."

"Does it matter?" Rachel demanded.

"Not to me, no." Jayne fixed her with a pointed stare. "But I think it does to you."

"We're going to Egypt."

"It's not your case any longer." But there was no heat in Jayne's words.

"Jamila's my asset. She knows where her father keeps his secret files."

"And she's not about to share that information with me," Jayne said before Rachel had to. "Naturally. *I* didn't save her from a man attacking her."

"I didn't go in after Jamila to flip her."

"No. You didn't, but that's not what my report is going to say."

"You want to save my career." For so long Rachel had thought she was alone, and now, suddenly, she was surrounded by people intent on helping and protecting her.

It was overwhelming.

"You're a damn fine agent, even if you are more emotional than is prudent."

Coming from this woman, that meant a lot, even with the caveat. "Thank you. I think."

"Whit and Beth think a lot of you." Jayne's tone said that meant something to her. "Both of them quite firmly asked me to watch out for you. They said they'd have my head if I didn't."

"They did?" Again, Rachel was surprised.

She'd tried to keep her boss's daughter at a distance since joining TGP. But Beth never recognized boundaries, even when Rachel was constantly setting them.

Now she couldn't help wondering if maybe she shouldn't be so careful to keep people out.

It was a startling concept for her.

"Yes. The Old Man himself is worried about how the torture you endured might affect you."

Rachel shrugged. "There are worse things in life than physical pain."

"Yes," Jayne agreed. "But that doesn't mean that going through the pain, and the realization that death is probably your only way out, doesn't have a profound effect on you. It does."

"You sound like you've been there."

"I have."

"I didn't know."

"Most people don't. Just like most people in Jamila Massri's life from this point forward will never hear about what happened to her before you got to that room, but it will be with her all the same."

"How do you know . . ."

"I've seen that look in a woman's eyes . . . more than once. Cover like mine has a dark side few women want to talk about."

"You?"

"Would kill a man who tried."

Rachel believed it. "Jamila wants to be like me."

"She could do worse for a role model."

"Danger is inherent in our lives."

"But we're prepared to deal with it."

"Even torture."

"Even that."

Rachel nodded. "Kadin has Roman Chernichenko working on transport to Egypt."

"I'll fly with you. I assume the others will be coming, as well."

"Yes."

"Jamila can stay with Beth and Ethan."

"Jamila wants to be the one to get the files from her father's house."

Jayne didn't look surprised, or even resigned. If anything, her expression was approving. "She needs to take back the power."

"Yes."

Jayne nodded her assent. "Keep an eye on her."

"Better than I have so far."

"Bullshit," Jayne said succinctly. "The woman's alive and a lot less damaged than she could be."

"If I'd gone in sooner—"

"Chuma wouldn't have been otherwise occupied when you shot Lavigne. He'd have gotten to the Viper in the drawer that much faster. Both you and Jamila might well be dead right now."

"You were listening in when I told Kadin what happened."

"It's what I do."

"Well enough that I didn't even realize you were there."

"You were talking with the door open."

Rachel laughed a little.

"What?"

"I thought Neil and Wyatt were being sloppy, talking about the case with the door open. Even in a safe house."

"And then you did it. Says something for how secure you feel around these Atratis," Jayne opined.

"They stayed to help me."

"Different teams of the Atrati have different reputations."

"Oh?"

"Kadin's team used to be led by Roman Chernichenko. They had a reputation for doing what they wanted but always getting the job done. They still do."

Rachel could see that. Easily. "Kadin's pretty stubborn."

"I'd say pot and kettle, but I think you know that."

Rachel sighed and nodded. "I do."

"That's not the only thing you two have in common."

Rachel knew Jayne wasn't talking about the mind-blowing sex. "What do you mean?"

"You both lead with your emotions. For each other."

"He doesn't have feelings for me." Not real ones. "He still sees me as some fantasy he created in his head when we were kids."

"You're wrong about that." Jayne sounded so certain.

"How would you know?"

"Because a man like Kadin Marks doesn't lose his shit over a fantasy."

"You're right, Jayne. I don't."

Rachel spun around. "How long have you been standing there?"

"Too long for you not to have noticed. You're tired, angel. You'd better sleep on the plane."

She wanted to talk on the plane. Her emotions were leaking out around the edges, and she knew that the only way to get a handle on what was going on inside of her was to have it out with Kadin. Once and for all.

"Later, angel. We'll talk later. I'm not going anywhere."

"Are you reading minds now?"

"Just yours."

Jayne snorted, but she didn't say anything, just turned away. "I need to call the Old Man before we take off."

"When do we have to be at the airport?" Rachel asked Kadin.

"Roman has a jet scheduled with a takeoff slot in two hours."

"What did Jayne mean, that you lost it?"

"When I figured out you'd left on your own, I might have gotten a little loud."

"But you left the earbud in the Land Rover. You expected me to take off after Jamila."

"I wanted to be prepared for it; I didn't expect it. Those are two different things."

"Oh."

He sat down beside her and pulled her in to his side. Like a lightbulb coming on in a room that had been dark too long, she realized something. He was always touching her. If they were in the same room, he wanted to be next to her. Right next to her. Not just on the same couch but touching, and his hand was always reaching out to offer comfort.

Would a man be that attached to a woman he didn't really see, a woman who was no more than a fantasy?

"What's happening at Lavigne's house?" she asked, because as much as she wanted to figure out what was happening between her and Kadin, she still had a job to do.

Even if she was officially on leave.

"Nothing so far. We sent in a cleaning crew. When and if Dr. Massri goes to the house to collect his daughter, there will be nothing to see but a mansion completely empty of people."

"And Lavigne?"

"He'll be interrogated by your agency once his condition is stabilized."

"They're flying in another agent?" This assignment just kept getting bigger.

"Whit recalled Ethan."

"He can't do that, can he? Ethan took a leave."

Kadin shrugged. "He can if Ethan doesn't argue."

"So, Ethan's doing the interrogation?"

"Jayne would do it, but gathering evidence in Egypt is a higher priority because of the timing constraints."

"She's scary good."

"So is Ethan."

"How do you know?"

"The man worked FBI before TGP. He's got a rep that would make him a good Atrati."

"He's a spy."

"Who does whatever needs doing to get the job done."

"That can be bad sometimes."

"It can, but he's got a solid moral compass."

"Good to know, considering he's the father of my only friend's baby."

"Beth isn't your only friend."

"Until yesterday, I didn't even acknowledge she was one."

"Well, you can make it a banner day and admit I'm your friend, too, Rach."

She looked up at him, the malaise she'd been struggling with since the torture starting to melt away under the heat of the emotions in his dark eyes. "Are you?"

"You have to ask?"

"I think I want the words."

"Yes. Rachel, I am your friend, and if you let me, I will always have your back."

She nodded, her throat too tight to speak.

"He's not the only one." Neil came toward them across the rooftop garden, his eyes still bright with adrenaline, Wyatt close behind him.

"I thought you two were meeting us at the airport," Rachel said, having no idea how to respond to the mercenary's offer.

"And let this big lug pack up my babies?" Neil asked with horror lacing his voice as he waved toward Kadin. "Not a chance."

"I assume you delivered Terne Lavigne and Ralph Giroux into the appropriate hands." Kadin didn't seem offended not to be considered good enough to pack up his teammate's equipment.

"Lavigne is in lockdown at the secure medical facility. Ethan and Beth met us at the airport just like they promised and took custody of Giroux. He took a shine to Beth right away. He's currently bedeviling Ethan—in perfect

English, mind you—with the statistical probabilities of Beth having twins."

"How did he know she was pregnant?" Rachel asked.

Cowboy shrugged. "That man is scary smart."

"Did he seem okay?" Kadin asked. "Even a highly functioning autistic can get very agitated being taken out of his comfort zone."

"Oh, yeah. The thing he seemed most upset about was the food being so many different colors. Apparently, he's partial to green food."

"Well, that's healthy, I guess."

"I'm betting his caretaker keeps a bottle of green dye in her kitchen. That's all I'm sayin'." Cowboy winked at Rachel.

And she felt herself smiling in response. "I'm sure you're right."

"We're leaving in an hour."

Neil and Wyatt both nodded.

"We'd best get to it." Wyatt turned his attention to Neil. "I'm fixing to get our kits stowed."

"Thanks." The warm look Neil gave Wyatt surprised Rachel.

Wyatt looked shocked, but he was quick on his feet, and he leaned down to bestow a light kiss on Neil's cheek. "Get your toys packed up, baby."

Neil turned a little pink and waved the other man away. "Go on, hon, get out of here."

Cowboy stared. "You called me *hon*. You haven't done that in at least a year."

"I also told you to get going."

Cowboy left, a bemused smile on his rugged Texan features.

"You've forgiven him," Kadin said with more satisfaction and happiness than Rachel would have expected.

Neil nodded.

"You're going to give him a second chance?" Kadin asked in a tone that said the answer really mattered to him.

"Yes." Neil looked up, his expression quizzical. "You care about his happiness."

"I care about both of you, but, yeah, Cowboy's been a friend since our grunt days. You're good for him."

"I'll try to be, but if he tries to go back into the closet, I'm taping C-4 and a detonator to the door."

Kadin laughed. "I'll push the button."

Neil grinned. "Yeah."

Chapter Twenty-one

Neil walked into the room he'd been sharing with Wyatt. Though they'd spent the nights in separate beds.

"We're leaving in forty-five minutes." He'd packed his equipment in record time, even skipping a couple of steps on the less fragile of his "babies."

Wyatt looked up from Neil's duffel. "I'm almost finished here."

"Good. I've got something I need you to do."

Wyatt paused, as if he could tell by the quality of Neil's voice that what he was talking about wasn't work related. "Do you, now?"

"I do."

"What might that be?"

"Oh, I think you'll figure it out." Neil pulled his Ozzie T-shirt over his head and shucked out of his jeans.

Just in case the other man wasn't getting the right clue. "We're heading to the airport."

"We don't have time for everything, but we have time for something."

"Why?" Wyatt watched him warily. "Is this just sex? Because I don't think I can do that, Neil."

"This is me." Neil waved his hand toward his already hard cock. "Giving you another chance. Do not screw it up."

Wyatt's features spasmed, and he pressed the finger and thumb of one hand to his eyes. "Tell me I'm not dreaming, that you're saying this for real."

Neil crossed the room and laid his hand on Wyatt's chest. "I love you, *my* cowboy. It's not something I can stop, and my heart is more grateful than you'll ever know that you finally got your head out of your ass."

Wyatt's hand dropped, wet gray eyes glittering with a joy Neil never thought he'd be the cause of in another person. "Mine, too."

"Your mama may never change her mind about family holidays," Neil warned.

"Then we'll make our own holiday traditions."

"Your daddy is not going to let you come back and run the ranch."

"I'm a mercenary, not a cowboy."

"Oh, you're still my cowboy, but you're my partner, too."

"Then no more taking unnecessary chances with your life. You have a partner . . . a life partner . . . depending on you."

"I'm good at what I do."

"You're the best, but I'm not going to lose you now that I've got you back."

"I'll be more careful." Neil grinned. "Can you get naked now? The clock is ticking."

Wyatt tore off his clothes and then stood there, his whole body vibrating. "I'm afraid to touch you, afraid I'll wake up and this won't be real."

That was the second time Wyatt had said something like that. "You dream about us getting back together a lot?"

"For an interminable year, those have been the only good dreams I've had."

"You have a lot of nightmares?"

"Memories . . . the look on your face when I told you

about my engagement." Wyatt swallowed convulsively and turned his head away. "I'll never forget that."

"Yes, you will." Neil turned Wyatt's head back to face him with a hand on his chin. "Look at my face now, and dream about this."

He let all the love and bone-deep happiness he felt in that moment show in his eyes and the smile he didn't even try to dim.

Wyatt's breath caught.

Neil pulled the other man's head down, their lips coming together in a kiss so profound, it felt like vows were spoken.

Wyatt lifted his head, his breath coming unevenly. "I bought a little place in New York."

"Upstate?" Neil couldn't picture his cowboy living in the city.

"Yeah, but it's still New York."

"Good." Neil had never pictured himself living in New York, but he wasn't overly attached to his apartment in Maryland.

As long as he and Wyatt were together, out in the open, the *where* didn't really matter.

As an Atrati, he spent at least half the year away from home, anyway.

Wyatt shook his head, his smile crooked. "You can be really dense for such a smart man."

"Calling me names is not going to get you laid." Though Neil wanted the other man so much, if they didn't move this into the next stage soon, he was just going to tackle Wyatt to the bed and be done with it.

"Baby, I'm trying to ask you a question here."

"You are?" And then Neil got it. "Oh! I mean . . . well, damn it, ask, then."

"I'm a little nervous."

"You've got experience," Neil snarked, but the bitterness that might have been there even the day before was gone from his voice.

"Not in asking someone I love more than my own life, more than my old dreams, more than the regard of my family, to marry me." Oh, shit, he was going to cry. "Neil, I love you with every little bit in me. I will always be there for you if you let me; as long as it is within my power, I will never let you down."

"Yes." Neil absolutely believed the other man.

"Wait. Are you saying you'll marry me?"

"Yes." He threw his arms around Wyatt, knocking the muscled former Marines MARSOC soldier onto the bed. "My dad is going to be so happy."

Wyatt laughed, right before nearly kissing the life out of Neil. Kisses led to caresses. Caresses led to rubbing, and rubbing led to climaxes that left the rafters shaking from their shouts and a hot, wet mess on their bodies between them.

Wyatt looked down at Neil, his gray eyes soft with love. "Mine. My beloved is mine, and I am my beloved's."

Neil felt tears prick at his eyes. "For a lifetime."

"You're not getting rid of me through eternity, either." Wyatt leaned down and kissed Neil, his touch as gentle as the passion had been feral. "Thank you."

"Thank you for not giving up on us."

"Never."

Neil smiled.

Jamila returned from the depths of the house where she had been with Mrs. Abdul since arriving in her torn clothes and Chuma's suit jacket. Despite the late hour and everything that had happened that night, the young Egyptian woman looked tired but composed.

Mrs. Abdul had given her clothes to wear, and Rachel

was surprised to see that they were more Western than Moroccan.

But Jamila appeared comfortable in the Dior skirt that hit her calves only a couple of inches above the ankle and complementary long-sleeved raspberry-colored blouse by the same designer. It was by no means a revealing outfit, but it showed that Jamila wasn't seeking to hide behind the djellaba and *khimar* she could have worn.

Mrs. Abdul patted the young woman's shoulder. "You remember," she said in French. "The words I spoke will be as true tomorrow as they are today."

Jamila nodded, her eyes filled with gratitude and a peace that shocked Rachel.

Turning to Rachel, the younger woman even managed something very near a smile. "Madame Abdul has taken care of all my concerns. I am ready for our flight to Egypt."

"I didn't know she preferred French." Though some Moroccans did. Rachel turned mystified eyes to Mrs. Abdul. "Thank you for caring for Miss Massri."

She said the last in French, her accent not nearly as natural as Mrs. Abdul's.

"There is nothing for which to thank me. She is a remarkable woman and will one day make her mark on this world, I think."

"I'm sure you are right."

"She will heal. In all ways," the older woman said obliquely.

Rachel's heart constricted in thankfulness. "That is very good to hear."

They were settled on the private jet when Jamila asked, "Do you know if my father has learned of this night's events yet?"

Rachel turned to Kadin.

"Abdul's man reported that Dr. Massri returned to the hotel and has gone to bed. It doesn't look like he's going to discover anything until tomorrow, but by then all he'll find is an empty house," Kadin told Jamila.

"So, he will have no knowledge of what has become of Abasi or Mr. Lavigne?"

"Nothing he can confirm. Dr. Massri will probably think the worst when he realizes Giroux is gone, as well, and his cohorts don't answer their phones."

"But will he believe the worst in that they are dead or the worst in that they have absconded with me and left him for some nefarious reasons of their own?"

Kadin shrugged as if he didn't think it mattered. "You're pretty good at coming up with possible scenarios. That's a valuable skill."

"My father has always said I have too much imagination."

Neil said, "Dull people often say that of the highly intelligent."

Rachel was sure he had plenty of experience on that score.

"My father is very smart. He is a doctor, after all."

"He doesn't appreciate your worth—that makes him ignorant in my opinion," Cowboy said, his satisfied glow making Rachel smile.

It was clear that the two men had reconciled and both were incredibly happy about it.

"It is good of you to say so."

"I have a habit of speaking the truth, ma'am."

Jamila giggled and shook her head. "You are from the South, yes?"

"Actually, sweet thing, I'm from the grand state of Texas." Cowboy was playing up his accent and making Jamila smile.

"You Atrati are special men," Rachel said quietly to Kadin.

"You think so?" he asked, the question carrying a heavier meaning than the words implied at first.

She could see it in those beautiful brown eyes that had mesmerized her since she was a prepubescent girl.

"I do."

"That's good to know."

"I hope so." The words came out as a whisper against his lips as he moved close enough to kiss.

He completed the move, giving her a kiss that had more promise than heat.

Jamila gasped beside her, and Rachel looked over. "I'm sorry. We shouldn't have—"

"No. It is all right. You Americans are freer with your affections than we Egyptians, but there is such gentleness in this big man when he touches you. It is good to see."

Rachel reached out and took Jamila's hand. "A good man tempers his strength."

"And a strong woman seeks a *good* man in her partner."

"Yes."

Jamila nodded. "It is as Madame Abdul said. Strength is in the decisions we make."

"We all make mistakes."

"Yes, it is how we respond to those mistakes that defines our character."

"Mrs. Abdul tell you that, too?" Neil asked with warm curiosity.

"Yes. She is a very wise woman."

Everyone nodded, though Rachel doubted any of them had realized quite how invaluable that woman would be to them.

The flight to the airstrip outside of Helwan was a little more than five hours, and they arrived in the wee hours of the morning. Rachel had tried to sleep and had managed to doze in fits and starts but didn't feel particularly rested when the plane touched down.

Jamila had slept a lot more peacefully beside her, not waking once and barely shifting as the small Lear jet carried them to their destination.

Jayne wanted to go directly to Chuma's house. Cowboy offered to go with her as backup.

Because they had Jamila with them, Rachel wanted Neil to come to the Massris' house as extra protection for the young woman. He'd readily agreed. And Kadin had approved the plan.

Upon arrival, Jamila showed Neil to her father's office, where he immediately began a dump of the man's hard drive.

She then led Rachel upstairs to her bedroom, where she withdrew a small thin packet from between the mattress and box spring. "This is the key."

It looked like a sheaf of papers, but Rachel didn't doubt the other woman.

They returned to the office, which Kadin had clearly been searching. A framed Salvador Dali print hung out on a hinge from the wall.

Behind the painting was a state-of-the-art biometric-access panel.

Looking not in the least startled by what Kadin had discovered, Jamila opened the satchel she carried. She pulled out a clear sheet with a brown circle about half an inch in diameter in the center.

Jamila approached the retinal scanner and put the clear sheet in front of her own eye. Blue light flashed, and then a green indicator light flashed in the lower right corner.

She went back to her little cache, pulled out a flattened rubber glove, and then very carefully pulled it on over her own hand. She then pressed the index finger against the finger pad. A second green light flashed.

A whirring sound came, and then part of the wall simply swung outward, revealing a room no more than four feet deep that ran the entire length of Dr. Massri's office.

"How did you figure out how to do that?" Rachel asked, more than a little impressed.

"I have a friend on Facebook. He has odd ideas about alien conspiracies but tremendous knowledge about security features."

"Why did you even look for the hidden room?" Kadin wanted to know.

"I came into my father's office once when he was in there. That door in the wall was open, and I could hear him moving about. I am not allowed in his office, but I thought he was out of the house. He had not even locked the door."

The man had been too sure of his daughter's obedience.

Neil whistled appreciatively. "But you liked your bits of silent defiance, didn't you? Just coming in here to prove that you could."

"Yes."

"You didn't let him know you'd seen him in the secret room," Rachel guessed.

"Naturally not. He would have beaten me for being in his office to begin with. How much worse would the beating have been if he thought I had discovered something he hid from everyone else?"

"You are going to make one hell of an agent when you finish university," Neil said, his voice laced with an appreciation echoed in Rachel's own heart and clearly in Kadin as well, judging from the look he gave the younger woman.

"I believe I will enjoy the challenge of it."

"Have you gone through the files in here?"

"I only discovered the room a few weeks ago. It took me some time to get both a high-quality image of my father's eye and his fingerprint. And I do not have a great deal of time in the house alone."

Neil picked the lock on a filing cabinet but did not open the drawer when the lock popped. Rachel looked at him inquiringly.

"I make it a rule not to underestimate the wariness of my quarry."

"You think he set a snare on the cabinet?" Jamila asked. "My father is very arrogant. He will have assumed that this room is sacrosanct."

Neil shrugged, examining the cabinet closely. "It's always better to be safe than sorry."

Jamila seemed to consider that, and then she nodded. "Let me look, if you will."

Neil could have refused. Jamila was not trained, and she was barely twenty, but she'd proven she had a keen intellect and understood her father's mind.

"He likes Chinese puzzle boxes. I give him a new one each year for his birthday." She examined the solid wooden filing cabinet. "I never told him, but I always did the puzzles before giving them to him."

More silent rebellion.

"You are so much stronger than I gave you credit for," Rachel said, her voice tinged with awe and remorse for her own assumptions.

She still didn't regret refusing to flip the young woman. If Jamila had been caught trying to spy on him by Dr. Massri, what had happened to his daughter earlier tonight would seem like a walk in the park by comparison.

"I spend so much of my time keeping up the obedient and meek-mannered façade, I do not drop it for casual friendship."

Rachel would bet the other woman didn't drop it for good friends, either. "Does anyone in your life know the real you?"

"Abasi. He said he liked my spirit and understood why I hid it from my father. It gave him some kind of satisfaction to know my father was unaware. Now I understand that Abasi looked forward to breaking me. But he did not."

"No, he didn't."

Jamila pressed what looked like a solid piece on the cabinet, and it slid inward. Then she pressed against the side opposite, and another piece popped out. She frowned in concentration at the cabinet and then smiled. "It is modeled after the box I gave him five years ago."

Jamila dropped to a squat and pressed one of the decorative carvings at the base, and the second drawer down popped open two inches.

"Step back, honey. If he went to the trouble of making the cabinet like a puzzle box, it's definitely linked to a nasty surprise for anyone who doesn't know the secret."

Jamila's brow furrowed. "But it is open."

"Let's not take a chance on faulty wiring." Neil patted her shoulder. "Great job, by the way. You've got an amazing memory."

Jamila's smile said she was proud of herself, too.

Five minutes later, Kadin and Neil had removed a small bomb wired to the top drawer. It was set up so that it would have gone off if they'd opened that drawer instead of the second one down first. And the access drawer had been designed not to open from the outside. Only the series of moves Jamila had made would pop it open from the inside.

Without following that sequence, the C-4 would have exploded and destroyed the files, as well as most likely killing whoever opened the drawer.

The idea that Jamila might easily have been that person made Rachel go cold inside.

But she couldn't dwell on what-ifs. It was time to do her job. "We'll take the files and go over them later."

"This is not legal, is it?" Jamila asked, not sounding particularly bothered by the fact.

"It's not protocol search-and-seizure, no, but considering the imminent threat to our national security your father poses, our methods will not be held against us," Rachel said. "Besides, you gave us permission to come into your home, and, as a resident, you opened the locked entries."

"I like that."

"Working at this level has its perks," Rachel agreed.

"Along with its dangers," Kadin cautioned. "Those pictures Chuma showed you of Rachel were from when your father's men had her incarcerated and were torturing her with a car battery."

Jamila looked at Rachel, her expression concerned. "They hurt you."

"Yes." Rachel wasn't going to deny it. Jamila deserved the truth.

"That kind of torture, it brings great trauma to your mind and body."

"It does," Rachel admitted, for the first time making no effort to hide how bad it had been.

She didn't want Jamila thinking the job she wanted when she graduated from college came without its costs.

"But you survived."

"Only because Kadin and his team got me out. My plan was to tip sideways into the urine-and-water mixture on the floor when they were shocking me and fry my own brain." Not to mention her nervous system and heart. "Before I gave up my cover."

Kadin jerked. She'd told him this, but hearing it again wasn't sitting well with him.

She understood that. He loved her.

Funny that she would realize it before acknowledging her own feelings, but the certainty had been growing since he'd arrived at Terne Lavigne's mansion to help her rescue Jamila. He had never once tried to tell her she couldn't or shouldn't get the other woman out.

He'd only pointed out the potential cost of doing so.

And he'd never refused to help her. He'd put his own career on the line just as she'd done for Jamila.

Rachel had come to accept that he was motivated not by a fantasy but by a love that had never died. She could believe in it because hers hadn't, either. Despite everything.

It never would. She loved Kadin Marks today. She'd loved him ten years ago. And she would love him ten years from now.

She honestly didn't know what was going to happen between them, but that tiny spark of hope she'd thought snuffed out was burning brighter and brighter with every passing moment.

Chapter Twenty-two

"You would have died rather than betray your government," Jamila said with deep respect.

"Or you. They wanted me to confirm I wasn't just a tourist."

"But you would not expose me to harm."

"No."

"You are a strong woman with great moral character." Jamila smiled at Rachel, a genuine smile Rachel wasn't sure she would have been capable of in the circumstances. The Egyptian woman's own strength shone in her dark brown eyes.

Rachel didn't see herself that way. "I am what I need to be."

"And we are never going to get out of here if you don't start packing these files." Kadin's tone was indulgent, his hand once again reaching out to touch her.

To remind her that he was there. And maybe to remind himself that she was, too.

When they finished, they put the physical evidence into the trunk of the car their contacts had provided. Rachel appreciated a criminal who didn't trust computers completely and therefore kept a paper trail. It would make their job that much easier.

Jamila had packed some clothes and a few items of sentimental value while the mercenaries and Rachel emptied the filing drawers in Massri's secret room, as well as combing it for any other possible physical evidence.

"He will not even notice I have taken these things. He knows so little about me and shows even less interest," Jamila said as she and Neil carried her single suitcase and a medium-size box out to the car.

They collected Jayne and Cowboy, who seemed pretty pleased with what they had found in Chuma's office and the safe in his bedroom, and headed back to the landing strip where their private jet waited.

Once the plane was airborne, Rachel immediately started going through Massri's files while Jayne dug into Chuma's hard drive with Neil's help. Their plane landed in Morocco nearly five hours later, but only to refuel before taking off again for the U.S.A.

By the time they arrived in DC, Rachel could barely keep her eyes open, but she was confident she and Jayne had catalogued enough documentation to not only bring Dr. Massri to justice but to get Terne Lavigne put up on charges of treason in France.

And the Egyptian politician, even if he was not imprisoned, at the very least would see his career in the political arena annihilated.

There were others involved, as well, and they would take a fall, too, but one thing was clear. This information revealed the true head of the Hydra and how to cut it off so the organization would die.

Kadin didn't ask if she wanted him to go home with her. He just got into the SUV Andrew Whitney had sent to take her to her small apartment in Maryland.

Housing costs were too high in DC for Rachel to even contemplate keeping an apartment there, especially considering how little time she was at home. However, she was regretting the choice now, when she had a forty-five-minute car ride between her and her bed.

Rachel had offered Jamila a place to stay, but the younger woman had refused, saying she was fine with the protective custody Whit had arranged.

Rachel felt a lot better about it when she discovered that the FBI protection detail included an agent she'd known since her DEA days.

"We'll meet in the office tomorrow to go over evidence and information," Whit instructed. "Tonight, get some sleep."

It was early evening, but since Rachel hadn't slept except fitfully during that first plane ride in over thirty-six hours, she didn't argue.

She was still nodding her assent as Kadin pulled her into the back of the SUV and buckled her seat belt for her. "Lean on me. You can sleep on the drive into Maryland."

"You've got my back," she slurred tiredly.

"Always. If you'll let me."

She didn't answer, just snuggled into his side and let her head fall onto his shoulder. She was only vaguely aware when he carried her from the car to her apartment and then proceeded to tuck her into bed.

She didn't slip back into full sleep until he joined her, though.

It was still dark outside when Rachel woke up. Kadin's body was wrapped around hers, one big hand in firm possession of her hip.

She turned a little, so she could look up at his face in the light cast by the streetlamp outside. He hadn't shut the blackout drapes over her window.

The sheer voile curtain did little more than diffuse the glow.

His body tensed subtly, telling her that even that small movement had woken him. His eyes opened, their sherry brown depths indiscernible in the shadows.

"Please tell me you don't normally wake up at . . ." He looked over at her digital alarm clock. "Four-thirty in the morning. I thought I gave up those kind of insane hours when I left the military."

She smiled at the cranky rumble to his voice. "Only when I go to bed before the time I usually eat dinner."

"Dinner's supposed to be eaten at six o'clock. No later. A man could faint from hunger if the chow's not on by then."

"Oh, really?"

"Really." He made an X sign over his chest. "Cross my heart."

"And does this man cook?"

"Of course. I'd pretty much starve otherwise. I live alone."

"Good, because if you want to eat by six, you'll be making dinner more often than I will."

"I can live with that."

Rachel stilled and then shared her greatest fear. "I'm afraid you still have an idealized view of me. I don't think the real Rachel Gannon will be able to live up to that woman on a twenty-four/seven basis."

"Would you say you had an *idealized* view of Jamila?" he asked.

"No." Rachel stopped and thought. "Not that, but I did underestimate her."

"And that's what I did with you ten years ago, but, my sweet angel, I haven't underestimated you since carrying you out of that cell in Morocco."

"You said that perfect image of me had sustained you through the ugliest parts of war."

"*You* sustained me, thinking of you somewhere safe in

the world because I was willing to fight for freedom. That's what sustained me."

"I can't be less than I am, but I can't be more than I am, either." Would he understand that?

He rolled over on top of her, holding the bulk of his weight up on his arms. But then he lifted a little, reaching toward the table beside the bed.

A second later the lamp clicked on, its yellow glow revealing Kadin's expression. His brown gaze was filled with an emotion she'd once believed in. Could she again?

She'd already accepted that he loved her, but could she trust that love to endure? The two of them together, so close they shared everything in their lives?

"I don't want you to be anyone but exactly who you are," Kadin said with unshakable confidence. "And I damn well don't want to live another day of my life without you in it. I screwed up ten years ago. So badly. And it makes me ashamed to admit I didn't even realize how bad my choice was for both of us until Morocco."

"You left because you thought I couldn't handle what you'd become."

"Yes, but you were right the other day. I left because *I* couldn't handle what I'd become, either."

"You were worried that you'd been used as a weapon against targets that shouldn't have been casualties of war."

"I was." His voice was raw, his expression totally open, and she could see that it ravaged him to admit this. "One of my first kills. He was a political target, not a military one. I figured it out when I saw his picture on the local news. I couldn't understand the language being spoken, but I got that he was dead. I asked somebody exactly who he was."

"Not military."

"Definitely not."

"Kadin, military assassins aren't always given other military as targets."

"I know, but back then, I was such a kid, and I really believed I was fighting for our freedom."

"You were."

"But I was also fighting for political leverage."

"War is like that, ugly and multifaceted and very, very costly in so many ways."

"It cost me you."

She finally understood that it had. Kadin had done something that his twenty-year-old self could not reconcile with his beliefs and sense of honor.

"You gave me up in penance."

His throat convulsed, his face twisting in pain every bit as deep as her own had ever been. "I think I did."

"You didn't believe you deserved to be happy anymore."

"But I destroyed your happiness along with mine. I destroyed Linny's life." He buried his face in her neck. "How can you forgive me for that?"

Two weeks ago, she would have said simply that she couldn't. But a lot had changed inside her in the past days. "I already have. And the truth is, it wasn't you . . . or even me . . . who destroyed Linny. Arthur Prescott destroyed Linny's life, and she helped him do it."

It was so hard to admit that, but Rachel wasn't going to live her life with any more lies. Even ones she told herself.

"Jamila could have curled up into a ball after what happened, but she's going to fight for a better life."

Kadin lifted his face, their eyes meeting again.

It felt so good, Rachel sighed.

He smiled and then said of Jamila, "She took back her power."

"And she'll keep on taking it. Linny gave up, and that

was her choice. It will always hurt, and I'll probably always believe I could have done something if I'd been paying better attention, but she hid her sadness too well."

"Prescott played with her mind."

"Men like him do, but my sister could have reached out to me. She knew that. She chose not to. She chose to give up when he dumped her."

"She was a sweet girl, Rachel, but she liked things easy."

It hurt to hear, but she couldn't deny the truth. "And she drank too much. You can't make good choices when your brain is pickled half the time. I didn't know that, either, you know? I didn't find out until I started investigating after her death."

"She made mistakes, but she loved you."

"And she knew I loved her," Rachel admitted for the first time in four years. "It hurts so much to know that wasn't enough."

"You're enough for *me*." Kadin pressed his forehead to hers. "You're exactly what I need, what I want, and every dream I let myself have."

It was so much, this acceptance that had been ten years in the making. She didn't pick it to death, and she wasn't going to let Kadin overthink their reconciliation, either. They were moving forward. The past had claimed too much of both their lives.

"I don't want to raise our kids with one or both parents gone for indeterminate periods of time," she said with certainty.

Kadin's body tensed, and then she felt hot wetness rolling from his temples to hers. "I love you, Rachel. I don't know how to stop. And I'll do whatever it takes to finally convince you of that."

"Good. Remember that the next time you decide to punish yourself."

He chuckled, his breath hitching a little.

"I love you, too," she whispered against his lips as she pressed their mouths together.

They made love like they hadn't in ten years, with full certainty of their future and the love that bound them together.

Afterward, he cuddled her close. "So, no more mercenary?"

"No. I'm sorry."

"No more secret agent?"

"Nope. I'm not sure if I even still have a job, but it doesn't matter. I've spent ten years more alone than I ever want to be again."

"My family wants me to move back home," he said.

"Sacramento's a pretty good place to raise a family."

"Yeah."

"Yeah."

"I need to go into TGP's offices today."

"I have to write my reports for Roman."

"Maybe the Atrati could use a training facility on the West Coast."

No one could have been more surprised than Rachel to come home from a grueling day going over evidence and assessing how complete the picture they had was, to find out that her parting shot that morning to Kadin had been nothing short of prophetic.

"The facility is north of Sacramento, almost at the Oregon border. It's small town out there, but we'd be closer to my family, and I'd get to hire my own instructors."

"They're making you the head of the facility?" she asked in shock.

"No way. Chief gets that job. But I'm in charge of sniper training and tactical warfare."

"That's kind of amazing."

"Yeah. Maybe someone up there doesn't think I screwed up too badly after all."

Rachel found herself smiling. "I'd say that's a given."

"I want you to come on as an instructor."

"I'm a spy, not a soldier."

"You're an expert marksman and have sniper training as well as covert ops. You're exactly what I need out there."

"As one of your instructors?"

"As my everything."

"No one should be someone else's everything." But for a lucky few, the love was so deep, it would always feel that way.

"Okay, but can I just feel like it?" he asked, echoing her thoughts.

She grinned. "Yes."

What else could she say? She and Kadin had both built lives without each other. There was no question they could survive on their own, but to be deep-down happy? They needed the other half of their souls.

"I'm glad to have mine back," she sighed against him as he kissed her.

"Your what?"

"Soul mate."

"Me, too."

"Always," she said the way she used to.

"Forever," he replied as he always had. And now she knew that he meant it.

Even if they'd had a detour to their future, they were still twined together with love so deep, it hadn't died despite ten years of pain, loneliness, and even sometimes hatred.

True love had that power, and it was a power Rachel was never letting go of again.

Epilogue

The news reported that a certain Egyptian politician was sentenced to death for treason and acts against allied nations. Jamila Massri could not make herself mourn the man's coming demise, any more than she mourned her own father's incarceration and being stripped of all his money, luxuries, and freedom for the rest of his life.

Dr. Massri hadn't even discovered his empty filing cabinet before he was arrested upon his arrival at the airport in Cairo.

He'd never tried to find her, never brought her up during his interrogation. Both Jamila and her protectors had come to realize that her father assumed Abasi Chuma had eliminated her.

Stupid, arrogant man.

Some men, especially bad men, were like that. Some men, like Mr. Andrew Whitney, were good men and helpful.

He'd arranged for her transfer to a university only a few hours' drive from her new friend Rachel's home with her husband, the big ex-mercenary, Kadin Marks.

Jamila was majoring in criminal justice and minoring in psychology. She was going to be an amazing undercover agent someday.

And she would never forget what Rachel had done for her, saving her life and her sanity.

The world had many good people in it, and Jamila wanted to spend her life protecting them from the ones bent on destruction and pursuing their own selfish purposes no matter the cost.

Maybe one day, she would even be a TGP agent like Rachel, or an FBI agent like the ones who had protected her until it was determined her father believed her to be dead.

Whatever she became, her future was hers to plan.

Just as it should be.

Also available this month from Brava, *Demon Hunting in a Dive Bar* by Lexi George.

She was wiping down the bar when she saw *him,* sitting in his usual spot at a table in the corner, surrounded by shadows. Shadows that he brought with him, Beck thought with a surge of annoyance. Conall Dalvahni carried his own black hole of gloom wherever he went. With his dark hair and eyes, and his brooding expression, he was the freaking Grim Reaper, if Death were a demon hunter.

Beck couldn't stand the guy, and the feeling was mutual. So, why was he back? He'd made it clear he thought she was pond scum, an insult to decent, right thinking creatures everywhere.

He was a demon slayer and she was a demonoid. Polar opposites. Oil and vinegar. TNT and a lit match.

It had been nearly a month since she'd last seen him. Twenty-one days, to be exact, three whole weeks without Mr. Dark and Gloomy, and good riddance. She should have shrugged off his icy disdain by now, forgotten about him and moved on. But his obvious contempt for her had stuck in her craw. She couldn't stop thinking about him, and that pissed her off.

Everything about him pissed her off. His forbidding, humorless demeanor and his arrogant, holier-than-thou attitude.

And now he was back. Not for long, though. This was her place. She'd kicked him out once and she'd do it again.

Hefting a liquor bottle with a metal pour spot in one hand, she stalked over to his table.

"What do you want?" she demanded.

"That depends." His deep, rough voice grated on her nerves and made her stomach knot. "What have you to offer?"

"Nothing you're interested in."

His dark gaze raked her up and down, casual and insolent. Infuriating. Beck's grip tightened on the bottle.

"You are mistaken," he said. "You have information about the demon activity in this area, information that I require."

"Get your information someplace else, mister."

"I am more than willing to recompense you for your trouble."

A flat leather pouch appeared in his hand. Opening it, he tossed a thick wad of hundred dollar bills on the table between them. Beck stared at the pile of bills. It was a lot of money, several thousand dollars at least.

"There is more where that came from, Rebekah."

Something hot and hurt flared inside her. On top of being lower than dirt, he thought she was for sale. She pushed the feeling aside. It didn't matter what he thought. She was an idiot for letting the guy get under her skin.

"The name's Beck and I don't need your money."

"Your name is not Beck. It is Rebekah Damian."

"Who told you my—"

"You are thirty-one years old," he continued, as though reciting a series of memorized facts. "Although you appear much younger, no doubt due to your demon blood. Your father is Jason Beck Damian, a nice enough fellow, but otherwise a quite unremarkable human. This bar belonged to him—thus the name—until he married and started another family. His wife does not drink and disapproved of her husband running a tavern. At her encouragement, he sold the place."

"Encouragement?" Beck made a rude noise. "Brenda nagged his ass until he caved."

"At eighteen, you were too young to purchase *Beck's* on your own," Conall said. "So you bought the place with the help of your partner, Tobias James Littleton, and turned it into a bar that caters to your kind. The name you kept."

"My goodness, Daddy's been running his mouth, hasn't he?" Beck drawled. She clamped down on her rising temper. "At his age, you'd think he'd know better than to talk to strangers."

"I have supped at his eatery several times in the past few weeks," Conall said with a shrug. "The name of the place eludes me."

"Beck's Burger Doodle," Beck ground out.

"Ah, yes. The Party Burger is a favorite of mine."

"Daddy makes a good hamburger. So what?"

"Your father has told me much about you." Conall reached across the table and toyed with the salt shaker. The sleeves of his Henley sweater were pushed back, exposing his strong forearms. His shoulders were broad and heavily corded with muscle. He had beautiful hands, strong and bronzed; the hands of a warrior. And not just any old warrior, Beck reminded herself; a demon killer. "He confided, for instance, that he had a three-day dalliance as a young man with a woman named Helené."

Her mother? Daddy had told Conall about her *mother*? Beck stared at him in disbelief.

"She was a dark haired beauty like you," Conall said, his gaze on her face. "He did not know it at the time, but she was demon possessed. Some months later, Helene returned, changed almost beyond recognition from the excesses of the demon. She had a child with her, an infant girl with a strawberry blotch on one shoulder, a birthmark common in the Damian family. That baby was you. She shoved you into your father's arms and left, never to be seen again."

"Daddy told you all this?"

"Yes."

"Bullshit. My father never talks about his freak of a daughter. He's an upstanding citizen now, a member of the Civitan Club and a good Baptist. What did you do to get him to spill the beans?"

Conall sat back in his chair. "You think I wrested the information from your parental unit by supernatural force?"

"Figured that out by yourself, did yah? My, you are the bright one."

"You do not like me."

"Ding, ding, ding," Beck said, tapping her forefinger in the air. "Right again."

Conall's black gaze slid from her face to the bottle in her hand. "I see. And what do you plan to do with that flask?"

"I was thinking of bashing you over the head with it if you don't leave."

His black brows rose. "You wish to hit me? Why?"

"Mister, the last time you were here, you all but said you think the kith are nothing but vermin to be exterminated, and now you're back. Seeing as how I'm kith and you're a demon hunter, I take your presence here as a threat."

"Kith? This is the term for your kind?"

"It's *our* term," Beck said. "For some reason, we like it better than scum sucking demon spawn."

"Are you always so sarcastic?"

"Only when I'm awake."

He regarded her without expression. Nothing unusual

about that; the guy had about as much expression as a two by four. "You think I came here to kill you."

"It crossed my mind."

"And yet you confront me with nothing but a bottle in your hand, and I a demon slayer."

"I can take care of myself," Beck said. "I've been doing it a long time."

Conall sprang at her in a blur of movement. The bottle in Beck's hand clattered to the floor as she was swept up and pinned against the nearest wall by more than six feet of hard muscled male.

"You fascinate me," Conall said. His voice was dark and rough. "I cannot decide whether you are brave or foolish. Perhaps both."

Beck went still. The heat from his big body and his crisp, woodsy scent surrounded her. He smelled like a little bit of heaven, she'd give him that.

"Let go of me." She felt the weight of his stare, but kept her gaze fastened on his wide chest. He was too close. He was too big, too everything.

The alpha male jackass ignored her and bent closer. The air froze in her lungs.

"You smell of jasmine and spices. Sweet and exotic," he murmured. His warm breath whispered across her skin. To Beck's horror and chagrin, she began to tremble. "How . . . interesting. I expected the stench of demon to be upon you."

His last words hit her like a slap in the face. Anger washed over her, bright and hot, followed by an overwhelming urge to escape. Shifting into a column of water, she flowed from his grasp. It was easy, this close to the river. Water strengthened her powers. It was one reason she hadn't wanted to sell the bar and move into town.

The stunned look on Conall's face as she poured out of

his arms was priceless, almost worth the aggravation of being around him.

Almost.

She glided across the wooden floor and resumed her former shape, taking care to place the table between them before she reshifted.

"Out." She pointed to the door. Her chest heaved and angry tears burned the back of her eyes. She would not let him see her cry. She refused. "And this time don't come back."